DOUBLE DOWN

VICTORIA PRATT

Entangled Publishing, LLC
2614 South Timberline Road
Suite 109
Fort Collins, CO 80525
Visit our website at www.entangledpublishing.com.

Select Contemporary is an imprint of Entangled Publishing, LLC.

Edited by Alethea Spiridon Hopson
Cover design by Louisa Maggio
Cover art from iStock

Manufactured in the United States of America

First Edition October 2015

To my mom and dad, who ignited my passion for books. Thank you for teaching me that being easily amused is indeed, a very good thing. And most of all, thank you, thank you, a hundred times thank you, for your unflinching support of my wild weirdness.

Chapter One

I hate being on time.

Not always, but when it comes to our morning briefing, I'd rather be in my seat before the sausage parade begins. This morning, however, thanks to last night's poker extravaganza and subsequent hangover, I'm one of the last ones in. Fantastic. Don't get me wrong. It's not like I have some OCD compulsion that makes me want to be the first one in the room. It's just that this particular room full of cops likes to try to make me squirm, and trust me, that is no easy feat. I'm a fast-driving, sharp-shooting, type-A ballbuster, but sadly, my long blond hair and obvious lack of penis are viewed as an egregious insult to these good ol' boys, and they make every effort to make me feel like "a girl."

I ran a bloodshot eye over the sea of blue uniforms and bad haircuts. Yep. Last one in. But, like my mother always said, never let them see you sweat. Chin up, shoulders back. She called that "assuming the position." We always giggled about it when I was a kid, although looking back I was probably giggling because my mom was giggling. The memory still brings a smile to my face to this day, although when I'm assuming the *other* position, it is a little weird to be thinking of my mother. Regardless, a hint of a smile replaced my hangover grimace as I walked down the center aisle and began the slow cut through the row to my seat. I've been here a couple of months now, so the comments are beginning to subside, but there are still a few who won't quit.

Case in point—Detective Jay Coleman. "Sweet ass, Jones," he whispered as I crossed in front of him.

I've decided to treat these daily offerings as compliments, instead of the misogynistic belittlements they're intended to be. After all, I do have a nice ass. "Thanks, Princess," I chirped. "I've been working out. Nice to see those charm school lessons are paying off for you." This earned me a few snickers from the boys. I even got a sliver of a smile from the only other female cop in the station, Lisa Miller. It did not, however, endear me to Detective Coleman.

"Princess" had become Coleman's nickname, thanks to me, doubly funny since he was probably the most manly man I've ever met—sandy blond hair, green eyes, big rough working hands, and perma-stubble. On my first day, they paired me up with another new officer, who, although he does have a penis, is similarly handicapped in that he is the most beautiful person I've ever seen. He's much prettier than me. I'm not half bad, but he's ridiculous—six feet, five inches of caramel skin, thick black hair, brown eyes, and a perfect mouth. Not handsome, beautiful. To make matters worse, his name is—wait for it—Ken. Detective Coleman thought he was being clever by introducing us to the rest of the force as Barbie and Ken. But anyone who has grown up with a brother knows that two wrongs most definitely do make a right, so I retaliated in the only way I knew how—I called him Princess and insulted his manhood. Funny, nobody calls me Barbie anymore, but Princess really stuck.

Ken turned his big doe eyes to me as I sat down beside him, and I was struck, as I always am, by the obscene length of his lashes. I wouldn't say I'm jealous of his beauty, but I do think it's kind of a shame to use up so many great features on one human, especially a male one. If I had the power I'd take his hair and give it to Ross. Then I'd give his eyes to Watson, and his body to Terry. I wouldn't give shit to Coleman, though. He'd probably go out and get himself syphilis, then come back and blame it on Ken. Frankly, Ken might benefit from an imperfection or two. Ever since the great Dave debacle of 2010, I've decided never to date anyone who is prettier than me. Ken could never tempt me, anyway, no matter how unattractive he could manage to make himself. Fishing off the company pier is a monumentally bad idea. It's hard enough to be taken seriously in this cop shop without adding "badge bunny" to my list of defects.

I pulled out of my reverie. "Morning, Ken. You good?"

"Can't complain, Cassidy. Can't complain." He probably would have complained if he knew that I had just mentally dismantled his body and distributed his goodies like Santa Claus.

"How's my partner doing today?" he asked with a smile.

"Well, I lost my shirt at poker last night, then I tripped and fell into a bottle of tequila, and it all went inside me. But other than that…it's all good."

Ken shook his head with mock disapproval. "I don't

know how you do it."

"It's kinda like riding a bike," I answered. "Except there's no bike. And there's booze. And you have a better chance of getting laid."

"Did you?"

Before I could answer, I heard Captain Rye making his way into the room and down the aisle. I could tell it was the captain without looking. He had a very distinct footfall— there was a stomp-drag to his gait. Heavy, tired, graceless. Today, though, those footsteps came to an abrupt halt at my row. I looked up to see what had stopped him. Apparently I was the object of his attention. I swung a look behind me to see if I was missing something, but there was no mistaking it. His humorless eyes were fixed on me, his expression a mixture of contempt and disbelief. This was actually an interesting development. Until this very moment, I had thought he only saw me as boobs, a badge, and a ponytail, in that order. Apparently today, I was something else to Captain Rye.

Could I be in trouble? I couldn't imagine how. Ever since I had arrived, or should I say, ever since I was foisted onto the department because of equality hiring, they had used my carefully honed bad guy–nabbing skills for playground duty. At least that's what I call it. Writing citations to drunks, putting Band-Aids on kiddies, tracking down truants and prank nine-one-one callers. You know, real crime fighting. It's actually pretty hard to screw up playground duty. The litmus test for a successful day is making it through your shift without getting flashed or peed on. A couple of months ago I would have thought that getting peed on would be the worst, but I've seen some things recently that have made me rethink.

Could I be getting praise? Also doubtful. It's kind of

hard to make a mark in the department when you don't get the opportunity to use your skills. So what had gotten Captain Rye's panties in a twist this morning, I wondered. I was about to find out.

"Jones, Miller, in my office."

He turned on his heel without waiting for us to follow. This was either going to be a good thing or a bad thing, but judging from my reception at the station, I was banking on the latter. Miller didn't seem fazed, though. She was the only other woman on the force. You'd think that fact would have worked as a bond between us, but sadly this was not the case. Lisa was a joyless woman with a seemingly endless supply of disdain for the human species. Physically she was quite… impressive. My mother would call her sturdy. There was a thickness to her that can only be attained through unfortunate genetics and a lifetime of heavy weight training, but her tragic hair was the result of pure neglect – lifeless and dull, and the color of damp hay. Her eyes might be pretty if she smiled, but since I'd never borne witness to such a thing, I wasn't holding my breath.

The door to the captain's office was open, and he gestured us inside, then pointed at the door, the universal symbol for "close it" used by power trippers all over the world. Sitting behind the desk was Police Chief Thompson.

Chief Thompson was the silver fox to Captain Rye's silverback gorilla. Thompson was lean and sinewy, with bright blue eyes and close-cropped silver hair. Captain Rye, on the other hand, was meaty and sweaty, with dark gray hair, beady dark eyes, and a bulldog underbite. I guess I'd be miserable, too, if I looked like that.

Beside Chief Thompson sat a redheaded woman with a

sad face and eyes red rimmed from crying. She was wearing a simple black sheath dress under a fine-knit black cardigan. I'd put her somewhere in her mid- to late forties. She looked familiar to me somehow, but I couldn't quite place her.

Captain Rye, finding himself without a seat in his own office, shuffled over to lean against the wall with his arms crossed over his chest. Whatever was going on, Captain Rye was not happy about it.

"Chief, these are Officers Miller and Jones," growled Rye.

I gave the chief the customary nod. "Chief."

He took a moment to look at us both then spoke. "I trust you both heard about the murder last night."

Lisa jumped in smugly. "Of course, sir."

The chief hesitated, only for a second, but long enough to underline the fact that he did not want to be interrupted. From the corner of my eye I could see Lisa wilt a little. It's amazing how much a person's shoulders can betray them. God, would I love to play poker with her.

"Last night," continued the chief, "Jimmy Polonco was murdered in one of his own establishments." He paused to let the information sink in, then added, "I'm sure I don't have to tell you what kind of shitstorm we're in for if we don't find the doer. Fast."

My skin was tingling. This was huge news. Jimmy Polonco was one of the most influential founding fathers of Sioux Sands. It was a new city, sprouted from nothing in the middle of nowhere, snuggled up to a huge Indian reservation on the edge of the North Dakota oil sands. When I was growing up, this was all farmland. Then, about ten years ago, Jimmy Polonco of the Chicago Polonco crime family rolled onto the reservation in a big black SUV, had a powwow with George

Bloodgood, one of the tribe elders, and hatched a plan to build a casino on Indian land. Somehow he had anticipated the oil boom, but instead of speculating on oil, he threw his money into the infrastructure that would support it. It had been a very lucrative decision for him.

Three years later, Polonco Casino was born. And where there's a casino, there are strip clubs, and hotels, and restaurants. Lo and behold, before our very eyes, a city was born out of the dirt, nourished by crime, gambling, sex, and money. It had really exploded in the last few years. That's why I'm here.

When a city arrives on your doorstep, it either absorbs the small towns around it or it crushes them like grapes. My tiny hometown, population eighteen hundred, was all but crushed. It lies on the opposite side of the reservation from the casino, so it wasn't swallowed up by the city. But, having lived out in the middle of the dirt for so long, most of the people in our town decided they wanted to live closer to the action, so they picked up and moved. As the population dwindled, many of the stores and restaurants on the main street shuttered. Eventually our little town could neither justify, nor afford, having its own police force, and I was suddenly out of a job. So I did what everyone else did—I looked for one in the city.

Luckily, due to the population explosion and an inordinately large amount of crime, they were in desperate need of more police officers, and I was given a job. If they'd bothered to ask, they would have found out that I had graduated at the top of my class and that I was an excellent police officer, a better shot than anyone in the Sioux Sands Police Department. I'd bet my life on that. But they didn't ask. This was the new wild frontier, the future of oil in America, a testosterone playground where, at best, women were tolerated but never appreciated.

The chief gestured to the redheaded woman at his side. "Mr. Polonco's wife came to see me. She's worried it could be an inside job. She's afraid, and so am I, that if we don't find out who did this, every mobster in Chicago is going to descend on our city, and they won't care what kind of collateral damage they do. They'll just start whacking until they figure they've got the right guy. Mrs. Polonco has asked me to put someone in undercover to find out who killed her husband."

Lisa and I traded a look. There was an entire room full of men out there, and Captain Rye liked every single one of them better than us. Why would he bestow the honor of solving a high-profile murder case on a *girl*?

"I'd be happy to do it, sir," said Lisa, shooting me a dirty look. *What an idiot*, I thought to myself. It's not like we were a couple of kids calling dibs. At least I really hoped it wasn't.

Chief Thompson and Mrs. Polonco traded a look.

"Actually, I don't know if that'll work," he said. "I'm thinking Officer Jones might be a better fit."

He looked uncomfortable saying it. Captain Rye, on the other hand, looked angry, and Lisa looked like she'd been punched in the stomach. I'd managed to make three people very unhappy without saying a word or moving a muscle. My mother would be so proud.

I waited. When you keep your mouth shut, people tend to either volunteer information or dig their own grave. Biting my tongue around people who have control over my career was one of my best features. I could feel Lisa looking at me. I didn't give her the satisfaction of returning that look, but I could tell it wasn't a pleasant one. Her breath was coming fast and sharp, and her fingers, balled up into meaty fists at her sides, clutched the heavy wool of her trousers, as though their release might trigger a cyclone of violence directed specifically at my face. It had been a long time since someone had wanted to punch me that badly. Finally, she couldn't take it anymore.

"With all due respect, sir," she said gritting her teeth, "I have to disagree with your decision. I can handle anybody and anything, and I've been here longer than her."

She was really going for it.

"She doesn't even want this!" She jabbed a fleshy thumb in my direction. "You offered it to her and she hasn't said anything!"

The room fell silent, all eyes on Lisa. Her face was flushed to a dark pink, interrupted by little blotchy white patches, and a film of sweat covered her upper lip and forehead. All in all, not a good look. When I was sure her tantrum was over, I turned to the chief. "May I respond, sir?"

Chief Thompson gave me the nod to continue, so I turned my gaze back to Lisa. "With all due respect, Officer Miller, unless you're a freaking wizard, or you have a crystal ball up your ass, you have absolutely no idea what I want, much less what I'm capable of. As for not responding to Chief Thompson, he hasn't made me an offer yet. You didn't give him the chance. And from the look on his face, I'm guessing that this assignment isn't going to be a pleasant one. So why don't you do us all a favor, and shut the hell up?" I paused for effect, turning away from her. "Chief?"

"Um... Thank you." It took him a moment to gather his thoughts. "You're right about the assignment. I hate to ask it of anyone, but…" He stopped again. "Understand, you're not obligated to take the assignment."

"Just tell me what it is, sir."

"Jimmy was killed at Double Down, one of his strip joints. We want to put someone in there undercover…as a stripper."

I didn't know whether to be flattered or offended. "And what makes you think I'm suited for that?"

He looked down at his shoes, suddenly finding something very interesting on the floor. He kicked back and forth for a second, gathering the courage to continue. "My, uh, wife said that you were…you know, into that."

My eyes grew wide. "Excuse me?"

"She said her cousin saw you doing the, what do you call it? The stripper pole stuff?"

Now it was my turn to blush. My best friend Bobbie had bought us pole-dancing lessons for my birthday last year. Every Tuesday night we'd grab cocktails—liquid courage, we called it—then go to our pole-dancing lessons. It was an amazing workout, much harder than it looked, but you try explaining that to a fifty-year-old cop. It sounded fishy, even to me. If I'd known that the chief's wife's cousin would be watching, I would have traded them for square dancing lessons.

"I've never been a stripper, if that's what you're thinking," I said weakly. "It's just…it's good exercise." I heard a little snort of derision from Lisa, and it took all my willpower not to elbow her in the trachea. I thought briefly about taking the high road, but I couldn't let it pass unpunished.

"Too bad Jimmy wasn't murdered in a cookie-bingeing club, Miller. That way all your special training could come into play." Lisa's eyes widened with anger, but I dismissed her by turning my attention back to the chief. "Why do I have to be a stripper? Can't I be a bartender?"

The chief turned to Mrs. Polonco. "What do you think, Leora?"

Mrs. Polonco took a deep breath and spoke with a low and quiet voice. "I'm told the bar staff is pretty stable, but the strippers come and go all the time. Nobody would question the presence of a new one." Her eyes started to water, and she pulled a tissue from her purse. "Forgive me," she whispered. "I'm afraid I'm a bit of a mess."

"I think we can take it from here, Mrs. Polonco," said the chief. "Why don't you go home and get some rest? We'll speak later."

"I think that might be best," she said, rising from her chair. "Thank you very much, all of you."

Chief Thompson nodded solemnly and helped her to the door. Once she was out of earshot, he continued. "Apparently, every Thursday night is amateur night. All you have to do is put your name on the list, and then you can…do your thing." He paused for a second while I digested the information. "And we can send someone else in undercover to watch your back. Detective Coleman and Detective Watson just closed a case. We could send in one of them."

My stomach lurched. If he was trying to sweeten the pot by adding a couple of good ol' boys to the mix, he had failed miserably. I'd rather die than let either one of them see me naked, especially Detective Coleman. I could picture him roaring back to the station spewing all the gory details to his buddies. I'd never live it down. Still, I needed to get off the playground-duty rotation. It was killing my soul. "I'll do it,"

I said. "Under two conditions."

The room fell silent. Captain Rye and Officer Miller visibly stiffened. Chief Thompson, on the other hand, looked a little intrigued.

"Go on," he said.

"I go in alone. I'll wear a wire or a tracker, whatever, but Detective Coleman looks like a cop, and he acts like a cop, and his presence would put me in danger."

"What about Watson?" asked the chief.

"Him, too. Plus he smells like deli meat."

"That's ridiculous," said Captain Rye.

"Fine. You'll go in alone," said the chief, cutting him off. "What else?"

"I'm assuming that this is a promotion?"

Captain Rye was apoplectic. "That's ridiculous! You've got some nerve, making demands like that. You should be grateful for being given this opportunity."

I was temporarily shocked into silence. There were so very many ways I would like to have responded to the captain, yet they all seemed to end with my boot stuck up his ass and a gaping, bloody hole where his teeth had been. As angry as I was, though, I was still able to comprehend that breaking your boot off in your boss's ass is not the key to job preservation, so I took a steadying breath and faced Captain Rye. "I'm sure there are a lot of women dying for the opportunity to grind their naked bodies into the laps of greasy old perverts, Captain. But I like to think I've been fairly selective up till now as to who gets to see me naked." That last part wasn't necessarily true, but they didn't need to know that. I turned from Captain Rye to Chief Thompson.

"Here's the deal. I've been a cop for eight years. Not at

this station, but eight years all the same, and I have a perfect service record. I've put in my time, I've been a good cop, and I deserve it. Now, I'm willing to do this for you, but you have to do for me, too. Otherwise, it's not worth it. You decide."

The chief looked at me appraisingly. I had either done a very good thing for myself, or a very bad thing. I knew which side Rye was on. He looked like he wanted to rip my badge off and cram it down my throat. Lisa was wide-eyed, as if she was waiting for lightning to strike me dead and didn't want to be standing too close when it happened. The chief, however, was the one I was worried about. I was either in or out on the basis of his response.

"Fine," he said. "Effective immediately."

"Thank you, sir. And I'm assuming there's a pay increase with that?"

"That's enough!" bellowed Captain Rye. He was furious at having his authority circumvented, but I could tell from the smile on Chief Thompson's face that I would be getting the raise.

"Thank you, Jones. You'll start tomorrow." He handed me a thick file. "Take the rest of the day to familiarize yourself with all the players, and get yourself sorted. We'll meet here tomorrow morning, eight a.m., to go over the details... Detective."

"Thank you, Chief." I gave Captain Rye a nod. "Captain." I gave Lisa a little smile. "Officer..." I said it so sweetly, but there was no mistaking the dig. I turned on my heel and left the room.

Chapter Two

I drove home from the station in my black Jeep, doors off, radio cranked up to eleven, pounding out the bass beat on my steering wheel. The wind picked up my hair and threw it into a rebellious cloud around my face, the only thing keeping it out of my eyes a pair of dark-tinted aviator sunglasses.

I glanced into the backseat, where a huge file box sat waiting for my attention, a huge file box that marked the start of a brand-new career path for me. I checked myself in the rearview mirror, gave myself a satisfied smile, and took a mental photograph. I felt like a bona fide, notarized, card-carrying badass. I wanted to remember this moment forever.

I pulled up the long gravel driveway to my house, and bless her heart, Bobbie was already there, waiting for me. I liked my house. It was one of the nicest ones in town — just on the outskirts of town, actually. I remembered being a kid and thinking that it was some kind of castle. It wasn't, of course, but it was always stately looking somehow. Two stories of light yellow brick, big windows framed by big black shutters, a great black door, massive shady trees, a huge yard. I think the beauty came from its proportions, though. There was even a little house out back. Most people called it a guesthouse, but my grandma had had one on her property, too, and she had always called it "the little house."

The main house was bigger than I needed, but I didn't care. After the mass migration to the city, lots of houses went up for sale, flooding the market. If you were willing to stay in town, you could have pretty much any house you wanted, dirt cheap. When I drove by one day and saw the FOR SALE sign, I knew I had to have my castle. It was close enough to the city if I felt the urge to go shopping or bar hopping, but I liked the five-mile cushion of separation that the Indian reservation provided.

I hopped up the steps and joined Bobbie on the big wraparound veranda. She'd been there long enough to make it through half a bottle of Mike's Hard Lemonade. She tossed me one as I reached the top step, and I used the bottom of my T-shirt to squeeze off the cap. "Chuck," she said, lifting her bottle in tribute.

"Bob," I answered with a big satisfied smile, clinking my bottle with hers. We had called each other Bob and Chuck since we were little kids. No one else was allowed to use those names—it was part of our own secret language with each other. We could have almost an entire conversation just with our eyes. We'd finish each other's sentences and laugh at the exact same things. A lot of people assumed we were sisters, and in truth, we were closer to each other than most sisters are. Although we look like mirror opposites—she had long black hair to my blond, blue eyes to my brown, and white skin to my buttery tone — we were very much alike in all the things that mattered.

We literally grew up together. Our parents were the best of friends and had built houses next door to each other when we were babies. Our dads had both been cops together on the reservation, one of the many things that set us apart from the other kids, and they thought it was important to live as close to the Indians as possible. If the Indians had allowed it, I'm sure our parents would have built on the reserve, but apparently there were rules forbidding such things. So they settled in as close to the reserve as they could get and tried their best to have us blend in to both communities. Bobbie and I loved it. We learned lots of cool things, like how to shoot moving targets, clean a fish, dive off the cliffs. Important stuff. It's even where we both saw our first...wiener. That's what you call it when you're five. In fact, that's what we still called it when we were inebriated. Which happened regularly.

Yeah, Bobbie was definitely the one to call in an emergency, and what I was about to embark upon definitely counted as one. Bobbie tossed me an old shopping bag. "You're in luck. I found it," she said. "You're gonna look purdy."

I reached into the bag and pulled out a pile of black vinyl. "There's not much to it, is there?"

"That's kinda the point." Bobbie giggled.

I couldn't help but laugh with her. She was right, and I was suddenly struck by the enormity and the hilarity of what I was getting myself into. It was one thing to go to a gym and flop around on the pole for an hour. It was quite another thing to do it in public. My mother would *definitely* not approve.

"Okay," I said, downing the rest of the bottle. "Let's try this bad boy on."

After another hard lemonade and no small amount of tugging, lifting, and squeezing, Bobbie turned me around to face my full-length bedroom mirror. "Open your eyes!"

"Holy crap. I look like a hooker."

"Again," Bobbie said with a dramatic flourish, "that's the point!"

I wasn't kidding, either. I really did look like a hooker — a hooker with a twist, though. We decided that if I was going to feel comfortable, I'd need a theme, a costume. Lots of strippers picked a disguise. Maybe pretending to be a pirate or a cowgirl made it easier for the psyche to accept the fact that you were showing a bar full of strangers your pink parts. Whatever worked. I decided on the classic yet oh so ironic Slutty Cop. Sure, it was a Halloween costume, but really, how choosy were guys who had beer, boobs, and a buffet to distract them?

"I think we should make it shorter," she said. "Up to about here." She was standing behind me, hiking the vinyl police skirt even farther up my thigh. "If you do that, nobody will think it's a Halloween costume."

"It'll be a turtle skirt!" I said.

"Honey, they're gonna see your snapper one way or another."

"Yeah." I sighed. "I suppose. I do love the boots, though."

The black leather was soft, climbing well over my knee and up the thigh, and they made my legs look fantastic. More importantly, I'd be able to jury-rig one of the leather straps to act as a holster for my tiny pink North American Arms Guardian .32. At four and a half inches in length, the casual observer would assume it was a toy gun, but they would be mistaken. It wouldn't drop a deer, but it would definitely be a fight ender in close quarters. My father had given it to me as a present for my senior prom. He'd had it custom made to match my prom dress. It might be the most thoughtful gift I'd ever received. Bobbie's dad had given her an equally sentimental gift—a tiny canister of Mace, disguised as a tube of lipstick. We were so badass. If my dad could see me now, he'd be so proud. Horrified, but proud. Dads should never see their daughters in side-snap G-strings.

Bobbie had some bodies to tend to, so she left me to my homework. I sat in front of the couch with my file box and a glass of Bailey's. I had a special cocktail for every occasion, but the captain of my heart was, and always would be, tequila. Tonight, however, was a comfort night, and that meant something sweet and creamy.

I fished some files out of the box and began sifting. Double Down was the name of the strip club where Jimmy had taken his last breath of recycled air. It was one of the more exclusive strip clubs in the city. Translation: very expensive dancers, very expensive VIP rooms, and a very discreet staff. You paid for discretion, and Double Down was discreet with a double D. Visiting dignitaries spent good taxpayer dollars there, along with the local businessmen and the odd celebrity. You never heard stories, which meant that secrecy was paramount at Double Down.

The crime scene photos weren't pretty. Dead people don't photograph well. It's like all of a sudden they stop hiding their bad angles and disguising their bad habits, and you're just left with the truth. And let me tell you something—the truth isn't everything it's cracked up to be. Jimmy was no exception to this rule. He'd been sitting at a table with a bottle of scotch in front of him when he'd been popped between the eyes with a .38. He looked surprised in the photo, as if someone had just wished him a happy birthday six months early. I suppose when you think about it, most people would look surprised if they were staring down the barrel of a .38.

The autopsy and toxicology report would normally take up to a week to get back, but Bobbie said she'd put a rush on it. Oh, yeah, besides being my very best friend in the whole world, Bobbie was the chief coroner for our charming little city. We had been quite the team when we were kids. I killed things, and she pulled them apart and studied them. We'd called her Frisbee "the slab." Now we called her slab "the Frisbee." Full circle.

There were a lot of players to get acquainted with, so I used the photos to make myself a little Polonco family tree on my living room floor. Jimmy had been the eldest of five siblings, at forty-seven years old. He had two brothers— Giovanni, forty-four, and Lorenzo, thirty-eight. Giovanni was cute in a thuggish kind of way, but Lorenzo was in a league all his own. He looked more like an Armani model than a gangster. Maybe it was the perfectly chiseled cheekbones, or the full lips. Or maybe it was the fact that every photo showed him on the verge of a smile. Whatever it was, it was good. He was popular with the ladies, it seemed. Every photo showed a different woman on his arm, all of them magazine-cover beautiful, tall and skinny, with that gaunt, hungry look brought on by purposeful food deprivation. I took another swig of my Bailey's, savoring the sweet taste.

I'd never be supermodel skinny, but then again, they'd never be able to wash clothes on their abdomens or break a man's nose with a flying spin kick. I considered that a checkmark in the win column for me.

All in all, it was an attractive family, but Jimmy had been the only one of the sons to get married. I blame *The Sopranos* for making marriage to mobsters look so unappetizing. In the photographs, Jimmy's wife, Leora, was a hard-looking woman, not at all like the woman I met today, softened by grief. Of all the photos, there was only one that had captured her smiling, and to be honest, it could just as easily have been a sneer. I was more than willing to overlook her sour personality, though. The pressure she was putting on the police department to find her husband's killer was the one and only reason behind my promotion. I preferred to look at Leora Polonco as a grouchy fairy godmother.

Of the surviving siblings, Lorenzo was the only one who was local. He'd moved here years ago to help Jimmy run his various businesses, but Giovanni had stayed in Chicago to help his father, Enzo, run his criminal empire. The sisters, Gina and Lorraine, were both married with children and living in Florida, so I doubted they were involved.

There were a lot of uncles, courtesy uncles, and cousins in the picture, too. I read the jacket on every one of them, researched their businesses, and inspected their credit ratings. I even Googled them to study their dating preferences and social activities. I wanted to know everything.

The Polonco family had their fingers in a lot of pots — gambling, nightclubs, restaurants, protection companies, limo services, and a host of other fishy-sounding enterprises. I was willing to bet that some of the companies were shells for drug running and money laundering.

When I'd gleaned all the information I was going to glean, I dragged myself up the stairs for bed. Didn't want to look tired and make a bad impression at my new stripper job.

Chapter Three

The next morning, Chief Thompson had already made himself at home inside Captain Rye's office. The door was slightly ajar, and he was leaning back in his chair studying a thick report, the fingers of his right hand laced through the handle of a coffee mug. My heart raced for a second, wondering if I'd mistimed my arrival, but the wall clock said 7:54 a.m., and so did my cell phone. I was six minutes early.

I heard Captain Rye round the corner at the end of the long corridor. He had a big black gym bag in one hand, and he balanced a big brown plastic coffee mug, which he had obviously filled too full, in the other. He was giving all of his concentration to the ugly brown mug, shuffling along at a snail's pace in an attempt to stop the seesaw tide of coffee from sloshing its way over the rim. It wasn't working. He looked up in irritation as his navy pants took a hit. When he saw me, it was as if I had magically reached out and pushed his invisible dickhead-reset button. He set his shoulders back and his jaw forward and continued toward me in what he probably fantasized was an intimidating march. To me, though, with his arms jutting out at right angles from his bulky torso, and his simian architecture accentuated by his clunky gait, he looked like a big stuffed ape that I'd gotten as a Christmas gift from my weird uncle Joe one year. I'd never liked that thing.

Chief Thompson's voice pulled me from my thoughts. "Detective Jones, come in," he said quietly. I glanced down the hallway again at the rapidly approaching Captain Rye, and stepped inside. "Shut the door, will you?" I reached back with my foot and tapped the door shut. Bad timing. I heard plastic make contact with the glass pane of the door.

"Shit! Jones!"

I turned around. Captain Rye was red faced and scowling, and a big coffee stain about the size of Australia covered his front. Chief Thompson walked over to the door, opened it, and stood in the doorway, blocking Captain Rye from entering. "Captain," he said. "We'll be a couple of hours." He eyeballed Captain Rye's now empty coffee mug. "Was that fresh coffee? I'll take one, if you don't mind." He turned to me. "Detective, you want a coffee?"

Captain Rye's face flushed purple, and the angry look on his face told me that for the good of my health I most definitely did not want coffee. "No, thanks," I said, looking down at the floor, pretending not to notice the pissing match.

"Just one then. Black. And a muffin, if you find any." He shut the door, dismissing the captain like a bratty child, and turned his attention to me. "Have a seat, Jones."

If I hadn't already accomplished it, this last interaction had sealed it. I had made an enemy out of Captain Rye. I would be a fool to expect any support from him or his boys on this assignment. Nothing would make him happier than my screwing up this case. There was no way in hell I was going to give him that satisfaction.

I sat down across from the chief and waited for him to speak. He had a serious look on his face, and I wasn't sure if it was his natural expression or if he was really worried.

"Are you sure you're okay with this assignment, Jones?" he asked finally. "There's no shame in walking away from it."

"Trust me, I couldn't be more sure. If I have to direct traffic at one more concert or respond to one more stolen bicycle report, I might kill myself, and everyone within a five-mile radius."

He raised his eyebrows in surprise, although I'm not sure if he was surprised that I had been relegated to such menial duties or that I was threatening to off us both by sheer virtue of geography, or that I kinda, really, definitely didn't look like I was kidding. "Well, we wouldn't want that," he said quietly, a quizzical expression on his face.

I'd seen that look before, many times, in fact. I knew I wasn't the type of woman people expected to see in a police uniform. At five-six, I was petite by police standards, although I did have an athletic frame. I was also blessed in the genetics department, with perky boobs, good skin, wide-set brown eyes, a small upturned nose, and full lips. A lot of men didn't care to look beyond that, and I could tell that Chief Thompson hadn't. Until now.

I gave him a smile, hoping that it was telegraphing the fact that I wasn't a complete nut job, and waited for him to continue. He gave me a fairly grim smile in return and pulled a couple of worksheets from the folder. "When we put someone in undercover, we need to create an identity."

"You mean a stripper name?"

"Among other things," he replied. "We need a backstory, a name, that kind of thing. Sometimes we need to provide our UCs with a different address, credit cards, but I don't think that's going to be necessary here."

We spent the better half of the morning working on my cover story. I picked Brandi as a stage name. Brandi had been the name of one of my roommates in college, and I'd always thought it would make an excellent stripper name. Plus, I knew it was a name I could remember, even if I got nervous. When you needed to lie, it was best to add just a little truth, because it made it easier to keep your story straight. I picked Hammer for a last name, in honor of Jennifer Hammer, the town slut from my high school, or as my mother and I liked to call her, the town philanthropist. That sounded classier. Of course, her charitable donations to mankind consisted mostly of blowjobs, but never mind. And come on…Brandi Hammer? What a cool-sounding stripper name!

On the uncool side, the department had issued me an '87 Camaro as part of my undercover disguise. It was a piece of crap from the police impound. Bright red, checkered with rust spots, and full of dents. Handing over the keys to my pretty black Jeep in exchange for that junker felt like a betrayal, but the chief assured me my Jeep would be safe in the impound lot until I could retrieve it. I wasn't sure the same could be said for me, though. Even if by some miracle the bucket of bolts managed to get me to work, I had serious doubts as to whether or not it would have the strength to get me back home again. Back in the eighties, it had probably been a real panty remover for some mullet-wearing, pimply teenager, but the decades had not been kind to this poor Camaro.

I guess I must be a pretty shitty stripper if that's all I could afford, I thought to myself. At least I'd probably be able to pull off that part of my cover story.

We also decided that I would be Canadian. It would make sense that I would want to be paid in cash under the table, no paperwork. Also, Bobbie and I had spent many summers up in Toronto when we were teenagers—some second cousin connection that I never fully understood—so I knew a lot about the city if I were pressed for details. And let's face it, if you were trying to gain the trust of people, what better way than by telling everyone you're Canadian? Well, Canadian or Swiss, but I'm terrible with accents. My accents always tend to sound like the drunk version of its bordering country. Besides, everyone knows that Canadians are trustworthy, gentle, safe, benign—great qualities for strippers.

It was just before noon when the chief dismissed me to get ready for my new assignment. He handed me a card with his direct line and his cell phone number, and we agreed to touch base every morning at ten, unless there was urgent news to report.

I picked my way carefully through the station toward impound, listening for any sounds of Captain Rye. He was a buzzkill I didn't need to encounter again today. I whizzed through all the paperwork, traded my Jeep for the hideous Camaro, and headed home to get ready for my grand stripper debut.

Chapter Four

The sky was just beginning to darken as I chugged and sputtered my way to the late Jimmy Polonco's strip club in my "new" car. The poor Camaro was in worse shape than I had originally thought, its ripped vinyl interior having absorbed the funk of nearly three decades of teenage boy secretions. The effect, amplified by the car's lack of air-conditioning and the late summer heat, was that of driving inside a sweaty can of tuna, only not as pleasant.

I pulled into the parking lot of Double Down. The big fuchsia neon sign loomed high over the building, making it visible to the cars passing by on the freeway. It featured two boobacious girls on their knees, clutching onto a big pole. Double Down. Hmm. Naive me. I had once thought it was a blackjack reference.

I circled around to the employee entrance at the back and turned off the motor. Dancers never used the front door. I guess management didn't want the girls to be harassed on their way in and out of the club. Or maybe they didn't want the patrons to see them in broad daylight. Either way, the back door suited me just fine. I was banking on the fact that the back door wouldn't have a metal detector and a bouncer like the front entrance. I wouldn't want to have to explain a gun and a knife on my first day.

I took a deep breath to muster my courage. "Be bold and mighty forces will come to your aid," I muttered on the exhale, as I kicked open the door to my shitty Camaro. It was a quote I'd found in an old *Cosmo* magazine when I was a teenager. For some reason it stayed with me all these years.

I repeated my mantra a few more times as I picked my way through the parking lot in the thick evening air, and by the time I reached the door, I was feeling like a badass again. I was ready to turn on the red light! I was feeling inspired. "Roxanne!" I belted out. "You don't have to put on the red light." Sting had somehow managed to make the whole harlotry thing sound sexy, but then again, he probably hadn't approached it from the employee entrance. I was about to launch into the chorus when the back door to Double Down opened, bringing me face-to-face with the very handsome, very amused-looking Lorenzo Polonco.

Standing in the doorway, lit by the magic light of the setting sun, he looked dreamy, like a movie star—an airbrushed one, in an impeccably tailored suit. His hair was dark brown and thick, perfectly tousled, as if he had just taken a walk on the beach, and there was a hint of a five o'clock shadow darkening his ridiculously square jaw. He was tall, too—well over six feet, and broad in a way that suggested he hit the gym on a regular basis. He was also *way* more handsome in person than he was in his photos. I looked down at my ripped-up jeans and white T-shirt, feeling suddenly under-dressed. Bobbie had actually predicted that this would happen, that one day I would meet some gorgeous stranger, and he would see me dressed like a street urchin and run in the other direction. I watched him discreetly clock the pink plastic sheriff's badge that Bobbie had pinned to my overstuffed bag. It said "Deputy Hotpants" on it. Awesome.

"Do I get to hear the rest of the song?" he asked.

A warm flush began to creep its way up my neck toward my cheeks. I would rather chew off my arms and legs than sing "Roxanne" to the handsome Lorenzo Polonco.

"I think I'll exercise my right to remain silent," I mumbled, an embarrassed smile pulling at the corners of my mouth.

"Really?"

I bobbed my head up and down. "Yup. Pretty sure that's my best move right now."

A slow, sexy smile spread across Lorenzo's face. "Well, only a fool would argue with Deputy Hotpants," he said. Oh, the irony. "Are you here on official business then?"

"Yes, sir. Reporting for duty."

Lorenzo raised his eyebrows.

"Amateur night," I said, opening up my bag to show him my costume.

"Ah, I see. Well, Deputy…" He paused for me to supply my name.

"Brandi," I said, inwardly cringing as it rolled weirdly off my tongue.

"Brandi. I hope you have a good night." He stood to the side, holding the door open for me to enter. "Maybe having a deputy in the lineup will help keep the fellas in line tonight."

I laughed. "Or maybe I'll lose my nerve and spend the night writing up fashion citations by the buffet."

"You'd be doing us a service," he said, laughing. "And just an FYI, I don't think strip clubs have had buffets since the fifties. I'd hate for you to be disappointed." Seeing me safely inside, he gave me a friendly, "Good night," and, still chuckling, strode out into the parking lot.

I watched him walk away, half hoping he would turn around, until the door finally shut with a soft thud. Damn, I hadn't been expecting that. My research had told me he'd be attractive, but it hadn't prepared me for whatever *that* was. A lone drop of sweat trickled its way down past my cleavage to find refuge in my belly button. Lorenzo Polonco had made me sweat. But I didn't have time to think about that. I had a job to do. I released the breath I hadn't realized I'd been holding and turned to take in my surroundings.

I'm not sure what I had been expecting—some dark, sexy antechamber, a mysterious hallway, dramatic lighting. I guess I'd been expecting anything besides stepping directly into the kitchen. Nothing like overhead fluorescents and the smell of frying meat to make a girl feel sexy. At least no alarms had gone off, no metal detectors. No burly gate-keeper to frisk me.

The kitchen staff looked tired and bored, barely looking up to register my presence. There were three men working in the kitchen, one cooking and two cleaning. The door to the walk-in freezer flew open beside me, spilling a gust of cold air out into the hot room, and a big hairy guy in a paper hat emerged carrying a bin of some kind of meat. He stopped short, looking a little startled when he saw me, not that I blamed him. I had been a little startled myself when

I saw the hair/makeup job that Bobbie did on me. She had called it pageant chic, which was French for "big hair and tons o' makeup."

"You lost?" he asked.

"Kind of," I said with a smile. "It's my first night. Can you point me to the dressing room?"

"No problem." He set down his load, rubbed his hands quickly down the front of his generously stained apron, and extended a meaty hand. "I'm Roger."

I slapped my hand into his and gave it a good, firm shake. First rule of Stripperdom — be nice and make friends, especially with the rest of the staff.

"Nice to meet you, Roger. I'm Brandi." I gave the air a little sniff. "Damn, it smells good in here. Whatcha cookin'?"

"Well, I whipped up a little roast beef and new potatoes for a special." He leaned in conspiratorially. "If you're good, I'll save some for you back here in the kitchen."

"You better be careful, Roger. You start feeding me, you won't be able to get rid of me." I was flirting shamelessly, but Roger didn't seem to mind.

"I don't think I'd get sick of seeing your face, sweetheart." He was grinning from ear to ear. I had an ally in the kitchen.

"Well, I guess I'd better get ready. I'd hate to get fired on my first day."

"No. We wouldn't want that at all. That would be a terrible thing. Follow me."

He led me through the kitchen and out into a dark narrow hallway with two more doors. The bass was pounding against the wall, and I could faintly hear the DJ announcing the next act. Shit. I was really doing this.

"That's the door into the club, and down there's the

change room," Roger said, pointing to the shiny black door at the end of the hall. "Nobody's allowed back here that doesn't work here, but sometimes the customers get a little carried away and try to follow the girls. Now if that happens, you just yell and I'll come and take care of him."

He gave me a big fatherly grin and a pat on the shoulder, which helped calm my nerves a little. I'd bet a month's salary he had teenage daughters. I liked him immediately.

"Thanks, Roger. I appreciate it," I said, heading off toward the dressing room. "Now get back to the kitchen! If I find lumps in my gravy tonight, I'm gonna put you over my knee." I could hear him chuckle as I pushed open the door to the dressing room.

It was a dark room, painted in high-gloss black with chrome fixtures and a big, shiny chandelier. Two of the walls were completely mirrored and outfitted with vanity stations and movie-star lights. There were at least two dozen girls, all in varying states of dress and undress, fixing themselves up for work. I hadn't realized that amateur night would be such a big draw.

The amateurs were easy to spot. They were the ones who were excited to be there, giggling and nervous, as if the thought of teetering into a bar full of men and showing them their boobs was the be-all and end-all. Most of the newbies looked more like they were dressed for a day at the beach than a shift at Double Down. You could get away with a bikini and short shorts if you were just trying out, I suppose. I bet a third of the girls would be too overcome with nerves to actually get up on stage, and another third would be too drunk by the end of the night to even finish their shift. The other third would either have found their calling or would be enrolling in night school tomorrow. These were not the girls I needed to get to know.

I was looking for the lifers, the girls who were here every night, raking in as much money as they could before gravity took hold of their goodies and put them out of work. These girls would look bored, and maybe a little pissed that their space had been invaded by a bunch of fresh-scrubbed neophytes looking for a thrill. I spotted six lifers. One looked like a queen-size bitch. No need to go there unless I had to. One was wiping furiously at her nose, the flecks of white powder curiously eluding her tissue. Her spiky blond hair looked fun and playful, but years of booze and drugs had taken a toll on her face. I doubted she'd be much help, either. Two more were leaning into each other, whispering and laughing. I might get to know them later. Then I spotted a tired-looking redhead, rifling through her purse for something.

"Anyone got a spare ponytail?" she called out, her head still buried in her purse.

I fished my hairbrush out of my bag and unwrapped two elastics from the handle. "It's your lucky day," I said, dropping them onto the counter.

"That's great. Thank you. I'm always losing these stupid things."

"I know. Me too. That's why I always carry tons. You never know when you'll need one."

I sat down on the stool next to her, pulled out my makeup bag, and started adding more eyeliner to Bobbie's masterpiece. What had looked like a ton of makeup in my bathroom suddenly looked conservative next to these girls. "They make me wanna stab myself in the eye," I said low, pointing at the newbies with my eyeliner pencil.

"Ugh. I know!" she replied, gluing on a strip of false eyelashes. "I hate being here on amateur night. I just really need the money."

"Yeah, I know what you mean." I turned my attention back to the mirror. "I'm Brandi, by the way."

She chuckled. "That's funny. I'm Sandy, and that piece of work behind you is Candy."

The spiky blond cokehead whipped her head around. "What? What did you say?"

"This is Brandi. Sandy, Brandi, and Candy. Get it?"

From the blank look on Candy's face, I could tell she really didn't get it.

"It rhymes," said Sandy. Still nothing. "Never mind." She turned back to her makeup and rolled her eyes. "Wait till you see her in a couple of hours."

"Sloppy?" I asked.

"More like zombie apocalypse."

I pulled the little bits of costume out of my bag and started to get dressed. I had an ex-boyfriend with a lingerie fetish, so my undergarments were kinda spectacular. I had decided to go with my lucky push-up bra. It was black and lacy, lined with a deep scarlet satin. The push-up was quite… pushy, turning my full B cups into generous C cups. My cop top was a tiny sleeveless blouse with little snap buttons that ended just underneath my boobs, leaving my stomach bare. I didn't mind, though—my stomach was my best feature, flat and lean, with the outlines of a six-pack, the by-product of years of running and kickboxing.

I slipped the tiny skirt over my tiny matching thong, and pulled the soft leather boots up and over the knee, adjusting my hidden gun so it didn't dig in. I stared at myself in the mirror. Not half bad. If I were a guy, I'd probably want to see me naked. At the very least, I think I had managed not to look like one of the newbies. I could see Sandy looking at me out of the corner of her eye.

"This your first night? I've never seen you here before."

I answered her as I hiked up my boobs to sit even higher in the cups. "Yeah. The last place didn't work out. The manager was a real perv, so I thought I'd come and check out this place. I wanted to come on amateur night so I could get a feel of the place without committing to anything. You know what I mean?"

"I suppose," said Sandy, "but to tell you the truth, I've only ever worked here. Been here for three years."

"Wow. They must treat you really well."

She gave me a little smile that I couldn't quite interpret. "I guess. And I finally made it upstairs to the VIP, which is where the real money is. You don't give that up if you don't have to."

I gave a theatrical sigh. "Bummer. You won't be schlepping it on the floor with me tonight then."

"Believe me, I wish you were upstairs with me. The girls up there are such bitches. I'd like to be able to enjoy one night with no drama."

Before I could respond, the dressing room door flew open, banging into the wall. I whipped around on my stool, my hand automatically reaching for my little pink Guardian. An overly tanned man stepped through the door with a big smile on his face.

"Knock-knock, ladies!"

Sandy rolled her eyes and turned back to the mirror. "Don't worry about him. He just likes to barge in every now and then to make sure nobody's doin' coke off the counter. Such a dick."

If I hadn't already known he was a dick, his little "knock-knock" maneuver would have tipped me off. Any guy who yells, "Knock-knock," after he's entered a women's dressing room earns instant dick status in my book.

"I can see that," I said, studying his face. He looked about fifty, with big bright perfect teeth, dressed head to toe in black. I recognized him as the club manager, Gary Baresco. He was on the cusp of greasy. "Slick" might be the word. He had more hair in the picture that I had studied—an old photo, I guess. Gary had been a police officer on the vice squad many years ago but quit due to a disciplinary dispute. According to the rumors, he and his partner had created quite a lucrative side business with several of the prostitutes they'd been watching. They denied it of course, but there was an avalanche of evidence against them. They were never convicted of wrongdoing, but once the media got hold of the story, the department had no choice but to put them on suspension. Turns out his forced "vacation" let him find his true calling, managing a strip joint.

"Nice to see so many sexy girls here tonight!" he said, rubbing his hands together as if he were about to dive into a plate of cookies. "I just wanna go over a few of the rules for all you newcomers. First, I'll be calling you up onto the side stage in groups of three, and there are three poles up there, so how 'bout that? Everybody gets her very own pole. The main stage is for the featured dancers, but maybe one day you'll earn your way up there."

I rolled my eyes. Yeah, that sounded like quite the promotion.

"Second," he said, "lap dances are twenty bucks a song. They don't touch you, but you can touch them. Everybody clear on that? Third, we don't go full bottomless here, okay? Panties stay on. That means you, Candy. Got it?"

I glanced over at Candy, who was slumped in her stool, giving him the finger. Classy.

"And last but not least," he yelled with enthusiasm, "let's have some fun out there, ladies! Now let's get a move on!" Gary thumped his clipboard with authority. "I need all my amateurs to sign in with me!"

There was a flurry of nervous chatter and squealing as the girls jostled for position in front of Gary.

"Give me your name for my list, then wait out there in the hall so I can take you all up together!" he yelled above the giggling herd.

I sprayed a coat of hairspray onto my extra-large hair, added a final layer of lip gloss, and bundled all my belongings into my bag.

"Well, Sandy, I guess I better get a move on. See ya later."

"Later," she said.

I shoved my bag into an open locker, made a mental note to bring a padlock with me next time, and joined the end of the line. Sara and Wendy, the last of the newbies, teetered past Gary and out the door. I stepped up to Gary and gave him a smile.

"Hi there."

"Hi yourself, sexy," he said. "What's your name?"

"Brandi. What's yours?"

He gave me a smile, as if the question had caught him off guard. "I'm Gary. I manage this place." He leaned in close, tracing his fingers down my arm. "Glad you came tonight.

I'm looking forward to watching you dance."

When his fingers reached my elbow, he gave a gentle squeeze and stepped back just a fraction, holding me in place to take in the entire view. His gaze lingered for a moment on my chest before he finished his inspection and brought his eyes back up to meet mine. I made a mental note to boil my arm when I got home. If any guy had looked at me like that on the street, I would have kicked him in the Scrabble tiles. But when in Rome... I swallowed my bile, and managed a smile. "Do I pass inspection?"

"With flying colors, babe."

"Then let's go!" I said, extricating myself from his damp grasp. I darted through the door in front of him, but I hadn't been quick enough to avoid a little pat on the ass. I cringed. Dickhead.

Chapter Five

The club was already bustling; men didn't wait until late at night to go to a strip club. The girls were always there, a lot of them would be wasted, and if you paid them money, they'd be nice to you. It was a good deal, really, much easier than going to a real nightclub, unless you actually wanted to take a girl home with you. That just didn't happen. Once a man puts away his wallet in a strip club, he becomes invisible.

The place was dimly lit, with those black lights that made everyone look super tanned. It made me feel somewhat better about the fact that I would be shaking my ass in front of a bunch of strangers. Mirrors lined most of the walls, making it easier for the men to ogle the dancers without the nuisance of having to turn their heads. Heavy swatches of burgundy fabric hung from the ceiling in strategic places, creating private areas for God knows what. The furniture was covered in red velvety baroque fabric, making it look regal somehow. It was what I imagined a New Orleans jazz club would look like, minus the naked women.

Gary parked us at the side of the stage and signaled to the DJ, and when the song was over, he hopped up onstage, and grabbed a microphone. "Good evening! I hope everyone is having a great time tonight."

There was a smattering of applause.

"I want to introduce our lineup of lovely amateurs for tonight. Please make these girls feel welcome. We do want them to come back. And remember, nothing says lovin' like money does, so let your wallet do the talking! Here they are. Ladies, come on up here and join me!"

He held out his hand for us to join him on stage, and the giggling procession wobbled its way up the steps, flocking to him like a bunch of baby chicks. The audience clapped and hooted for us, which was kind of them.

"Spread out, ladies. Don't be shy," Gary said encouragingly.

I'd been to enough cattle auctions as a child to know that you can't start bidding on a cow until you've seen the goods, so in the spirit of nabbing bad guys, I put some space between me and the other girls and gave a little twirl. The crowd showed its appreciation by whistling and making those strange grunting noises that only drunk boys who are faced with the possibility of seeing boobs can make. How sweet. I gave a little curtsy in appreciation.

"Whoo, whoo! Go Brandi!"

I looked out into the crowd, trying to see beyond the blinding stage lights, and saw Bobbie. Bless her heart. She was whistling and waving like a proud parent at her child's first dance recital. Momma maybe didn't realize she was probably going to get a lap dance.

Gary told me to get ready because I'd be going up in

the first group. *So much for easing into things*, I thought to myself, fighting a sudden urge to bolt. I had never tried approaching a stripper pole without at least two stiff drinks in my system. Bobbie and I had always pre-medicated for our pole-dancing classes. The pole just looked different to the sober eye. I swallowed my panic and scanned the room, zeroing in on a table of frat boys. God bless frat boys. They're so predictable. These boys were no exception—half in the bag and horny, with a row of shots lined up in front of them. I made a beeline over to their table and flopped down in the closest lap. "You boys drinking tequila?" The one whose lap I was occupying gave a huge grin.

"Hell, yeah! You want one?"

God, did I. I raised a shot glass for a toast. "Here's to seeing triple, sleeping double, and staying single!" I yelled. We threw back the tequila and cheered. There was a leftover shot on the table, so I picked that one up and put it back, too.

"I'm up first, boys. Wish me luck."

With that, I planted a big kiss on my frat boy's forehead, and headed back toward the stage. I could feel the tequila heating me up, feel the tingle spread outward from the center of my body to the tips of my fingers. God, I loved tequila. Bobbie and I call it "te-kill-ya," but tonight, it was my salvation.

Gary was purring my name into the microphone, which was my cue to come up onstage and join the other two girls for what would probably feel like the longest song in the history of recorded music.

I climbed the stairs, sending up a prayer to the patron saint of strippers that I wouldn't forget the routine I had learned in my pole-dancing class. As I reached my pole, a red stage light bounced off the chrome, highlighting a veritable cornucopia of smudges, smears, and prints. In mere moments, I'd be mashing my scantily clad body into that venereal stew. I stifled a gag.

Gary hopped off the stage and the music started up, "Pour Some Sugar on Me" by Def Leppard. Sweet relief! We had used this song in class. It was a classic stripper piece. I waited for the second big drum punch and launched myself onto the pole with enough momentum to send me in two complete circles. I touched down gently, wiggled around for a bit, using the pole as my personal back massager, then leaped onto the pole again, wrapping my legs around it this time and turning myself upside down. It was like riding a bike, only very different. Everything was going according to plan. I wiggled, twirled, and grinded my way through my workout/routine until I finished with a flourish, sweating, smiling, and winded. If only the music had ended at the same time, I would have been golden. *Shit!*

I looked around at the other two girls on stage with me. They were nervously shuffling their feet to the music, expressions of terror and excitement alternating across their faces. They seemed to be using their poles more for balance than anything, but what they lacked in technique, they definitely made up for in skin. They were both down to their panties. *Double shit.* I had been so deep in concentration that I had forgotten to take off any articles of clothing. Fantastic.

In my defense, we hadn't really covered the actual stripping part in our pole-dancing classes. I had half a mind to write a note to Lady Donna at the gym and tell her that my prized stripper diploma wasn't worth the cheap pink paper it was printed on. In the meantime, I still had one entire chorus left, and fleeing the stage didn't seem to be an option, so I fumbled at my buttons and yanked off my shirt. This brought a cheer from my frat boys, who had moved up to the edge of the stage for a closer look at their new friend. I tossed my cop top onto my frat boy's head and knelt down in front of him. He passed me another tequila shot, which I downed immediately. I ripped off my skirt, and, lacking a better idea, gave it a Tarzan swing over my head. This earned me another round of hoots and grunts, but I was in the weeds now.

The song was in its final stages, but I was starting to get cold feet about getting any more naked. I looked down at my frat boys, who were now lined up with rolled-up dollar bills between their teeth. Didn't take a brain surgeon to know that those George Washingtons were meant for me, so I swallowed the vestiges of my pride and crawled along the stage in front of them while they stuffed bills into my thong. There was probably a better way to collect, but thanks to Lady Donna's negligence, I'd never know. The song wailed to its conclusion, and I was saved. I blew my frat boys a big kiss, gathered my clothes, and sprinted off the stage to a chorus of claps and whistles.

The backstage area was shockingly cool after the lights of the stage. I took a deep breath and relaxed into the concrete wall, tuning out the giggles of the girls next to me. The bills were itchy against my skin, so I pulled them out and smoothed them into a tidy pile. Twenty-two bucks. Damn. That was the hardest twenty-two bucks I ever made. I probably would have made more if I'd shown my boobs, I thought regretfully. God, what was wrong with me? Badass detectives weren't supposed to worry about how much money they could stuff into their underwear. I needed to focus, get to work, and find a murderer, and none of that was going to be accomplished hiding back here, contemplating my bleak earning potential in the skin trade. I yanked my outfit back together and headed out onto the floor to find Bobbie.

Bobbie was on her feet clapping and whistling as I made my way over to her table. She looked fantastic as usual, in a tight slinky micromini dress. "That was great, honey! I'm so proud of you!" she said, giving me a big bear hug. "Take a load off!"

She pulled out a chair for me, and I dropped into it. "Yeah, I'm a superstar, all right. Made a whole twenty-two bucks." Bobbie had the good grace not to comment further. "Have you seen any murderers wandering around?" I asked.

"Sorry. My eye's only trained to spot dead guys. Drink? I seem to have acquired quite an assortment."

There were five drinks on the table, all of which were hers, none of which she'd had to pay for, I'm sure. People always felt compelled to keep Bobbie hydrated, and God bless her, she could hold her liquor as well as I could.

"I'll pass," I said. "I've already had three shots of tequila. It's probably harder to spot murderers when your head's in the toilet."

"Copy that," she said.

"Oh, before I forget, do you have my spare house key on you? I forgot to take it off my key chain at impound. I had to break into my own house today."

Bobbie fished through her purse and slid a key across the table. "Do you have a place to put this?"

"In my magic pocket," I answered, slipping the key into the tiny side pocket of my long leather boot.

I scanned the room for possible bad guys, ruling out the

men in pervert's row. Those were the ones sitting right in front, at the edge of the stage, looking for intimate details on the strippers. The thought made me cringe. I ruled out the frat boys and anyone else who had that glazed-over horny look. The drunkards were out, too, as well as the bachelor parties and birthday parties. That left…no one. Shit. I needed to check out the VIP rooms, but it had been made painfully clear that we had to "earn" our way up there. Whatever that meant. I could feel my shoulders slumping forward, my body already conceding defeat.

"He's not here," I said to Bobbie.

"Who's not here?"

"My murderer."

It's not like I was expecting to find the actual murderer. I'd have been happy with anyone involved in the crime. I was looking for someone brooding and mysterious, someone like the guy who just sat down at twelve o'clock on the opposite side of the stage. Where had he come from? He was wearing a hoodie, a baseball cap, and a mustache—three suspicious-looking items on one guy. Mustaches were especially suspicious on guys under forty-five, and this guy looked to be in his thirties. I squinted my eyes, trying to get a better look at him through the strobe lights. There was something familiar about him, his posture or his jawline, something. He caught my stare, registering something close to surprise, and quickly looked down. No way! I jumped to my feet. It was Detective Coleman.

"Bobbie, you better go. This is gonna get ugly."

I took the route that would block his exit to the door if he decided to bolt. Didn't matter anyway, because his reflexes were shitty, and I reached him quickly. Detective Coleman looked up at me and swallowed nervously, looking genuinely surprised that I'd seen through his clever baseball hat/mustache disguise. "What the hell are you doing?" he asked in a quiet voice.

"I could ask you the same question," I said, matching his flat tone. "Who told you I'd be here?"

He was so busted. Confusion flitted across his face as he culled the shallow furrows of his mind for a plausible excuse. Confusion was one of my favorite expressions on a man's face. It made them vulnerable, pliable. I dropped down into Coleman's lap, slipped my arms around his neck, and whispered into his ear. "You want me to give you a dance, Jay?"

He was speechless, and he held himself stock still, like a deer caught in headlights right before he makes his mad dash into oncoming traffic. I had never seen Jay at such a disadvantage, and it filled me with a terrible happiness.

"Why else would you be here if you didn't want to see me naked?" I brushed my lips against his earlobe, and felt his entire body tense.

"Are you drunk?" he asked.

"Yep," I said, lying. I leaned back with my arms still clasped around his neck and looked at his mouth like it was a big thick steak. He cleared his throat and licked his lips. I was making him nervous. How cute. I moved my glance down his body, stopping deliberately at his zipper. Apparently I was making him more than just nervous.

"I like it," I said, dragging my eyes away from his zipper. He gave a nervous chuckle. "You like what?"

"I like that you can't hide how you feel." I pulled back to look into his eyes again, playing my hand through the back of his hair. "Mmm. It's soft," I whispered.

His eyes widened, and I let out a laugh. "I meant your hair!" I looked down at his lap again. "Obviously I was talking about your hair."

It was Coleman's turn to laugh. His look of confusion was melting into something else.

"Let's make a deal," I whispered.

"Okay," he said roughly.

I took his hand in mine as if to shake it then brought it up to my lips. "I've been curious about you from the moment we met. The first time I saw you, I wondered what it would be like to kiss you. Every time I see you, it's all I can think about." I slowly ran my tongue between two of his fingers. "You know what I mean?"

"Yeah, I know what you mean," he said, his voice a husky whisper.

I pressed myself into him, trapping his hand between my chest and his, and brushed my lips against his ear. He held himself perfectly still, avoiding any unintentional nipple contact. Strange that he would pick this venue to act like a gentleman. Guess he saved his pig act for work. "What I want to do right now," I whispered, "is pretend that we don't work together." I pulled back to look into his green eyes and gave him a serious look. "You can't tell anybody at the station about this. Not anybody."

Coleman swallowed his breath. "I promise. I promise it'll stay between us."

A slow sexy song started, and I slid out of his lap to stand in front of him. I closed my eyes and let my hips move to

the music. I could still feel the warmth of the tequila coursing through my bloodstream, my liquid courage, and I ran
my hands slowly up the length of my body, grazing the sides
of my breasts with my fingers. I looked at him through my
mane of blond hair and started to undo the buttons on my
shirt. His eyes darted down to my fingers, then back up. I
wondered if he was conflicted or if he was checking to see
if I was bluffing. I undid my last button, letting my shirt fall
off my shoulders onto the floor. Bluffing is for poker. Now
I definitely had his attention. I leaned over him, resting my
hands on the arms of his chair, putting him at eye level with
my very expensive bra. "You like?" I asked.

I could feel his warm breath on my skin as he answered
me. "I do."

I lowered myself down into his lap again, this time with
my back against his chest. I could feel his heart speeding as
I melted my body into his, gently grinding myself into his
lap. I slowly arched my back, reaching my arms up to circle
his neck, and ran my fingers through his hair. I angled my
face so I could watch him as he snaked his eyes down my
outstretched body. I knew this was my best angle, so I let him
take his time. His eyes lingered on my breasts, probably wondering what they looked like out of the lingerie. I led his gaze
slowly down my stomach with my fingers, pausing at the top
of my skirt to play with the tiny ruffle, then slid a finger under
the fabric and pulled it away from my body, not enough for
him to see anything, but enough to make him wonder. "Do
you want to see what's under there?" I asked in a whisper.

"Yeah," he replied.

My fingers found the snap that would undo it, and I gave
it a little pull. The skirt spilled open, revealing my tiny lace

panties. His pulse sped up against my cheek, and I turned in to his neck, giving him a soft bite, which turned into a lingering kiss. I let my fingers play under the elastic of my panties.

"God, you're beautiful," he said softly into my hair.

I pushed myself harder into his lap. "You think so?"

"Yes." His voice was a raspy whisper.

For a fraction of a second, I let my guard slip, let my body respond to him. Between the tequila, the music, and the fact that I was grinding myself into the crotch of a handsome man, I figured I was entitled to at least a tiny bit of slack. Besides, this was pretend. I despised him. And, I rationalized to myself, I was working! One might even argue I was performing a public service. *Snap out of it!* I gave myself a mental shake. Flesh. It had always been my weakness.

I dragged myself out of his lap, giving him an eyeful of my backside, and turned in a slow circle until I was facing him again. He was white-knuckling his armrests in an attempt to keep his hands from reaching out to me. I smiled a catbird smile, enjoying the feeling of power, and leaned in to him, straddling him in his chair, grinding myself into the rough denim of his jeans. I kept the rhythm of the music with my hips, torturing myself against his zipper just a little. I leaned into him again, using my hair as a shield from prying eyes, and brought my mouth to his neck. I ran my tongue down the length of his carotid and sucked on the tender skin until he groaned. Then I raked my nails down his thigh until I reached my own ass, and grabbed a handful, squeezing as hard as I could.

"God, I want you to touch me," I whispered into his ear, locking his fingers into mine. "I want to feel you inside me." I drew his hand down my thigh, cupping it around my freshly squeezed cheek.

"What did you say?" He gave me a searching look, wondering if he'd imagined my last words.

"I said you're a pig." I gave him a sadistic smile.

The smile vanished from his face. "What?"

"You pig!" I screamed. "Get your hands off me!" I slapped his face with enough force to rattle his teeth, and reared back off him, leaving him stunned.

Two bouncers appeared out of nowhere, one of them grabbing Coleman by the collar and yanking him out of his chair, the other one coming to my side, his eyes wide with concern.

"Look what he did to me!" I cried out in my best damsel in distress voice, tears welling up in my eyes. I showed the gathering crowd the angry welt that was rising on my rump. I had done a real number on my ass. It looked like a big nasty paw print. "It's gonna leave a scar!"

Coleman's eyes were wide with shock as he eyed my injury. He hadn't seen that coming at all.

The bouncer grabbed him by his hood and his belt, and started dragging him to the door. "Come on, asshole! You're lucky I don't call the cops, hurting her like that."

"Wait!" I yelled, halting their progress toward the door. Coleman turned to me and heaved a sigh of relief. "He owes me money."

Coleman's look of utter disbelief filled me with a morbid satisfaction. He was truly shaken. His hands were trembling as he reached into his wallet and pulled out a twenty. I shook my head at the bouncer. Not enough. The bouncer thrust his meaty hands into Coleman's wallet himself and pulled out a wad of cash.

"This should cover it," he said, holding the money out to me.

I walked up to them, wiping the tears from my eyes, and took the money. There was a lot of it. Apparently I was getting a very generous tip for my exertions.

"One more thing." I reached out and ripped the fake mustache off his lip and got up in his face. "If you tell anybody about this," I hissed, "I'm going to tell everyone we know that you're hung like a light switch...Princess."

Coleman gave me such a look of hurt surprise that I almost felt bad. Almost. But the fact was, he had come in here to humiliate me. That had been a bad idea. And whoever had told Detective Jay Coleman I was going to be here was going to get an ass kicking, too.

Coleman was almost to the door when Candy spotted him. "Hey! Steve! What happened?" she asked as she ran over to him, trying to pry him out of the bouncer's grip. "Why are you guys throwing him out?"

"Don't worry about it, Candy," replied Coleman.

"Hey, you shaved off your mustache!"

"Just shut up, Candy, okay? Leave it alone." The bouncer dragged him the final few feet to the door and yanked it open.

"Wait!" yelled Candy. "Have you seen Amber? She didn't show up for work today, and she's not answering her phone." Before he could answer, he was hustled out the door and tossed onto the sidewalk.

Holy shit, I thought to myself. They know him here. He's a bloody regular. He wears a fake mustache and goes by a fake name. And who the hell is Amber? I would have to get to the bottom of it later. Meantime, I had attracted quite a crowd with my little drama, not the least of whom was my friend Roger from the kitchen, who figured I might need a piece of cake to make me feel better. He was right about that. Cake made everything feel better. The two bouncers were back, and concerned about my injuries. Seems they admired the way I handled my aggressive "customer." Gary, the manager, on the other hand, looked less than pleased. A flock of newbies had also gathered around, offering comfort and admiration for my apparent bravery. Lorenzo Polonco chose that moment to glide back into the club with his entourage.

"Did I miss something?" he asked coolly, taking in the activity.

"Some asshole got rough with Brandi here, but she clocked him one," said my new bouncer friend. "Ripped his mustache off, too. It was so cool."

At the mention of my name, Lorenzo turned his full attention to me. Somehow he'd managed to become even more handsome in the last two hours. He had a presence about him that commanded respect, and made people want to stare at him, me included. *Animal magnetism*, I thought to myself. "Are you hurt, Brandi?" he asked, his voice low and buttery.

"I'll be okay," I answered. "I'll have a few bruises, I suppose, but it could have been worse." I looked into his eyes, which were a deep chocolate brown and full of sparkle and mischief. I was surprised to find concern there, too, and it made me feel suddenly shy.

He gave me a gentle smile. "May I see your injuries?"

Logically I knew that I was in a strip club, surrounded by nearly naked women, and not five minutes ago, I'd been grinding myself into Detective Coleman's lap like a champ. But for some reason, the last thing I wanted to do right now was to show this man my bruised bits.

"It's my bum," I mumbled into his expensive necktie. "It's probably all purple now."

He cupped my chin with his fingers, lifting my face gently so I could meet his twinkling eyes, then with a serious voice he said, "I'm very sorry you hurt your bum."

The corners of his mouth were twitching in an effort to keep a straight face, making it impossible for me not to smile. "All in the line of duty."

"Ah yes. Deputy Hotpants." He leaned in conspiratorially. "No offense, but you're really terrible at keeping the peace."

I nodded in agreement. "I knew I should have hunkered down at the buffet. You should always trust your gut, huh?"

"Yes, you should," said Lorenzo. "Look, I know for some reason you were really hoping to get a buffet out of this, but would you like to join me for dinner upstairs instead?"

Hmm. This was a pickle. On one hand, I did need to check out the VIP area, but on the other hand, I'd just had a traumatic experience and wasn't sure how much more strippering I'd be able to handle for one evening. There was also the issue of boundaries upstairs. That's where the even more morally ambiguous stuff happened.

My face must have betrayed my thoughts, because Lorenzo said, "Just dinner. Scout's honor. I've had the worst two days of my life, and it looks like your day hasn't been a real picnic, either. What do you say?" To highlight his good intentions, he took his jacket off and slipped it over my shoulders. "You can even bring your cake."

I looked down and realized that I was still clinging to my piece of cake. No surprise there. "I better ask Gary."

"Don't worry about Gary. This is my bar, not his, and I say you've just been given the night off."

Chapter Six

The upstairs looked much the same as the downstairs, with the exception of the clientele. Rich guys just dress differently. Downstairs catered to the jeans, T-shirt, and running shoe crowd. Upstairs it was all silk shirts, custom-made suits, and soft leather shoes. Lorenzo definitely belonged upstairs. His suit, part of which I was wearing, was a midnight-blue silk Versace that probably cost more than what I made in a month. He'd paired it with a bluish-purple silk shirt and navy tie. I buried my face into the collar of his jacket and took a deep breath.

"Oh my God. This smells so good." His cologne was amazing—earthy and expensive, yet manly. "If you tell me it's not cologne, and it's just the way you smell, I might pee my pants."

He gave me a playful smile as he guided me to a quiet booth. "I'll make things easier on both of us then, and tell you that it's just my cologne. But I'm glad you like it."

I scanned the club as I slid into the booth. Sandy was entertaining an accountant, I assumed, on the other side of the room. He looked like he had enough money to blow on women, but not enough to spend on an expensive briefcase. There was no one else up here that I recognized, no one from my thick file. I did, however, spot the murder table. You could tell the chair had been replaced; it was the same fabric, only newer, unworn.

"What's your drink?" asked Lorenzo, drawing my attention away from the room and back to him.

"Ah, sadly you don't have my drink here," I said.

"Really? I find that hard to believe. What is this mysterious drink of yours?"

"It's only mysterious here in the States. In Canada it's almost a national treasure."

"Is that so?" he asked with mock surprise. "Then I must have one." He caught the bartender's eye and flagged her over. "Let's get to the bottom of this."

The bartender, a beautiful, busty brunette in a tight little black dress, sashayed over to the table, working her hips like a champ. If the show was for Lorenzo, it was lost on him, because for some reason he was focusing all of his attention on me. I had to give him kudos for resisting. If I were a guy, I would have felt compelled to take in the view. She fired me a nasty look, and leaned onto the table in front of Lorenzo. "Hey, Lorenzo, what can I get for you? Your usual?" It was obvious what she wanted to give him—a heaping helping of her DDs.

"Well, Catherine, my friend Brandi would like to know if you can make her an extra-special cocktail."

"I'd be thrilled," she replied with a thinly veiled sneer.

Yikes. Even if she could make it, I would be too afraid to drink anything she served me. Sitting with Lorenzo had landed me on her shit list. Or maybe her natural expression just made it look like she had a mouth full of piss. Either way, it didn't inspire a lot of confidence. "Can you make a Caesar?" I asked with an extra dose of sweetness.

"You mean a salad?" she asked, countering my sweetness with venom.

"No." I'd given her a chance to be nice, but she didn't take it. I turned my body away from her to face Lorenzo, casually resting my hand on his arm. I didn't need to look at her to know that she was shooting daggers into the back of my head, and that was fine with me.

"I have an idea," I said to Lorenzo. "If you have Clamato juice, I'll make 'em myself."

"Deal," he said with a smile as I started out of the booth. Catherine, not realizing that she'd been dismissed, had no choice but to skitter out of the way.

"Thanks anyway, Cathy," I said, and headed to the bar. It was so fun to mess with the bitchy ones.

I rimmed a couple of highball glasses with lemon juice then dipped each glass into celery salt. I scooped ice into each glass, and reached for the vodka. "Do you have a preference?" I asked.

"The good stuff," he said, pulling a bottle of Clamato from the fridge and giving it a healthy shake.

"Of course." I plucked a bottle of Belvedere from the shelf and free-poured into the glasses. "Spicy?"

"Of course," he said.

I shook Tabasco and Worcestershire into the vodka, added the Clamato juice, gave it a little stir and handed him the magic elixir.

"You've done this before," he said.

"Yeah. I used to bartend up in Toronto." Not a total lie. I had bartended my way through college, just not in Toronto.

"Lucky for us," he said, raising his glass. "A toast...to Canadians and their strange cocktails."

"Hey, check yourself," I said, raising my glass to touch his. "You Americans gave us Honey Boo Boo." It took him a moment to stop chuckling, but eventually he took a drink.

"Oh, wow, this is good," Lorenzo said once he could tear his lips away from the glass. "This is so much better than scotch. I want about a dozen of these, then I might actually start feeling like a human being again."

"Wow! A dozen," I said. "That's serious. We'd better sit at the bar then." I placed the necessary ingredients on top of the bar and settled into a bar stool. "So who goes first?" I asked him earnestly.

Lorenzo looked a little puzzled. "What do you mean?"

"Well, when you're drinking your pain away, you have to lay it all out on the table. That way you can leave it there when you're done. It's kind of like therapy, but with booze, which makes it way better. So...what's your damage?"

"Okay," he said tentatively. "I got a sixty-dollar parking ticket this afternoon."

Hmm. Not useful. It was barely even interesting. Maybe this wasn't going to be the most productive interview, but I was already invested and after my copious shots of tequila I couldn't imagine trying to follow another lead this evening, so I plowed on. *Lead by example*, I thought to myself. *Ah, Mother, you'd be proud.* I took a healthy swig and laid out one of my grievances. "All right. My turn. Tonight I showed a bunch of frat boys my boobs for money. Twenty-two dollars, to be exact."

He met my grimace with a sympathetic nod. "That's not good."

"Nope. Your turn."

Lorenzo smiled, getting into it. "Okay, yesterday my cleaning lady dropped an open bottle of Pine-Sol on my laptop, which was also lying on top of my backup memory drives. Gone," he said. "All of it."

"That sucks!" I reached for the vodka and starting mixing another round. "Well, today my dog rolled in shit, but I didn't discover this until he'd already taken a nap on my bed. And unlike some people, I don't have a cleaning lady. How's that for shitty luck?" That wasn't a total lie, either. When I was ten my dog Daisy pulled just such a stunt on my brand-new flowered comforter. I was getting altogether too good at this half-lying maneuver.

"Two nights ago my brother was murdered."

I stopped mid-stir and looked into his face. He looked so sad all of a sudden, like a little lost boy, and I felt a twinge of guilt at my act of deception.

"Oh my God," I said. "I'm so sorry. That's awful. Do they know who did it?"

He shook his head no.

"Were you two close?"

"Yeah, we were," he said. "I don't know how much you know about my family…" He paused, giving me a questioning look. I shrugged my shoulders, letting him know that I was a blank slate, and he continued. "Most of my family is still in Chicago, where I'm from. And let's just say they're very… connected, if you know what I mean. They're old-school the way they do business, you know?"

I did know. "Connected" was the polite society word for *Mob*. "I think I get what you mean," I said.

Not seeing any judgment on my face, he continued. "My brother Jimmy and I moved out here because we wanted to get away from all that. Start businesses that were legit. Get away from that life where you're always looking over your shoulder, everybody either afraid of you or out to get you. And we were doing it, too. But now…" He trailed off, suddenly aware that he'd been confiding in a perfect stranger.

"Now you're worried about what your family will do?" I asked.

"I don't know," he said, taking a deep breath. "Enzo washed his hands of us a long time ago. I have no idea what he makes of all this."

I raised my eyebrows. "Enzo?"

"My father. We've always called him Enzo, even when we were little kids. He thought it sounded more professional, with the family business and all." He shook his head. "Jimmy was the only real family I had." He paused, deciding how much more he was going to share. "And that's my shitty luck." He rubbed his hands on his trousers, as if to wash his hands of the conversation, and just like that, confession was over.

There was a moment of awkward silence as Lorenzo contemplated his tragic family, and I contemplated the handsome Lorenzo. He seemed genuinely devastated at losing his brother, and while that didn't make him innocent, it certainly didn't put him at the top of my suspect list (impressive, since my suspect list was quite empty).

I pushed another cocktail in front of him. "You definitely

win. I was going to whine about my bruised ass some more, but somehow that pales in comparison to losing a brother."

"Hey," he said taking my hand. "Thanks for listening. And I really am sorry about your night. That's not something a lady should have to endure."

"Oh, yeah, I'm quite the lady," I said with a laugh. His brown eyes held such sincerity that I had to look down. "I guess I kind of asked for it, though, right? I mean, it's not like I was expecting unicorns and rainbows when I signed up for amateur night."

Lorenzo rubbed his thumb reassuringly over my knuckles. Damn, he was good.

"If you don't mind my asking, why did you sign up for amateur night? The whole stripping thing doesn't really seem like you."

"It's not," I said, taking a swig of my cocktail. "But I don't have my working papers, so I need to make my money under the table. Tonight was my first time trying the stripping thing. Unfortunately, what they teach you at the gym doesn't really translate that well in the real world."

He gave me an incredulous look. "So, you got up there on stage and did…"

"A workout routine," I said, cutting him off. "Yeah, pretty much."

Lorenzo dropped his head, and his shoulders started to shake.

"I can't believe you're laughing at me!" I said with mock indignation.

"I'm sorry," he said, wiping tears away from his eyes. "It just feels so good to laugh right now." He pulled my hand up to his lips and gave it a chaste kiss. "Please don't be mad."

Of course I couldn't be mad, looking at his handsome face, seeing the tension draining away. He suddenly looked years younger, and I gave him a big grin. "It's okay. You look good when you laugh, and I think you needed it, even if it was at my expense." I looked down at his hand, which was still holding mine. "Can I be honest with you?"

"Please," he answered, his smile turning curious.

"Well, I hope you don't mind me saying, but this whole strip club thing doesn't really seem like you, either."

Lorenzo cast a look around the room and nodded his head ever so slightly. "You know the first thing they teach you in business school? They teach you to invest your money in recession-proof business."

"And strip clubs are recession-proof?"

"Strip clubs and casinos," he said. "When times are good, men turn to women and gambling. And when times are bad, they turn to women and gambling even more. Either way, they both cash in on the arrogance and ignorance of men. And in an oil town, as I'm sure you've noticed, there's no shortage of arrogant and ignorant men."

"True story," I said.

"Having said that, you're right. Before Jimmy died, I was running the casino. I was never very involved with the day-to-day operations of Double Down. This place was always Jimmy's deal. I guess I never really felt comfortable here." He smiled, giving my hand a gentle squeeze.

"Until tonight."

It was an unexpected compliment, and I felt it take root somewhere south of my waistband and work itself up to my face. I couldn't help but smile. Before I could embarrass my-self with an awkward response, Sandy appeared at the bar looking for Catherine. Crisis averted. Thank God. Or shit. Either one.

"Great," she muttered to herself, "where the hell is she this time?"

"You okay, Sandy?" I asked.

"Oh!" she said with surprise. "I didn't expect to see you up here, but it's nice to see a friendly face."

"What do you need, Sandy?" asked Lorenzo.

"I need a drink for my customer," she replied.

"No problem," I said, hopping off my stool. I smoothed down my skirt, feeling very grateful not to be a boy at this moment. "What can I make for ya?"

"Really? I need a Manhattan."

"Not a problem. I can make those in my sleep." I fixed her cocktail and handed it to her.

"Thanks, Brandi."

"You got it." Two thirsty customers seeing signs of life behind the bar hustled up with drink requests. I smiled at Lorenzo, who was watching me with amusement. "What can I get for you gentlemen?"

When the rush was over, I climbed back onto my bar stool.

"Please tell me you can come back and bartend for me tomorrow night," Lorenzo asked. "I can pay you under the table, and the tips are good up here."

"I noticed," I said, holding up the wad of bills that had been left for me on the bar. "Good thing I didn't try to show them my boobs."

Lorenzo laughed. "I'm sure they're lovely."

"They are."

"So how about it? Do I have a new bartender? And

you'd have your weekends free," he added. "Our weekend bartender's pretty good. She actually shows up and tends bar, if you can imagine."

I laughed. "How novel! What about Catherine, though?" I asked, feigning concern.

"She's probably passed out in a booth somewhere. Doesn't usually make it past eleven, from what I hear. I have no idea why Jimmy kept her on." I had a pretty good idea, but I kept it to myself. "So what do you say?"

This was a fantastic turn of events. I'd be able to snoop around *and* keep my clothes on. "I'm in," I said smiling up at him. "And thank you."

"No. Thank you," he said holding my gaze, and I was suddenly aware of his leg touching mine, and his long fingers holding onto my hand, and his soft chocolate eyes staring at my mouth like it was dessert. I wasn't really known for my impulse control, and under any other circumstances I probably would have let myself be swept away in the moment, but I was working now. I was Kevin bloody Costner in *The Bodyguard*. I had to get out of there before I acted on my animal instincts, or before he acted on his. God forbid.

Chapter Seven

I woke up (alone, thank God) to a warm beam of sunlight that had filtered its way through my curtains to spill across my bedspread. I hadn't gone with a traditional girlie theme in my bedroom. After all, I wasn't exactly a girlie kind of girl. I'd painted the walls a beautiful leaf-green color that matched almost perfectly to the leaves of the huge maple tree outside the window.

My bed had been made from an old, intricately carved Moroccan bench that I found at an estate sale. My carpenter/friend Carl had taken it apart and reconfigured the beautiful dark wood into a gorgeous king-size bed that had to be anchored into the wall with huge screws. This had raised a few eyebrows, but what are you going to do? If you can't stand the screws, stay out of the bedroom. That's what I always say...now.

I'd even found a beautiful Louisville Slugger in the same deep rich wood tone to stand in an equally elegant umbrella stand beside my bed. This was my dad's idea. Actually, he wanted me to sleep with a .22 under my pillow. The baseball bat was our compromise. At his urging, I also installed a security system in the house. One of the control panels was mounted beside the front door, while the second one was mounted beside my bed. I had argued with my dad on this one. It didn't exactly match the serene decor of the bedroom, but I'd learned to pick my battles. And if I were to be completely honest, the security system did make me feel more secure when I went to bed at night, like a watchdog that I didn't have to feed.

The duvet cover and the rest of the fixings were all in shades of off-white, feminine enough to be pretty, but not so girlie as to scare away potential visitors. Besides, if my visitors were there to check out the decor, I was bringing home the wrong visitors.

I padded downstairs to my cheerful kitchen, put the coffee on, poured myself a bowl of Raisin Bran, and stood eating it over the sink, looking out the window. No neighbors. I still had to get used to that. I poured myself a cup of coffee, milky and sweet, and headed outside with the phone, letting the screen door slam shut behind me.

The warm morning air felt like magic on my skin. I loved August. Loved being able to take my morning coffee out onto the veranda in my T-shirt and underwear. The only thing standing between me and utter serenity was my memory of last night. I was still tingly from my non-date with the handsome Lorenzo Polonco. Just the thought of him sent shivers through my body. Wow, did I need to get my act together! It wasn't like I was a stranger to lusty behavior and poor judgment, but I usually managed to keep it free of my work environment. Bobbie would give me a free pass. She'd assign some hormonal explanation to my behavior and blame everything on science—something to do with the way female animals seek out dominant males when they're in heat. Hmm…I had been acting a little Animal Planet last night, from my lap dance with Jay, my archenemy, to my near miss with Lorenzo, an honest-to-God reformed mobster. If I'd been some jungle creature, I would have had a go at both of them and thought nothing of it. As it was, I silently cursed all of those perfectly placed chromosomes that made me a full card-carrying, top-of-the-food chain, guilt-feeling human woman.

Murder waits for no one, though, and animal needs aside, I had a crime to solve. My new status as undercover detective on nights got me out of the tedious morning briefing, meaning there would be no confrontation with Detective Coleman this morning. I was more than a little relieved. The thought of seeing him after what had transpired last night made prickles of sweat appear at the base of my skull. No animal instincts at work there. Still, the cop in me wanted answers from him. I wanted to know why he'd been at Double Down last night. Why did they know him there? Why did he go by an assumed name? I'd get answers, all right. They just might not be from Jay.

I had agreed to check in with Chief Thompson at ten o'clock for a progress report. I would have given my right arm to be able to reveal the killer's identity. As it was, I had made at least some progress, so I dialed his direct line and waited.

"This is Thompson," he barked into the phone.

"Hey, Chief. Jones here."

"Oh, good morning, Detective. I thought you were somebody else." His tone lightened and he continued. "How, uh…how did it go last night?" he asked.

"Well, it was pretty productive. I've been promoted to night bartender in the VIP area, and my new best friend is Lorenzo Polonco. Not bad for one night's work. Oh, and I made twenty-two bucks. I'm keeping that, by the way."

"Oh, yeah, of course." He paused awkwardly, then said, "You earned that fair and square."

"Another thing," I said, "now that I have you on the line. I'm wondering who else might have known about my being at Double Down last night?"

"Nobody except the people who were in the room with us when you got the, uh, promotion," he said. "Why?"

"Just wondering." I decided to keep Jay's presence at the club to myself. Tattling on a fellow cop was a sure way to get oneself blackballed at the station. You needed to be really certain of wrongdoing before you went mucking around with a fellow cop's career, and unfortunately, being a grade-A asshole didn't fall under the umbrella of wrongdoing. Besides, after the way I handled him last night, I was betting Jay would keep quiet about the whole thing, too. "Anything else I need to know?" I asked, changing the subject.

"I'll let you know when we learn anything new. Touch base tomorrow, same time. Got it?"

"Got it, Chief." A soft click on the line let me know Chief Thompson had moved on to other business, which was exactly what I wanted to do.

I pressed one on my speed dial and waited for Bobbie to pick up.

"Cassidy Jones! Tell me everything!" she yelled into the

phone. "Last I saw, you were dry humping that dude with the mustache!"

I told her all the events of the previous evening, with embarrassing detail, and when she finally stopped laughing, I asked if she'd found out anything interesting from Jimmy Polonco's autopsy. She assured me that I would be her first telephone call when she got the lab results back, and we signed off.

There wasn't much I'd be able to do until I got back into the club that night, so I decided to go for a run to clear my mind. I pulled on a pair of black running shorts, a white tank top, and some running shoes, then hit the road. Running had always been like a tranquilizer for me. When I was a kid with an unexplained sleeping disorder, I would regularly abandon my bed for the open road at two in the morning. It was my thinking time. I'd put my brain on autopilot and let my feet decide where to take me. Every now and then my dad or Bobbie's dad would drive by in their patrol car. "You need a ride?" they'd always ask. "Nah. Just getting some exercise," I'd always answer. It had been comforting to know there was someone out there looking out for me, but it was equally comforting to know I was trusted to look after myself.

Today my feet were taking me on a familiar route through the reservation, toward the city. I knew these roads like the back of my hand. They were gravel, packed down hard after years of use. It was a money thing, I supposed, why they had never been paved, but I liked the dirt and gravel. It was softer on the joints and didn't give off that horrible tar smell in the hot summer months.

I passed by the swimming hole where Bobbie and I had learned how to swim as kids. There was a lesson underway.

Six intrepid youngsters had made their way out into the deep part of the river and were treading water between the boat launch and the floating dock, their little heads bobbing up and down, trying not to swallow water. One terrified kid was clinging to the side of the boat launch wall, wailing. Poor little guy. That was my friend Marvin twenty years ago. Nothing could get him off the wall, either, not the name-calling or the bloodsuckers that would attach themselves to Marvin's white belly every week. Some people just weren't meant for deep water.

I ran past the reservation school. It looked dark and empty and unkempt. They weren't wasting any precious re-sources on maintenance during the summer months. When we were kids, Bobbie and I would visit the playground at night to play *Charlie's Angels*. Every now and then we would coerce another little girl to come and be our third angel, but usually there were only the two of us. My brother, Butch, would come out and be Charlie for us sometimes, although in retrospect he would probably rather have been angel number three. My parents had named us Butch and Cassidy in honor of my dad's favorite movie. My mother, ever the practical one, had put her foot down and gotten her tubes tied after I was born, for fear that their third child would be named Sundance. Fair enough.

I sailed past George Bloodgood's house. It was dark and empty looking, too, with a FOR SALE sign out on the front lawn. That was very strange. As tribe elder, where would George have gone? I couldn't imagine he would have left the reservation, since he and Jimmy Polonco were the co-founders of the Polonco Casino that sat on George's ances-tral land. What impact, I wondered, would Jimmy's death have on George? On the casino? Would he be happy or sad at his passing?

I jogged by the Polonco Casino on my way out of the reservation, and wondered if George had ever been angered by the fact that the casino bore Jimmy's last name and not his. I continued on into the city, through the cookie-cutter subdivisions into the city proper, finally realizing that my feet were guiding me toward Bobbie's lab. Surely she would have found out something by now. Besides, I had already covered about eight miles on my run, and I wanted a ride back home.

I hustled into the building and bypassed the usual security process with a wave to the guard. I was a regular fixture here, not to mention the fact that it would be hard to smuggle anything interesting into the lab in my scanty outfit. It was just past noon, so I went straight to Bobbie's office. She was double tasking as usual, pushing a sandwich into her mouth with her left hand and entering data into her computer with her right. When she saw me, she stopped typing and flagged me over with the other half of her sandwich. She knew when a girl needed a snack.

"Listen to this," she said, wiping her mouth with a napkin. "Wow! You're sweaty. Anyway, so we know Jimmy was shot, right? Well, get this." She leaned in conspiratorially with her autopsy photos. "I thought he smelled a little…sour when he came in."

I wrinkled up my nose. I'd seen Bobbie do the sniff test on her corpses before, and it made me want to retch.

"Oh, stop it," she said, giving me an elbow in the ribs. "I decided to do a little swab, and I found traces of vomit on his chin and clothes. Weird, right?"

"If you say so."

"Well, let's just say getting shot in the forehead doesn't make you vomit. It just makes you dead. So I did a little digging, and it turns out Jimmy had been poisoned before he was shot. Isn't that crazy? Someone poisoned his scotch."

That *was* crazy. Either someone had wanted to make sure he was really, really extra dead, or there were two people out there who had wanted him dead. "Was he already dead when he got shot?" I asked through a mouthful of egg salad.

"Nope. There was only a small trace of vomit on him. I'd have to say that he had just begun to feel the effects of the poison. He was probably sitting there coughing and choking, wondering why the hell his throat was closing up."

"Prints on the bottle?"

"Just Jimmy's."

"What was the poison?"

"Cyanide, which was an excellent choice. Flavorless, colorless. He wouldn't have known until it was too late."

We sat in silence for a moment. "I need a ride."

B obbie loved blasting the air-conditioning in her white Escalade. She wasn't a big fan of sweating. I, on the other hand, was a huge fan of oppressive heat. I pointed all the vents on my side toward Bobbie and opened the window, letting the hot air rush over my face. "Turn left here," I said.

Bobbie threw me an inquisitive look. "I thought I was taking you home," she said.

"You are, after we visit Detective Coleman's house."

Bobbie giggled with excitement. "Detective Dry Hump?

Awesome! I love a road trip!"

"I'm never going to live that down, am I?"

"Nope."

"You mean, not until you do something stupider."

"Is that possible?" she asked.

I chuckled. We both knew that it was more than possible. It was only a matter of time.

I guided her turn by turn to Jay's house. I'd accessed his information from Bobbie's crime lab computer and printed out a map. Jay lived in a blandly nice suburban subdivision, the kind that boasts three different house styles and two different brick options.

"Don't you think it would be creepy to live in the exact same house as all of your neighbors?" asked Bobbie, wrinkling her nose at the thought. "I mean, can you imagine coming home drunk, wandering into the wrong house, and ending up in a stranger's bed?"

I would have pointed out that we did occasionally drink too much and wind up in a stranger's bed, but I let it slide, my mind on other matters. "I wonder if his neighbors have any idea that he likes to sit in dark strip bars wearing a fake mustache."

"Probably not," said Bobbie.

We turned off Birch Street onto Beech Street and cruised to a stop in front of Jay's house. "Here it is. Number eighteen." We sat looking at the house for a minute.

"What are we looking for?" asked Bobbie.

"I don't know." More silence. "Do you think I should go look inside?"

"Oh my God, yes!" cried Bobbie. "Oh, wait!" She whipped off her sunglasses and thrust them into my hands.

"You have to wear these. You need a disguise."

I looked at the glamorous, white-framed, oversize Chanel sunglasses in my hands and chuckled.

"Yeah, I should blend in nicely with these," I said flipping down the visor to take a look in the mirror. They looked ridiculous with my running attire, but what the hell? I'd just spent the last ten minutes with my sweaty head hanging out the window, catching wind like a Saint Bernard. My hair was an unmitigated disaster. I was going to look like a crazy person with or without the damned glasses.

I climbed out of Bobbie's SUV and the hot humid air closed in around me instantly. It was like wading into a massive bowl of hot Jell-O. I looked around to see if any neighbors were out being nosy, but it was too hot for any sane person to be outside if they didn't have to be. I made my way up the walkway and climbed the steps to the front door. There was a window beside it, but it was frosted and didn't let me get a good look inside. None of the shadows inside were moving, which was a good sign, but that's all I could tell.

There were several potted plants on the stoop in varying states of death and decrepitude. Would he be that stupid? I lifted one of them. Nothing. Then the next and the next. Nope, not stupid enough to leave a key. *Shit.* A swipe across the top of the doorframe yielded nothing but dirt. *Double shit.* If there were neighbors keeping watch, their curiosity would be piqued by my behavior, so I made a show of knocking on the door. *Nothing to see here. I'm not trying to break in*, I telegraphed to any possible onlookers.

I hopped off the steps, trying to look as nonchalant as possible, and trotted around to the side of the house. I peeked through the kitchen window, expecting to see a messy tornado of bachelor living, but I was surprised to see that it was very neat and tidy. Dishes, presumably from this morning, one bowl and one mug, had been washed and left to dry on a tea towel beside the sink. Hmm. Breakfast for one. Not that I cared, but it appeared that Jay shared my love for Raisin Bran. I made my way around into the backyard and peeked into his bedroom. It was a masculine room, with a huge wooden bed and a matching dresser. The door to his walk-in closet was open, giving me a partial view of his wardrobe. Wooden hangers. How very evolved of him. On his bedside table were two alarm clocks. His late-night habits were obviously making it hard for him to get out of bed in the morning. There was also a glass of water, a handful of change, a tube of Chapstick, and a VIP card for the Polonco Casino.

I jiggled the window to see if I'd be able to get it open. A loud *rrrouuufffff!* brought a startled scream from my lips as a huge German shepherd bounded out of the walk-in closet and ran toward me. I leaped away from the window as he launched himself up against the glass, barking and drooling, showing me his big white fangs. There would be no exploring Jay's house today, not with Cujo at home, but at least I had another tidbit of information to think about. Jay was a regular at Double Down, *and* a VIP at the Polonco Casino. No way was that a coincidence.

By the time I arrived home I was in a major funk, and it had nothing to do with the fact that I'd screamed like a little girl when Jay's big bad German shepherd lunged at me. He had just been doing his job. I couldn't fault him for that. No, there was something else behind my black mood, but I couldn't quite pinpoint the exact emotion I was feeling, or even the precise reason behind it.

I reached into the freezer and pulled out a little tub of comfort. Some people call it chocolate gelato. I fished a clean spoon out of the dishwasher and played back the events of the day in my mind. Somehow I had been able to wrap my head around the fact that Jimmy had been shot. Poisoning, though—that was so premeditated. Unpredictable, too. Jimmy could have easily shared that bottle with six of his closest friends. He could have used it to send drinks out to his VIP customers. Lorenzo could have joined his brother for a drink at the end of the night and been left choking on his own vomit in the dark empty bar, too. Hell, someone could have poisoned the bottle of vodka we'd polished off last night and I'd be a goner as well. I guess what was bothering me was my feeling of powerlessness. It was one thing to be attacked and given a chance to defend yourself, or at least to know who was the instrument of your demise, but to be struck down by some unknown element…well, that was just plain cowardly. I was pissed off. That was it. I just hadn't recognized the emotion because it was covered in a layer of fear. Scared and pissed off. What a combo.

I took my gelato into the living room and pored over the crime scene photos again, inwardly chastising myself for not being more thorough the first time. Nothing was going to get past me this time around, though.

The scotch wasn't a label I was familiar with. I punched it into my computer and found that it was a very premium bottle of thirty-year-old Springfield single malt, with a price tag of about seven hundred dollars. I made a mental note to check the scotch menu at the club tonight. If the expensive Springfield scotch was on the menu, chances were the culprit was a staff member, or at least a part of Jimmy's inner circle. If not, I was back at ground zero. It could have been from Jimmy's private stash, or who knows where else?

I examined a close-up photo of the scotch bottle. The back lighting from the bar lights showed the water line on the bottle to be just below the neck—a new bottle, minus one generous pour. If it had been a freshly opened new bottle, chances are there would have been a plastic security wrapper around the cap. I riffled through more of the pictures, and there it was by his shoe. At least it looked like a plastic seal.

I sat back against the couch. The fact that the security wrapper on the bottle was still intact meant that whoever had poisoned the scotch had not done it at the bar. Someone had gone to great lengths to pull this off. They would have had to reglue the cap and redress the security wrapper. The prints had been wiped from the bottle after this procedure, but there was a remote possibility of finding a print on the inside of the wrapper, and only one person's prints would be inside the security seal—the person who had tried to poison Jimmy Polonco.

My mind was racing with possibilities. Had they bagged the plastic security wrapper along with the bottle? Bobbie hadn't mentioned anything about it. She would have had time to make it back to the lab by now, so I pressed one on my speed dial and waited for her to pick up.

"What's up, Chuck?"

"Did they bag you a plastic security wrapper? Like from a bottle of scotch?"

"I'm actually looking at the inventory list right now, and I don't see one on there. Why do you ask?"

"Because there's one in the photo. Shit. I have to get to the club. See ya." I hung up without saying good-bye, but Bobbie wouldn't have cared. Good friends are like that. Besides, I didn't have time for extraneous words. I had to get myself tarted up for work.

Chapter Eight

The parking lot for Double Down was almost empty when I pulled in. Lorenzo's brand-new black Maserati wasn't there, not that I expected it to be this early in the day. Still, I felt a twinge of disappointment and wondered what he was up to at this very moment. Wherever he was, he was probably wearing something cashmere that I'd want to rub up against. Nah, in this heat he was probably wearing something lightweight, like linen or raw silk. He probably smelled like a million bucks, too.

The creaky groan of my rusty car door opening ended my musing on the matter. Just as well Lorenzo wasn't around. The fewer witnesses to my horrible rust-pocked Camaro, the better. It stood out like a postapocalyptic blight on the landscape. Camaros and cockroaches, I thought to myself, would probably be the only things to survive the apocalypse. I probably looked a little Mad Max myself. I had poured myself into a pair of tight black leather pants and topped it with a skimpy white tank top that showed off my well-defined arms, and thanks to yet another magical bra, a fairly bountiful chest. My tall leather boots kept my little gun hidden but handy, and my hair was blown out into a voluminous blond cloud. All in all, I felt like quite the badass. I hoisted my purse over my shoulder and headed inside.

I was really early for my shift. It was just after five and I wasn't scheduled until seven, but I didn't want to risk a cleaning crew coming in and sweeping up my evidence if they hadn't done it already. If anyone asked I would tell them I wanted to familiarize myself with the menu and the computer, which wasn't a total lie. I stepped into the kitchen and gave Roger a big smile. "Hey good-lookin! Whatcha got cookin'?"

Roger gave me a surprised look. "Oh, hey, Brandi! Didn't recognize you without all the uh…" He circled his face with his fingers to indicate that he had been talking about my war paint.

"Ah, yes," I said with a smile. "Turns out I'm better suited to bartending than…the other stuff."

"I'm glad," he said, giving me a fatherly hug. "I'll have dinner for ya whenever you want it."

"You're a good man, Roger. I don't care what everybody else says about you."

Roger chuckled and gave me a playful slap with a tea towel. "Cheeky," he said with a laugh.

I hightailed it upstairs to the VIP area. It was empty at this time of day. I imagined the high rollers would be getting off work right about now and heading to business dinners. In a couple of hours, they'd come rolling in looking for comfort.

The day bartender was behind the bar cutting up limes.

She had long white-blond hair and white-blond eyebrows and pale white skin. Her dark eyeliner stood out in shocking contrast, forcing your attention to her eyes, which were a glacier blue. If I believed in such things, I would have thought she was the human reincarnation of a wild husky.

I headed over to introduce myself. "Hi! I'm Brandi. The new night bartender."

"What's up? I'm Tara. I'd shake your hand, but…" She held up her knife and her juice-covered hand. "My hands are kind of full."

"No worries," I said. "I just came in early to get up to speed. I won't get in your way."

"That's cool. Let me know if you have any questions."

"Thanks, Tara." I swiveled around on my stool so I could see the murder table. It had been a couple of days since Jimmy's murder. What was the likelihood of finding a plastic security seal after so much time had passed? Surely the cleaning crew had swept it up by now.

There were a bunch of candles sitting on the far end of the bar. "Those need to go out on the tables?" I asked, pointing.

"Yeah."

"I can do that if you'd like."

"Thanks," she said. "And if you could light them, too, that'd be great."

I loaded up a serving tray with candles and started distributing them throughout the room, but I needed Tara to leave so I could search under the murder table. I headed back to the bar for more candles and threw a big smile at her. She smiled back. Sweet. I gave her a little "Oh" and pointed at my tooth. "You got a little something," I said. That was enough. She thanked me, mumbled something about a damn blueberry muffin and scurried off to the ladies' room.

As soon as she rounded the corner out of sight I sprinted over to the murder table and dropped down to my hands and knees. The tacky pull of the carpet under my fingers let me know it had been a while since any great pains were taken to clean the rug. I thought of all the various bits of DNA I was inadvertently collecting on my own skin and stifled a gag. I'd been doing a lot of that lately. What a delicate flower I was becoming. I was about to abandon my search when I spotted it. Instead of vacuuming, the cleaning staff had obviously opted for kicking larger items of garbage into corners or under pieces of furniture. The piece of plastic I had been searching for had been wedged under the far side of the table, out of sight. I took it gingerly by the edges and worked it out from under the table leg.

"You okay?" Tara asked from right behind me.

I bolted upright in surprise, banging my head on the underside of the table. "Shit!" I yelled. "You scared me." I backed out from under the table, pocketing the plastic with one hand, and producing a matchbook with the other. "I dropped my matches."

Tara eyeballed me dubiously. "I wouldn't touch that carpet if there was a thousand-dollar bill down there. That's so gross."

I gave her a weak chuckle. "You didn't grow up with brothers, did you?" I looked at my sticky black hands and felt a churning in my stomach. "I better go wash these bad boys."

Afternoon triple-washing my hands and dousing them with hand sanitizer I pulled out my cell and texted Bobbie.

FOUND IT!

I gently pulled the plastic wrapper from the pocket of my black leather pants, careful to only touch the very edges, and held it up to the light. It was a little on the mangled side, but sure enough there were several prints on it. I slipped the evidence into a sandwich baggie I'd brought with me, buried it in my purse, and headed out into the bar. Damn! This whole detective thing was all right.

The rest of the evening went on without a hitch. Tara showed me the computer system and menu. Things hadn't changed much since my college bartending days. The Springfield scotch, I noticed, was not on the drink menu, meaning that someone had given the bottle to Jimmy. But who? Had it been a liquor vendor? A gift from someone?

I didn't have too much time to dwell on it once the bar filled up and Tara took her leave. There were lots of drinks to make and lots of people to chat to. Everyone was very nice to me, especially Sandy, who was starved for non-bitchy female interaction. Not surprisingly, Catherine was barely missed at all. Apparently sobriety, friendliness, and a basic knowledge of bartending had been missing at the upstairs bar for quite a while. I was chatting to a stocky businessman when one of the waitresses handed me an order that made me smile. A Caesar. I looked around to find Lorenzo watching me from "our" table, a cell phone pressed to his ear.

He held up two fingers. "Make it two," he mouthed, his lips settling into the faintest smile.

I finished the orders that were coming in then fixed two Caesars. I told the waitress I'd deliver them myself, and she shrugged her shoulders and wandered off.

"Hey, stranger!" I said, sliding into the booth beside him. He was wearing a summer-weight navy cashmere sweater and perfectly creased linen pants. Cashmere and linen—called it. I'm good. "Are you checking up on me?"

He smiled. "Something like that."

"Really? You're worried I've forgotten how to pour a draft?"

"Actually, I was more concerned about my customers," he said, taking in the room with a chuckle. "They're not really accustomed to being served drinks."

I laughed, too, looking proudly at my fed and watered customers. "Don't worry. They seem to be adjusting nicely."

"Yes, they do," Lorenzo said, turning his warm brown eyes back to me, his laugh settling into a brilliant smile.

I took a swig of my drink and contemplated the handsome Lorenzo Polonco. Every fiber of my carbon-based being wanted to flirt with this man. I was willing to operate on the theory that a little harmless flirting could actually be considered part of my job description—get close to the victim's family, get the inside track, blah, blah, blah. So what if the mere sight (let alone the fucking amazing scent) of him made me feel funny in my general blue jean area? I was more than capable of limiting my flirting to harmless banter. My years of athletics proved I had a disciplined side, and although I rarely applied it to my dealings with men, I was fully confident I could withstand Lorenzo's considerable charms. Just because I *wanted* to slip under the table and wrap my mouth around his business didn't mean I *had* to. A romantic (okay, sexual) entanglement would be stupid, with a capital STUPID! Unethical, too. He was my boss (sort of), and technically still a suspect. It would be crazy to do anything that might jeopardize my new promotion. I took another sip. Besides, he was grieving. What kind of predator chases a man who's grieving? Actually, I didn't have to look past the mirror to find that kind of predator. But still, this man was off-limits, and the list of reasons was longer than my arm.

Lorenzo's buttery voice brought me back to the room. "Seriously, though, how's your first night going, Brandi?"

"Well, I didn't show anyone my boobs, so everything seems to be running smoothly," I said. So much for not flirting.

"Is hiding your boobs the secret to your success?" he asked with a smirk.

"No, not all the time. You should see what a tank top and a good push-up bra gets you at Home Depot."

He raised his eyebrows questioningly.

"I once got an entire barbecue for free at Home Depot."

"Are you serious?" he asked.

"Totally serious."

"Wow," said Lorenzo, "that must have been some push-up bra."

I peered down the front of my tank top. "I think it was this one, actually."

"I would have given you more than a barbecue," he said, gently brushing a blond hair away from my face. His fingers lingered there for a moment, barely grazing my temple as he looked at me with that devilish smile of his.

A little jolt shuddered through my body, ending south

of my belt buckle. I crossed my legs, hoping to stifle the feeling, but who was I kidding? That never worked. It was a chemical thing, practically science! How was a girl to resist the indomitable pull of science?

Someone shouted, "Order up," from the bar, and I chuckled, breaking the tension. "Duty calls," I whispered, and slipped out of the booth. I took a long pull from my drink to fortify myself and floated back to the bar on unsteady legs. Damn, that man had an effect on me. He made me feel like an unspayed cat, all giddy and wild. I couldn't remember the last time a guy had made me feel like that. Don't get me wrong—I was a very active…dater, but most of the guys were more pleasant diversions than anything else, and some not even that. Certainly none recently had made me feel all goofy like this. I sighed. Might as well enjoy it while it lasted, because once the case was solved and Lorenzo found out I was a detective, the fairy tale would be over. I giggled at the irony. Of course my version of a fairy tale would be played out in a seedy strip club. Freud would have a field day with that one, but Freud could kiss my ass. He'd had the hots for his mom, for God's sake. Who was he to judge?

I had only just reinstalled myself behind the bar when Lorenzo walked up and leaned against it. "Can you make me another Caesar, Brandi?"

I grinned and reached behind me for the expensive vodka. "Are you having another rough day?"

"Not particularly," he answered. "I've got a friend joining me, and I thought she might want to try your house specialty."

I felt the heat rising in my cheeks. I was an idiot, a

presumptuous ass. He hadn't invited me over to join him for a drink. He'd been trying to order one for his date. Well, he was an ass, too, I thought unreasonably. We had bonded over that drink. That was *our* drink.

I had successfully summoned enough indignation to swamp my embarrassment. "That's what you get for hiring a Canadian," I said, trying to sound blasé. "You can't leave your drink on the table all unprotected like that."

"Duly noted."

Over his shoulder I spotted a beautiful woman with poker-straight auburn hair. She was tall and model thin, with milky-white skin that had probably never met the sun unprotected. She wore a stunning gold cocktail dress and a pair of delicate gold strappy sandals. Definitely not a Double Down employee. The kiss she gave him by way of greeting highlighted that fact, and I felt a little stab of something. Jealousy? No way in hell, I reassured myself. It's not like we were an item or anything. We had shared one good conversation. *One.* Besides, I knew he liked the ladies. I had an entire folder in my living room full of photos of the handsome Lorenzo squiring a stream of undernourished giraffe women to one event or another. I pushed the drink toward him and gratefully turned my attention to the drink orders that had accumulated.

"Thanks, Brandi," he said. "I'll see you at cash-out."

"Yup. You bet."

Jerk.

It was eleven thirty when the bar crowd finally began to thin. I had seen neither hide nor hair of stupid Lorenzo and his stupid date since he escorted her away to his office, drinks in hand. In fact, he probably had her ankles pinned behind her ears right this very moment, not that I cared. I was, however, in a terrible mood for some other mysterious and completely unrelated reason. I was feeling antsy and useless. I mean, unless the killer decided to come back and take a crack at Lorenzo while I was actually there working, I couldn't imagine solving the case from behind the bar. In skintight leather pants and a tank top. It was official. I was in a funk. But it had nothing to do with Lorenzo.

I didn't realize how hungry I was until Roger appeared at the bar with a tinfoil-covered plate of food.

"Room service!" he said with a smile, setting the plate down on the bar and climbing onto a stool.

"Roger, you magnificent beast. Let me buy you a drink! What's your poison?"

"I'll just have a ginger ale, Brandi. I don't do much drinking anymore."

"Gotcha." I gave him his drink and pulled out some cutlery. "What did you bring me?"

It smelled amazing, and my stomach gave a grumble of anticipation.

Roger smiled and pealed the tinfoil back. "I thought you'd like some grilled chicken and steamed veggies. You look like the healthy type."

"That's perfect. Thank you, Roger."

He set another little plate on the bar. "And a little piece of my homemade rhubarb pie."

"You're talkin' dirty to me. Rhubarb's my favorite, but

nobody makes it anymore."

Roger gave me a happy smile. "I know. My wife loves it, but none of my daughters do."

I'd been right about him having daughters. I found it hard to believe, though, that a cook like Roger had been unable to convince them of the virtues of rhubarb. I switched gears and asked him how things were going downstairs.

"It's been quite the memorable evening," he said. "Candy went a little crazy, and they had to send her home."

"What happened?" I asked. "She violated the no-panty law again?"

Roger chuckled. "I'm not a hundred percent sure what happened, but she had a big meltdown, and when I came out to check on her she was crying over her roommate and her boyfriend. She was high as a kite though, so she wasn't making much sense."

Once Roger left, I went around cleaning up tables and slicing limes for Tara's shift in the morning. By the time I was ready to cash out, the bar was spick-and-span. My years as a bartender in college were certainly coming in handy, even if my degree wasn't. I had even managed to shake my crappy mood, thanks to Roger. And pie. I was willing to cut myself some slack, and blame low blood sugar on my momentary lapse.

At two a.m., Lorenzo jogged up the stairs with a bunch of cocktail waitresses in tow. It was a pretty bedraggled bunch. Most of them looked wasted, the rest wilted. Seven hours slinging drinks in high heels will do that to you, I guess.

He approached the bar as I was wiping down the salt and pepper shakers. "Are you ready to cash out, Brandi?"

He had a warm smile on his face. Men were always

smiley after sex. If we'd been standing on the same side of the bar, I might have accidently punched him in the nuts. Instead, I gave him a polite smile. "You bet," I answered. It had come out frostier than I had intended.

He beckoned for me to come along as he led the girls down the hallway to his office. *It probably smells like boring sex right now*, I thought to myself. Whatever, I didn't care. I'd been wondering how I was going to get in there. It was the only part of the club I hadn't searched, and it was the one part of the club where I felt I might find answers. I grabbed my cash drawer and my purse and followed the girls down the long, narrow hallway. The first two doors were the restrooms. The next door, I had discovered earlier, opened into a small storage room/janitor's closet. Lorenzo and Jimmy's office was the last door on the left, right beside the emergency exit.

I half expected Lorenzo's skinny friend to be in there, napping in a state of postcoital bliss, but she was nowhere to be found, not that I cared. The office was almost exactly what I had expected, a veritable man cave, with a heavy wood desk, a sumptuous leather couch, and several club chairs, all in varying shades of cognac leather. A beautifully polished liquor cabinet stood in the corner, appointed with a select few bottles of premium liquor. I noticed with the tiniest bit of satisfaction that there was a bottle of Clamato juice on the foldout bar top next to a set of heavy lead-crystal glasses. They matched the glass that had held Jimmy's last drink, I noted to myself, which meant the bottle had probably started out here in the office.

There was art on the walls, prints of old *Time* magazine covers that had been expensively framed. There were also plaques and photos from various sports teams thanking the Poloncos for their generous support. It looked like a business trying to take the straight and narrow route.

I looked over to Lorenzo. One of the waitresses, obviously high, was dumping handfuls of crumpled receipts onto his desk. He looked up and caught my eye, mouthing, "I'm sorry," with an apologetic smile, and I couldn't help but smile in return. I didn't envy his job at the moment.

The other girls watched me dully from the couch as I continued my inspection of the office. Years of late nights and booze had taken their toll. I was probably older than all of them, but I felt like a fresh-scrubbed teenager in their presence.

Once the last girl had left, I put my cash drawer in front of Lorenzo and took a seat across the desk from him.

"How was your first night?" he asked.

"It was good." I would love to have stopped talking and played it cool, but unseeable forces compelled me to add, "And yours? Did you have fun tonight?" I winced, hoping it hadn't sounded as needy to his ear as it had to mine.

"No more than usual," he said, a curious expression on his face.

"I hope it's okay I haven't used any of my credit card receipts as gum wrappers," I said, lightening the mood.

He laughed. "You saw that?"

"It was hard to miss. She was wasted. I don't know how half of those girls made it to the end of their shift."

"I'm sure half of them didn't," he answered grimly. "Now do you see why I'm so happy you're here?"

"It's not these?" I asked, pointing to my boobs.

He grinned. "Human resources says I'm not allowed to comment."

As he worked through my receipts, I nonchalantly eyeballed the items on his desk. It was an organized clutter of paperwork—inventory lists, liquor orders, a scheduling book, a wooden tray filled with letters and other sundry items. My eye caught a little gift card poking out between two letters, the kind that comes stapled to a gift basket or a flower arrangement. The message was hidden beneath an envelope, but it was signed, *Love, Dad.*

That's strange, I thought to myself. Why would Lorenzo's estranged father send him a gift? Stranger still, why would he sign the note from "Dad"? From what Lorenzo had told me, he had always insisted on being called Enzo. I looked up to Lorenzo. He gave me a smile. I wanted that card. Something about it was fishy.

He finished counting out bills and put everything into a big cash envelope. "Just give me a second," he said as he swiveled his chair around. "I'm going to put this away." He knelt down in front of his wall safe and punched in a security code. I stood up pretending to stretch my legs and perched on the edge of the desk. When I was sure he wasn't looking I reached over, snatched the card, and slipped it into my purse. My purse was becoming a bloody forensics lab tonight. I'd feel better once I got everything to the lab. As it was, my heart was racing with nervous energy. I had no idea that petty thievery would be such a rush. Lord help me, I was fighting the urge to pinch his stapler, too, just to see if I could get away with it.

Lorenzo locked up the safe, spun the lock, and rounded the desk to stand in front of me, and the look he gave me did nothing to quiet the thudding in my chest.

"You did a great job tonight, Brandi."

"Well, it's not exactly brain surgery. Did your girlfriend enjoy her drink?"

"She's not my girlfriend."

"I see." I didn't know what else to say to that. Lorenzo was obviously a man who liked to play the field. I don't think I'd ever met anyone who could go toe-to-toe with me in the casual sex department, and I found it unnerving, somehow.

"She's a business associate."

"And do you kiss all your business associates like that?"

A curious expression settled on his face. "Are you jealous?"

He had hit the nail on the head, but there was no way I'd give him the satisfaction of knowing that. I looked down at my manicure. "You flatter yourself, Mr. Polonco."

A slow smile tugged at the corner of his mouth. He was enjoying our little sparring match. "She kissed me, Brandi. I didn't kiss her," he said, his voice low and silky. "If you must know, she's a restaurateur. We're breaking ground on a new restaurant next month. It's going to be fine dining, very upscale." He lowered his eyes for a moment, something dark clouding his lusty mood. "I don't want to attach my name to it. I don't want people to think it's...part of the family business, you know? And I don't want anyone to associate it with all this."

It was the first time I'd heard him express any kind of insecurity about his family and his businesses. I smiled, weirdly honored to be someone he felt he could confide in. He returned my smile, pushing all thoughts of business away as he ran his thumb along my jawline, gently tilting my chin with his long elegant fingers. The shame in his eyes had been replaced by something else, something animal.

"Are you finished being angry with me?"

His touch, his voice, his scent, the look in his eyes—I could feel my body respond to him. A clenching in the pit of my stomach spiraled outward like a warm tide, teasing its way downward to that pure pleasure spot below my belt. He knew. Without saying anything, he lifted me to my feet and lowered his head, brushing his lips against mine in the sweetest, lightest whisper of a kiss.

A part of me wanted to pull away, and not reward his teasing, but then his lips parted mine so expertly, so gently, and his tongue found mine, exploring, tasting. God, he was a good kisser. When he finally pulled away, it took me a moment to open my eyes.

He took my hand and laid a lingering kiss across my fingers. "I don't want you to forget about me over the weekend," he said with a grin.

"I'm sure you'll find a business associate to keep you company."

And then his smile was gone. He curled his fingers around the nape of my neck, pulling me to him roughly. "I won't." He crushed my lips with a longer, harder kiss that left me shivering for more. His fingers twisted through my hair, locking me in place so he could work his way down my neck, his tongue hot and wet against my skin. At the base of my neck he bit down softly, making me gasp. I was in trouble. He had my number. He pushed the strap of my tank top down over my shoulder and kissed the exposed skin as his other hand cupped my breast, raking his thumb across my nipple. It ached and tightened under his expert touch, coaxing a moan from my lips. I was losing control to this man. I couldn't afford to do that.

By some miracle I was able to pull away, although I knew I'd be tingling in my nether regions for days. "I have to go," I said with an unsteady whisper and kissed him one last time. "See you Monday."

I was in a lust-induced fog when I pushed through the doors of the kitchen out into the back parking lot. The hot night air did nothing to cool my desire to turn around and run back into Lorenzo's office. I leaned against the side of the building and tried to collect my thoughts. I could still taste him on my lips and smell him on my skin. It was like a chemical reaction with him. *Pheromones*, I thought to myself. *Fucking Animal Planet!* I had an itch that the woman in me desperately wanted Lorenzo to scratch. The cop in me, however, told me to go home and scratch it myself, so it was with a Herculean effort that I pushed myself off the wall and forced my body toward my car.

The unsteady *click-clicking* of shoes on the pavement behind me pulled me out of my reverie. I turned around to see Candy speeding toward me in a full-blown speed wobble. *Note to self—cocaine, stupidity, and stiletto heels don't mix.* All I wanted to do was get into my shitty car and go home and curl up in my big soft bed with a book and a big glass of wine, and maybe imagine what could have transpired with the hunky Lorenzo. Apparently, that would have to wait.

Candy teetered to a rolling stop in front of me, and without warning launched her purse in an unwieldy arc toward my head. Unlike Candy's, my reflexes had not been impaired by recreational pharmaceuticals, and I ducked her purse easily. My training took over immediately, guiding my fist unthinkingly, yet squarely, into her jaw. She dropped to the pavement like a sack of potatoes. *Oops.*

As a rule I didn't like to hit women, and a tiny part of me felt a little bad. But the other 99.9 percent of me felt completely justified and more than a little satisfied. Normally the woman in me wouldn't wait around for her would-be attacker to wake up and try her luck again, but the cop in me who won every single inner battle, it seemed, would not abandon an unconscious, scantily clad stripper in a deserted parking lot. Besides, I actually did want to talk to Candy and I felt fairly confident I could handle anything she could dish out. To avoid any further altercations, though, I fished my plastic slutty-cop handcuffs out of my purse and trussed her up like a game hen.

It didn't take long for Candy to regain consciousness—her version of consciousness, anyway. She shook her head groggily, trying desperately to focus. It took her several seconds, upon registering my presence, to piece together the recent events that had led to her sitting against the side of my car with a bloody lip and perhaps a mild concussion.

"Why'd you do that?" she asked through trembling lips, tears springing to her eyes. I was silent, so she asked again, "Why'd you do that?"

"Oh, shut up, Candy," I yelled at her. "You're a woman, for God's sake. You should know better than to attack another woman in a dark parking lot. Grow the hell up!" I was really pissed off. Candy at least had the decency to look ashamed. "You're lucky I didn't do worse. I get really pissed off when people mess with me!"

"I'm sorry," she mumbled.

I took a deep steadying breath and knelt down beside her. "You ready to talk?" I asked her calmly. She nodded her head, sniffling. "Can I take these off?" I asked, pointing to the plastic cuffs.

"Yeah," she said softly, all the fight having left her.

I pushed the little release button on the cuffs and set her free, then pulled a pack of tissues out of my purse, offering one to her. She took it and thanked me. Next I pulled out a chocolate bar, unwrapped it, broke it in two, and gave her half. She took that, too, and gave me a questioning look.

"Go on," I said taking a bite. "Chocolate's the second best thing you can put in your mouth after midnight."

This earned me a little giggle, and she took a tiny nibble. Then suddenly, real tears started rolling down her face. I eased myself down onto the ground beside her and let her cry, watching as huge sobs racked her thin body. When the tears finally stopped, I asked, "Why'd you do that?"

"That was my question," she said with a shaky laugh.

"Yeah, but you know why I hit you. I'm not quite sure why you tried to hit me, though." She looked down at the tissue in her hands that she had been nervously shredding.

"I'm sorry. I didn't mean to hit you," she said. I raised my eyebrows. Really? "I mean, I shouldn't have done that. It was stupid. It's just…ever since you got here things have been really bad. You got my boyfriend kicked out and I can't find Amber and I don't know what to do."

"That Steve guy is your boyfriend?"

"Yeah," she said looking away from me. "Sort of." She drew in a raggedy breath and continued. "He's my friend, and he's my best customer. But when he comes in here, he doesn't want me to dance for him, he just wants to talk and buy me drinks and he worries about me. Why would he do that if he didn't like me?"

If he's here for your sparkling conversation, he's either

*mentally deficient or he's pumping you for information, or
he's staking out the place.* None of these things I said aloud.
Instead, I said, "I don't know, Candy."

We sat in silence for a moment. "What's the deal with
this Amber chick? She's your roommate?"

"Sort of. She stays with me sometimes. She lives a ways
away from here, so sometimes she crashes at my place after
work. But I haven't seen her for two days."

"I take it that's unusual?"

"Yeah," she said, "even if we don't see each other at
work, we text each other all the time. She doesn't have any
family around. Just that guy she's been seeing, but he's busy
all the time. So we're kind of like sisters, you know?"

I did know. If Bobbie went MIA for two days, I'd be
swinging at strangers in parking lots, too. I knew I'd regret it
later, but my heart went out to her and I offered to help. "Do
you have a picture of Amber?" I asked.

"Of course," she said, fishing out her phone. "I have
tons." She pulled up her photos and scrolled down. "There,
that's us," she said, showing me the screen. "We took that on
our last night off."

The photo was a little grainy, but I could see enough
to tell that she was a beautiful, buxom brunette with striking green eyes, probably in her early twenties. A tattoo of
a crown sat proudly on her ample cleavage, with the words
"Fit for a King" stenciled in bright turquoise underneath. I
bet her mother had loved that carefully thought-out decision. Amber and Candy were standing in front of a brightly
lit Indian sign, which I recognized to be the big tourist cen-
terpiece outside the Polonco Casino.

"You guys go to the casino a lot?"

"Yeah, when we're not working. Amber's been dating the manager there."

"Junior Bloodgood?"

"Yeah. I don't know why, though. He's not very cute."

I was inclined to agree. I had known Junior from a very young age. He was the only son of George Bloodgood, the tribe elder and cofounder of the Polonco Casino, but whatever handsome and charismatic genes George had been blessed with, they had obviously skipped a generation. Junior was short and stocky, with unfortunate proportions and an even more unfortunate personality. His skin was pocked from an acne-filled adolescence, and he tried to hide his divots under a mat of facial hair. The result was less than appetizing. His feeble attempt at a mustache looked like shrapnel from a lunch of black beans. How could Amber kiss him willingly, I wondered, my stomach churning at the thought. It wasn't as if he had overcome his unappealing appearance with a dazzling personality, either. He was as sour as a grapefruit, with no apparent sense of humor. My dad had had many a run-in with young Junior Bloodgood when he used to patrol the reservation. In fact, he was the only kid that my dad had asked me not to play with, and since neither Bobbie nor I particularly liked Junior, I happily abided by his wishes. Lucky for Junior, George Bloodgood had carved out a place for his misfit son at the Polonco Casino.

"So is he more like a 'boyfriend' boyfriend or a customer boyfriend?" I asked.

"You mean, does he pay her to be with him?" Candy asked.

I nodded.

"She's not a hooker!"

"No, of course not," I said.

"She met him one night when we decided to go to the casino, and it was like love at first sight or something."

"I'm sorry. I didn't mean to offend you. I'm only trying to figure this all out, okay? I'm sorry."

"Okay," she mumbled. "She's a sweet person. I'm worried that I haven't heard from her."

"Did you ask Junior if he's seen her?" I asked. Candy looked sickened and shook her head. I waited for her to elaborate, but she didn't. "That's okay, Candy," I said. "I'll check it out for you. Are you okay to drive home?"

She nodded her head, gave a last sniffle, and rose unsteadily to her feet. I watched her get into her brand-new Mercedes and drive off. *I'm in the wrong business*, I thought to myself as I lowered my exhausted body into my rusted-out bucket of a Camaro.

A Mercedes, for God's sake.

I felt a little less sorry for her than I had earlier.

Chapter Nine

I woke up earlier than I wanted to. My alarm clock told me it was seven forty-five a.m. I wasn't beating the early birds to the worm, but it had been a late night, and five hours of sleep was fewer than I liked to get.

I toyed with the idea of falling back asleep, but my mind was already fully awake. Saturday was usually my day to sleep in, but the sun was like a magnet to me. Already, I could feel the heat building, the humidity rising. It would be the perfect temperature outside right now. I'd have time to get in a good run and take the evidence I had collected last night to the lab before Bobbie and I started our Saturday summer ritual.

It was just before noon by the time I arrived back home, slick with sweat from my run, and the air already had that syrupy heaviness to it that I loved so much. Bobbie would be arriving at any moment, so I ran upstairs and slipped on my bikini—red, tiny, and perfect for minimizing tan lines.

There are bikinis that you wear in public and bikinis that you only pull out when you're alone or with close friends. This was definitely one of the latter. I pulled two fluffy beach towels out of my linen closet and headed outside to align the lounge chairs with the sun in the middle of the lawn.

I knew suntanning wasn't great for me, but I reconciled this with the fact that I didn't smoke crack, and was therefore entitled. This whole not-smoking-crack thing left me eligible to enjoy a whole host of vices that would otherwise leave me feeling guilty. When someone would say, "Hey, you drink a lot," or "You've slept with how many men?" I'd say, "Well, at least I don't smoke crack," and I'd happily carry on. It was genius, really.

I set up the stereo speakers on the deck, found my favorite radio station, and went inside to mix a pitcher of margaritas.

An "I'm here!" at the back door announced Bobbie's arrival. "Sorry, I couldn't get in the front door. Some stripper borrowed my key."

"You could have knocked. I probably would have let you in."

"I didn't want to risk it. I've been looking forward to this," said Bobbie, giving me a sisterly hug. "Wow. You're sweaty."

"Sorry. Just got back from my run. So did you have a rough week?" I asked.

"Ugh! So many dead people! For God's sake, why do people insist on doing sports in this crazy hot weather?" She gave me a pointed look. "Haven't they ever heard of heatstroke?"

"Yeah, whatever. Maybe they're afraid they'll get big

fat asses with all the drinking and eating they do if they don't exercise," I said. "Not everybody was born with your freakish genetics."

"Oh, please, Chuck," she said. "One day without exercise isn't going to kill you."

"Yeah, but why take a chance?" I answered grimly. "Besides," I said, handing her a margarita, "you don't want me to start feeling guilty for drinking these bad boys, do you?"

"Girl," she said, "you do what you gotta do. I'm not here to judge."

"And that's what I love about you. Now let's get out there."

Bobbie scooped up the drink tray and made her way carefully through the kitchen and family room out to the deck. I followed her with the phone and my police receiver. What better entertainment than tequila, good gossip, a country music station, and dispatch reports? Bobbie set down the tray, tossed her swimsuit cover-up, and settled herself into a lounge chair in her equally scandalous yellow bikini.

"You ready, Bob?" I yelled from the side of the house.

"Hit it, Chuck!"

I turned on the tap, sprinted over to my lounge chair, and stretched myself out before the water hit. The first couple of passes of the sprinkler were always wondrously warm from the hose sitting out in the sun, but after about a minute, the water became exquisite torture. Bobbie and I had been sunning under the sprinkler like this since we were little kids. We replaced the Kool-Aid with booze, our bathing suits got smaller, and our taste in music had changed, but aside from that it was a pretty solid tradition. It was on my second trip to the margarita tray that I heard a loud squawk from the police radio, a possible 187 on the reservation.

"Hey, Bobbie!" I yelled over the music. "Possible homicide on the reservation."

"Really? They sure it isn't heatstroke?"

I turned down the music and listened for more details. Some kids had found a floater at the swimming hole. My thoughts went to the poor kid I had seen clinging so desperately to the side of the boat launch yesterday during his swimming lesson. *Boy, I hope he wasn't the one who found the body.* If he'd been scared of the water before, he'd be terrified now.

"Let's go for a ride," I said, pulling on my cutoff jean shorts and a straw cowboy hat.

"But our pizza's coming," said Bobbie.

"That's why God created cell phones." I threw Bobbie her tiny beach cover-up. "Come on."

Five minutes later we were pulling into a growing line of vehicles that were trying to get into the small parking lot at the swimming hole. The park was swarming with cop cars, cherries on, and police officers trying to keep the spectators at bay. A small group of sobbing children and their parents were sequestered over on the picnic tables beneath a canopy of trees while two young officers worked on taking their statements. They must have been the ones who made the gruesome discovery.

When we got to the front of the line of traffic, a handsome yet slightly wilted-looking Ken signaled with his hand for us to stop. It was blazing hot out there in the dusty parking lot away from the shade of the trees, and a fine trail of sweat was fighting its way down past the brim of his hat and onto his beautifully sculpted cheek. I would have been right there with him, directing traffic, getting sunburned, and cursing Captain Rye had I not snagged my promotion. My heart went out to him, and I wondered if they would ever let this exquisite creature off playground duty.

Bobbie put her window down as Ken walked up to the car.

"Yum, yum," she whispered under her breath.

Bobbie had a thing for the pretty boys, thank goodness, which meant we never fought over men, not that we would anyway, since we had a dibs system in place for exceptions. Still, it was a good thing. Ken leaned his head in through the window and flashed us a smile. "Sorry, we can't let anyone in today."

"I bet you can make an exception for us," Bobbie said batting her eyes.

"Sorry. As much as I'd like to…" His voice trailed off when I took off my hat and lowered my sunglasses.

"Oh, come on, Ken!" I said. "Only two days and you've already forgotten about your partner? That's so cold!"

Ken turned red. "Aw, shit, Cass! Sorry about that. I've never seen you out of your uniform."

Bobbie flashed me a *why don't you introduce me?* look over her sunglasses.

"And this is my friend Bobbie," I said. "She's our friendly neighborhood coroner, accent on friendly. Bobbie, this is Ken, my partner."

Bobbie stuck her hand out through the window for a

shake. "Very nice to meet you. Cassidy didn't tell me her partner was a stone-cold fox."

I rolled my eyes. Bobbie was good. Ken looked like his pants were getting crowded.

"Hate to break this up, friends, but we got a dead body to look at," I said.

Ken broke out of his Bobbie-induced trance. "Right. Sorry. Why don't you pull up over there?" he said, pointing to a spot at the far end of the lot. "I'd let you park closer but…Captain Rye's here."

I'm sure if Captain Rye hadn't been here he would have let Bobbie park on top of the actual corpse, but nobody wanted to risk attracting the captain's ire if it could be avoided.

The coroner's van arrived just as we were parking and inched its way up to the chain-link fence. Bobbie and I made our way over to the woman who was exiting the coroner's van. "Hey, Andrea!" Bobbie called out with a wave.

Andrea was a serious-looking petite woman with a sandy brown bob and sensible shoes. Round spectacles underscored her bent for business. "Hello there, Bobbie," replied Andrea. "What brings you out on a Saturday?"

I waited for the inevitable upturn of the nose that many studious-looking women gave scantily clad coworkers, but it didn't come. I liked her immediately.

"Oh, you know, I was in the neighborhood. You've met Cassidy, haven't you? She's one of our girls in blue."

"I have now," said Andrea, offering her hand. "Nice to meet you."

She gave me a firm handshake, which I appreciated. "Nice to meet you, too," I said.

Andrea wasted no more time on pleasantries. She was obviously a woman who was very good at her job and wanted to get to it. "Let's go see what we have," she said, beckoning us to follow.

Bobbie and I followed Andrea, letting her take the lead. The body had been fished from the water and carried to the spotty shade of a poplar tree. Someone had thought to cover the body with a thin sheet to protect it from the sun. Heat and humidity were not kind to corpses.

Unfortunately, Captain Rye, who had been busy supervising a small team of forensic divers, took this moment to turn around and survey the rest of the scene. His eyes bulged with anger when he caught sight of us, and I watched with a certain amount of dread as he rearranged his jaw to highlight his mounting rage. He balled his fingers into fists as he hefted his bulk toward us with as much speed as his stocky legs would allow. He looked like a bull on a rampage.

"Hey!" he bellowed, flailing his arms. "Get the hell away from my crime scene!" He swung his big head from side to side, looking for someone to eviscerate for letting civilians inside the perimeter, but before he could make Ken's day worse, Bobbie fished her credentials out of her pocket and flashed them to Captain Rye.

"As chief coroner, I believe I have every right to be at this crime scene, Captain," Bobbie said calmly. "I'm sorry if my casual attire was cause for alarm, but it couldn't be helped."

I'd always admired Bobbie's diplomacy. Captain Rye allowed his anger to be tempered by Bobbie's charm. He even managed to forget about my presence for a moment, but just a moment. Once he managed to sever eye contact with

Bobbie, though, the spell was broken, and he immediately set his sights on me. Who knew a straw hat and sunglasses would be such an effective disguise? I lowered my glasses so he could identify me.

"Captain," I said, pushing my glasses back into place.

He lurched in close to speak. "What the hell are you doing here, Jones? This isn't a baseball game. What, are you gonna buy a hot dog and peanuts?"

"No, sir," I said, averting my eyes from the pocket of gooey spittle that had flopped out onto his lip. He needed a breath mint.

I looked from my flip-flops over to the body, which Andrea had just uncovered. It wasn't a pretty sight. A short plaid skirt barely covered her most intimate bits, and her tiny white blouse had been torn so badly that it was only staying on by its armholes, leaving her almost completely exposed. She had been petite, although the bloating had added inches to her girth. She'd had long brunette hair, breast implants, and long pink artificial nails, some of which had gone missing. My field of vision narrowed until all I could see was the woman splayed out on the lawn in front of me. I could hear Captain Rye hissing threats into my ear, but they were white noise to me. My eyes were drawn two inches farther north than most eyes would be looking, to the tattoo on her upper chest, a tiny crown and the words "Fit for a King."

"I know her," I said.

The white noise beside me that was Captain Rye stopped, and I was back in the real world.

"You know her?" Rye repeated stupidly.

"Yeah. She was a dancer at Double Down. Her name is Amber." *Guess that does make it my business.*

I knelt down beside Andrea and Bobbie, staking my claim to be there with the body, and gave Captain Rye a fleeting glance. I'm not sure what I expected, that maybe he'd at least be happy his Jane Doe now had a name. Not the case. He threw me one more dagger stare before resetting his face into an unreadable mask. His hostility toward me made me nervous. Aside from getting a promotion and being a woman, I couldn't figure out what I had done to make him hate me this way.

I turned my attention back to Bobbie and Andrea, hoping the captain would lose interest and leave me alone. "Looks like she was strangled," Bobbie said, pointing her gloved finger to the deep purple imprints on Amber's neck.

"So this wasn't a drowning?" I asked.

"Doesn't look like it. I'll be able to tell you more once we run our tests, but if I were a betting woman I'd say she was strangled to death then dragged by her arm to the river." She pointed to another paw print on Amber's arm.

"So they dumped her to make it look like an accident," I said. I pointed to her broken fingernails. "Looks like she fought back, though. Bet someone has some serious claw marks on him."

Bobbie gave a sigh. "Too bad she's been in the water so long. Any skin she may have been able to scratch off is probably long washed away. We'll be lucky to find any trace amounts of DNA from the killer."

Andrea pulled a file out of her kit and began working on Amber's fingers. "It's still worth a shot, but water's rough on DNA samples."

Captain Rye gave a gruff harrumph, stuffed his hands in his pockets, and turned on his heel. Bobbie, Andrea, and I bonded over a look. What an ass.

"Can you tell how long she's been in the water?" I asked.

Bobbie did some math in her head then answered me. "From the amount of decomp, I'd say she was in there for at least three or four days."

That would put her there close to the time of Jimmy's death. Somehow Amber's murder was connected to the murder of Jimmy Polonco. All I had to do was connect the dots. Before I could think on it further, I felt a tap on my shoulder. I whipped around, expecting to see Captain Rye's ugly red mug again, but was pleasantly surprised to see Ken's handsome face instead.

"I believe that gentleman is here to see you," said Ken, pointing to a slender, nervous-looking teenage boy in a bright orange shirt standing on the other side of the yellow tape.

"Thanks, Ken." I stood up slowly, giving the kid a wave of acknowledgment. Out of the corner of my eye, I could see Captain Rye watching my every move. I could only imagine the expression on his face right now. *Oh, well, in for a dime, in for a dollar.* If he disliked me before, he'd hate me now. I crossed the parking lot slowly, and when I reached the teenager, I dug a twenty out of my back pocket and gave it to him.

"Keep the change, Brian," I said.

"Thanks, Ms. Jones," he said, handing me my pizza. "Uh, enjoy your lunch."

I made myself comfortable on the hood of Bobbie's SUV with my pizza and my napkins. I had a great view of the entire park. Luckily, we had parked under a grove of shady trees and a tiny breeze had picked up. All in all, it was a fairly pleasant spot for an impromptu picnic, minus the dead body, of course. I felt a buzz from my back pocket and dug out my phone—a text from a number I didn't recognize. *What are you doing tonight?*

I frowned. *Who is this?*

Sorry. It's Lorenzo.

I felt a tiny jolt of pleasure at seeing his name, but couldn't resist. *Lorenzo who?* I giggled.

You forgot already!

Just kidding. You made sure I'd remember you.

That's a relief. Are you busy tonight?

A smile leaped to my face at the thought of seeing him. *Do you need me to work?*

No. But I could use your help with something else.

Sounds serious.

Is that a yes?

Who is this again?

Dammit, woman! Meet me at the City Center baseball

park, 6 p.m. Dress for action.

I was going to see Lorenzo tonight. A thrum of excitement coursed through my body. I couldn't imagine what
the hell we were going to do at the baseball diamond, but it
didn't matter. Lorenzo was probably going to kiss me again.
He was probably going to try to do unmentionable things to
me, an idea that was both wonderful and terrible, in equal
measure. The cop in me would try her best to keep him out
of her vagina, but the woman in me wanted to rip the summer-weight linen off his muscular body and work him over
like a rented mule. Choices.

I grabbed a piece of pizza, suddenly ravenous, and
turned my attention back to the proceedings. Bobbie and
Andrea were wrapping up their initial search of the body,
talking in hushed tones to each other, while Captain Rye
paced along the riverbank, throwing sullen glances between
the divers, the body, and me. He looked like a man who was
being tested beyond his limit. Maybe he was hungry. The
next time I caught him glaring at me, emboldened by my
Lorenzo-induced giddiness, I held up my slice and pointed
to it—an offering. How could he hate someone who was
offering him pizza, for God's sake? My offer was met with
a stern look, and he turned his attention abruptly back to
the divers. Apparently, he was more than capable of hating
someone who was offering him pizza.

What a dick.

I looked over to the kids and parents sequestered on the
picnic tables. I recognized one of the mothers as Rosemary,
one of the girls from the reservation who I used to play with
as a child. She had married another one of our childhood

playmates, an Indian boy named Reggie, and had a litter of kids. Seven, according to Facebook. I shuddered and said a silent prayer for Rosemary's vagina. It probably looked like a crime scene by now.

I watched as the police wrapped up their questioning and escorted the witnesses up to the chain-link fence. Rosemary waded her way to the parking lot, her progress slowed by the four little girls who were clinging to her like cat hair.

"Hey, Rosemary!" I yelled, jumping off the hood of the truck.

Rosemary turned around, squinting against the sun, trying to figure out who had called to her. I waved my hands over my head to flag her attention. "It's Cassidy!"

"Oh my God!" she squealed, steering her flock of kids in my direction. "How are you doing? It's been ages!"

"I'm doing great. It looks like you've been busy, though," I said, pointing to her little brood. They were gorgeous, all buttery bronze from a summer of swimming and playing in the sun.

"God, and that's only half of 'em," she said, sounding a little exhausted. "Reggie and the boys are off on their yearly fishing trip up at the lake. What about you? Still no kids?" she asked with a tinge of sadness.

People always asked that question with sadness once you hit your late twenties. As if your ovaries weren't sporty enough to muster up a healthy egg, or no man had found you worthy of bestowing his seed upon you. Truth be told, I just didn't want to have kids. Neither did Bobbie. You can't tell this to a mother, though, so I responded the way I always do, with a heavy sigh and a downturned shake of the head. Let her think what she wanted.

"You girls hungry?" I asked, pointing to the pizza box.

Rosemary's kids turned big imploring eyes to their mom, and she relented with a smile.

"One piece each, okay?" she told them, and they sped off toward the truck at warp speed, all knobby knees and squeaky.

"You guys found the body?" I asked.

"Yeah," said Rosemary, suddenly serious. "I can't believe something like that happened here."

"Did you recognize her?"

Rosemary shook her head. "No. Thank God. It was nobody we knew."

Just then, Bobbie made her way into the parking lot and gave a little shriek of delight when she spotted Rosemary. As we caught up, I watched Chief Thompson roll into the parking lot in his black SUV. He had a grim look on his face as he took in the scene. Without stopping to talk to anyone, he circled the lot and left. I could only imagine the type of pressure he was under. Another dead body in his district wasn't going to ease his workload any.

I turned my attention back to Bobbie and Rosemary. Bobbie was inspecting the pizza box—one piece left. She cast a glance over to the kids, noting the sauce on their faces.

"Dream killers," she muttered, pushing the last slice into her mouth.

"Well, Bobbie and I better run, but it was so nice to see you again, Rosemary," I said, giving her a farewell hug. "I hope we get to see you again soon."

"Me too, I'd love that," said Rosemary.

Bobbie gave me a grim look as we climbed back into her SUV. "I'm still hungry."

Chapter Ten

It took me approximately two hours to get ready for my date, a fact that the cop in me found more than a little mortifying. I told myself it was because I didn't know what the date entailed. I mean, "ready for action" could be interpreted so many different ways. I hadn't been this excited about a date in a very long time, which actually made the situation even more appalling. After all, this wasn't even a real date, and in my head I knew that…

Unfortunately, everything from the neck down felt conflicted on the matter. The sad fact was Lorenzo Polonco, despite his sketchy lineage, was kind of a catch, and even though I'd led him to believe I was a down-and-out stripper, he seemed to feel the same way about me. I hated to admit it, but it made me feel good, a deep-down solid good. Perhaps it wouldn't be the *biggest* disaster in history if I let myself enjoy a bit of harmless physical stuff, as long as my heart didn't get involved. The heart had terrible instincts.

Left untethered, it would follow the vagina to the brink of disaster, like a rudderless boat caught up in a riptide.

I shook my head and chuckled. I was getting ahead of myself. Things hadn't progressed that far, and for all I knew, maybe they never would. Anyway, I was a big girl and perfectly capable of steering my flailing heart away from the abyss.

The heat of the day was past, but the air was still warm and humid as I pulled in to the baseball park. The parking lot was teeming with minivans, the penalty, I fantasized, for contributing to the overpopulation of the earth. I clocked Lorenzo's black Maserati and felt a little flip-flop in the pit of my stomach. My excitement was somewhat tempered, however, by the prospect of being spotted in the hideous Camaro, so I crept along the perimeter of the lot, parking as far away from the action as I could, then followed the tide of children to the diamond. There were actually four baseball diamonds at this complex, and a sea of kids, all in different brightly colored jerseys, were sprinting over to their respective teams. A tiny human on Rollerblades teetered by me in a red jersey emblazoned with "The Pee Wee Gamblers" on the front and "Polonco Casino" on the back. I smiled. Now it was starting to make sense.

The sight of Lorenzo stopped me in my tracks. He was in the outfield, hitting balls to his ragtag team of tiny baseball players. He wore a Gamblers jersey, too, but his had "Coach" on the back. If there had been any part of me that ever wanted children, my ovaries would have been doing backflips. As it was, I did feel a certain sensation down there, related to—but very different from—the act of childbirth.

I sidled up to the fence and watched for a minute,

although I noticed I wasn't the only woman lining up to get a view of the handsome Lorenzo. I didn't think I was the only woman who had spent the greater part of the afternoon getting ready to see him, either. There were more than a couple of tube tops on display, not to mention a fair number of daisy dukes, a slew of elaborate updos that would have looked more appropriate at the governor's ball than the ball field, and one highly questionable sundress that, from my vantage point, revealed a stunning boob job, a discreet cesarean scar, and a pair of red lace panties. Now, *these* ladies were dressed for action! I looked down at my own wardrobe choice—a pair of ripped cutoff jean shorts, a white tank top, and a pair of leather high-top Converse sneakers. I needed to up my game.

When Lorenzo finally spotted me, he gave me a huge smile and waved. The woman beside me in the minuscule sundress waved back, emitting a satisfied purr. She fluffed up her hair with her fingers, and while Lorenzo's back was turned, hiked up her boobs. After all, how is a man supposed to find you interesting if he doesn't know the status of your areolae?

Lorenzo, oblivious to the mating dance on the sidelines, gathered a pile of baseballs, passed the bat to one of the taller kids, and jogged over. "Brandi! I'm glad you could make it."

"Me too," I said, matching his smile.

He nodded toward one of the benches. "Come with me. I've got something for you."

Beside me, I could see sundress lady deflate. I felt a stab of sympathy for her until I heard her mutter, "Nice shoes, bitch."

I leaned in close—"Your nip's out"—and followed Lorenzo over to the bench. I spared a look back to see sundress lady readjusting her cleavage. When she looked up to shoot me a dagger, I smiled and gave her two thumbs up. Making friends all over town.

"You know her?" he asked.

"She liked my shoes."

Lorenzo, bless his heart, was happy to take it at face value. He pulled his duffel bag from under the bench, fished out a red jersey, and handed it to me.

"Aw, this is sweet, Lorenzo. Thank you."

"Look at the back."

I flipped it around. *Assistant coach.* "Are you serious?"

Lorenzo shrugged. "I told you I needed your help."

I laughed. "You know, I used to play baseball when I was a kid. I wasn't half bad."

He leaned in close, placing a chaste kiss on my cheek. "I'll bet," he whispered.

I felt my cheeks flush and busied myself with the donning of my new jersey. The sundress was *really* gonna hate me now.

The umpire called out something loud and unintelligible, sending the players racing to their respective dugouts. The Pee Wee Gamblers made a beeline over to Lorenzo, crowding around him in a sweaty little huddle, wiggly and excited, waiting for their marching orders. They looked like puppies waiting for treats, which I guess wasn't too far off the mark, actually. Lorenzo waved his clipboard over his head for attention. "Hey, everybody, I want you to meet Coach Brandi. She's going to be helping me out tonight." He pointed at me with his clipboard, and I smiled at them, hopefully highlighting the fact that I didn't bite. "And if we have a good game tonight, and play our best, then we're going to have pizza afterward." This brought excited squeaks from the kids. "So I really hope you try your hardest, because I promised Coach Brandi I'd feed her, and she gets pretty cranky if she doesn't get fed." This brought a chorus of giggles from the kids and a belly laugh from me.

"He's telling the truth, you guys," I said. "Things could get pretty scary over here if I don't get me some pizza!" More giggles, and a grin from Lorenzo. This was already the best date I'd had in over a year, and I still had my clothes on.

Lorenzo read out the batting order while I made my way over to the third baseline. Any adult—any primate, for that matter—could be the third-base coach for a group of seven- and eight-year-olds. The ball never reaches the outfield, and only rarely is a ball ever thrown from one player to another. After the pitch, peewee baseball is essentially a game of projectile-enriched tag. But, as my dad always said, "If you don't have the goods, you'd better have a good plan." And I definitely had one of those. If my runner looked speedier than the kid chasing him with the baseball, I'd make him run for home. If he was chunky, I'd make him stay put until the coast was clear. Easy peasy.

My strategy worked like a charm. In the end, even my chunky guy was able to steal bases, blessed as he was with deceptively nimble evasive maneuvers. "Soccer player," he informed me when I complimented his swan dive/front roll into third. It was exciting, really. Even more exciting was watching Lorenzo doubled over in laughter as I waved kid after kid through to home base. Forty-five minutes later, the Gamblers were celebrating their landslide victory at the picnic tables with a cooler of Gatorade, awaiting the arrival of our pizza.

Lorenzo brought me a cup of Gatorade and sat down next to me on the bench, smiling. "I like your kamikaze approach to coaching."

I laughed. "Yeah, I can't help myself sometimes."

"Thank you for coming, Brandi. I know it wasn't the most romantic start to our evening, but I intend to make it up to you."

"Are you kidding me? This was the most fun I've had on a date in a long time." I pointed over to the kids. "I mean, it would have been better if those guys weren't here…"

"What?" His eyebrows shot up.

"I'm kidding!" I laughed. "Seriously though, I had no idea you coached a baseball team. I thought sponsors just kicked in cash."

"I've been doing it for years. I get a kick out of it."

"Well, it was really cool to see. And I'll be honest, I didn't think I'd ever get to see you in jeans and a T-shirt."

"Is that a good thing or a bad thing?"

"Oh, good. Definitely good." I leaned back and eyeballed his backside. "Super good."

Lorenzo laughed and shook his head, then after a moment, he closed his eyes against the setting sun and took a deep breath. "I can't tell you how good this feels."

I closed my eyes and leaned my head back, too, savoring the last few golden moments of daylight, and let out a contented sigh.

Lorenzo was looking at me when I opened my eyes. He was serious now, though. "I mean it," he said quietly. "It feels really good being with you." He shook his head softly.

"There's just something about you. You're…you're real." He looked over to where the kids were playing a lawless game of kickball. "You know, you're the first woman I've ever brought out here."

"Really?"

"There aren't a lot of girls like you, Brandi."

I felt strangely honored, and special, and flustered, and I felt a huge smile take over my face. "Thank you, Lorenzo." I looked down at my shoes, feeling some strange new emotion unfurling in the depths of me. "That was sweet of you to say."

We sat in amiable silence until a muffled buzz emanating from Lorenzo's pocket returned us to the real world. "It's you," I said.

"What's me?"

"You're vibrating."

"Oh." Lorenzo pulled his phone from his pocket. "It's work. I'm sorry. I should take this." He got up from the picnic table and walked to the fence. As he listened to the voice on the other end of the phone, the playfulness seeped from his face, leaving him tight-lipped and serious. I had a pretty good idea what news he was receiving—the news was out about Amber. He walked back to the table, his face all business. "Please don't hate me," he said.

"What's wrong?"

He stuffed his hands in his pockets and took a deep breath, deciding how much to confide. "There's been an emergency at work. I have to go." He looked over to the kids. "Shit."

"Don't worry about it, Lorenzo. Go do what you have to do. I don't mind staying for pizza duty."

Lorenzo smiled and took my hands in his. "You don't

have to do that."

"I know I don't, but I want to." Lord help me, I actually did, if for no other reason than to quash the nagging guilt I felt at having withheld my knowledge about Amber. "Now go."

"Thank you, Brandi." He reached into his pocket and pulled out a wad of cash. "For the pizza," he said, pressing the bills into my hand. He kissed my cheek and whispered in my ear, "This is *not* how I wanted to kiss you tonight."

"I had something else in mind, too." I looked down at the money in my hand—five crisp one-hundred-dollar bills. "My God, Lorenzo, how much pizza did you order?"

"Buy yourself something pretty with the rest."

I started to protest, but he wouldn't hear it.

"I'm not kidding, Brandi. I wanted to spoil you tonight," and he strode off into the parking lot.

D riving home, I gave my mind over to the mental math of my date. I had long ago discovered that assigning logic to my feelings made me feel like I had at least a modicum of control over them. In the plus column, my professional ethics were intact, the abrupt end to our date eliminating the need to choose whether or not to cross over the line with Lorenzo. In the minus column, I had *really* wanted to stone-cold screw the living daylights out of that man. In the plus column, unless Bobbie had made other plans, we'd probably still be able to go to the casino tonight, as was our original plan before I got "called in to work." But in the minus column, I had *really* wanted to stone-cold screw the living daylights out of that man. I was going to go ahead and call it a draw.

Bobbie pulled into my driveway just after I did, emerging from her Escalade in a slinky black dress with thin spaghetti straps and a plunging neckline. I looked down at my sneakers, now covered in dust. "I need to change, don't I?"

"Yes, Cassidy," she said, taking my arm and pulling me up the steps, like a wearied mother dragging her bratty child out of a candy store. She dragged me straight up the stairs, down the hall, and into the closet. Her fingers went directly to a strapless red dress, which she plucked deftly from the hanger. "This one," she said.

I laughed. Only best friends could get away with that shit. As I climbed into my dress, I told Bobbie to pull my wig box down. I needed to go incognito tonight. There were two people I wanted to spy on—the casino manager Junior Bloodgood, whose girlfriend had turned up dead this morning in our childhood swimming hole on the reservation (and the discovery of whom had effectively cock blocked me this evening), and Detective Jay Coleman, who for some inexplicable reason had a VIP casino card, was slimy as hell, and had unexplained ties to Double Down. Also, it wouldn't be the worst thing in the world if Lorenzo made an appearance at the casino. Call me crazy, but I wanted to watch him in his natural habitat.

I decided on a long, straight black wig with choppy bangs while Bobbie chose a long feathered wig in a shade of burgundy that had never been seen in nature outside the Amazon jungle. We stood back and studied the final result in my full-length mirror. Bobbie in her black dress and shock of red hair, me with my black hair and shocking red dress—we definitely weren't going to blend in, but then again, blending in had never been our forte.

The Polonco Casino was much the same as every other casino I'd been in. Bright flashing lights everywhere, designed to keep the eyes moving from one vice to the next, every twinkle a promise of fortune. Garishly patterned carpet underfoot, attempting to pull focus away from a multitude of drink stains and other sins. There were banks upon banks of slot machines up front by the door, ringing, clanging, and flashing. Those were the siren song of the casino. Come on over, it'll only cost you a quarter. Cheap thrills. Yeah, right. I could see half a dozen old-timers right now who were most likely pissing away their entire pension checks, one thrilling quarter at a time.

Once they had your purse strings loosened, they lured you into the higher-stakes action of roulette, craps (which nobody really seemed to understand, but which looked incredibly cool in a 007 kind of way), blackjack, poker—all designed to scrape away at the lining of your pocketbook. Ah, commerce, you beautiful bastard.

After trading four crisp one-hundred-dollar bills (thank you, Lorenzo) for chips, we wound our way over to the blackjack tables. Unlike the poker tables, which were housed in a private card room off to one side of the casino, the blackjack tables sat smack-dab in the middle of the action, up on a raised dais. Strategically speaking, this high ground was the best vantage point for spying on my various targets. Besides, blackjack was Bobbie's favorite game. At least one of us would be able to give Lady Luck a run for her money tonight. We circled the blackjack area looking for the perfect spot.

"That one," I said, pointing to a table where five reasonably attractive thirty-somethings dressed in suits and ties were plying their luck against a stone-faced dealer.

A couple of them had forgotten to take off their convention name tags, highlighting the fact that they were here from out of town. They would make perfect company for us this evening, even if they were insurance salesmen. Bobbie smiled in agreement, and we made our way over.

"Gentlemen," purred Bobbie, "may we join you?"

Five sets of eyes whipped around to see if the body matched the velvety voice, followed by a flurry of activity as the suits jumped to their feet, offering their stools.

"Good call on the dresses," I whispered under my breath.

"You should wear one more often," she said with a grin. "You might meet a nice respectable guy."

"That's what I'm afraid of."

We had been given our pick of seats, so we chose the two in the middle. No small coincidence, Bobbie found herself sitting next to a carefully manscaped slender gentleman in a perfectly tailored suit, while I found myself next to Rock. Lord have mercy, he was a brute of a man, with three days' scruff and a thickly muscled torso that looked like it wanted to fight its way out of the confines of his slightly rumpled sports coat. Bobbie's companion looked like he wanted to buy her the moon. Mine looked like he wanted to steal it.

I gave Bobbie a grin, and she rewarded me with an eye roll that would have blasted a lesser woman into outer space.

"What?" I asked. "He seems super nice."

A deep whistle and a wave from my new friend managed to get the attention of a tiny, scantily clad cocktail waitress, and we were off to the races.

It was a festive atmosphere at our table. Drinks were magically replaced every time we turned around, and the chips were flying. Every time someone at our table won a big hand, the table would erupt in cheers and high fives, and gradually, more and more insurance salesmen gravitated to our table to see what the ruckus was all about and to join in the fun. By the time an hour had passed, our ever-growing entourage had turned almost the entire blackjack section into one big party. It would only be a matter of time before the floor manager would come over.

Sure enough, a slightly built man with wispy blond hair and clear blue eyes approached our table with a new dealer and waited respectfully for the hand to conclude. As the new dealer took his post and unveiled two new decks of cards, the wispy blond man leaned in between us, handing each of us his business card, introducing himself as Bertrand, the floor manager. I recognized him from my files. He was Lorenzo's right-hand man. And while Bertrand's less than intimidating physique might lead some to believe that he was a pushover, I knew better. He was a master in many forms of martial arts. He was also a master marksman, skilled with guns, knives, bows and arrows—you name it. If he could hold it in his hand, he could kill you with it. And now, for one reason or another, Bertrand was the floor manager at the Polonco Casino. What a jack-of-all-trades.

I looked at his business card. "I thought Junior was the floor manager. Does he have the night off?"

"Actually, he's no longer with the casino," Bertrand answered with professional reserve.

"Wow! That must be a recent thing, huh? I mean, he was still working here last week, wasn't he?"

Bertrand smiled politely. If he objected to the questioning, he didn't show it, but he certainly wasn't forthcoming with information. "I'm not sure when he left, to be honest."

I was quite sure he wasn't being honest, but I guess I couldn't really blame him for not sharing personnel info with a complete stranger. He discreetly extended two VIP passes to us, threw a vague look of disdain in the direction of our newly acquired companions, and suggested that we might prefer the atmosphere in the VIP lounge.

"Thank you very much, Bertrand," I said, giving his arm a little pat. "We just might take you up on it."

"Will you be up there?" asked Bobbie, as she leaned across the table in front of me to present her shiny cleavage to Bertrand.

He smiled courteously. "No, ma'am. I'm working to-night." Then with a slight bow of his head, he issued a polite, "Good evening, ladies," and disappeared into the crowd like a shadow.

"He's cute," Bobbie murmured as she accepted another card from the dealer with a tap of her finger.

"Especially the 'ma'am' part."

"Shut up, Chuck." She delivered an elbow tap to my ribs. "That was completely uncalled for. Ma'am...please."

I giggled. I loved giving Bobbie the gears. I guess I shouldn't have been surprised that Bobbie had found Bertrand cute, though. He hid his killer very effectively underneath his metrosexual business suit, a wolf in lamb's clothing. I liked that. Lorenzo could have picked some muscle-bound goon to be his right-hand man, but he hadn't. He had picked an unassuming assassin with impeccable manners.

I tucked the passes along with his business card into my

clutch and swept the room for any sign of the subjects of my curiosity. Finding none, I turned my attention back to Bobbie and the blackjack table. She was playing both my hand and hers, as she had been doing for much of the night. Not surprisingly, she raked in yet another handsome pot for me. It would definitely serve my interests to let her continue playing my chips for me for the rest of the night.

"Hey, Bobbie," I whispered into her ear. "I need to go check out the VIP area. You wanna come with, or do you want to continue building our fortune?"

"I'll stay, if you don't mind. You're making a lot of money tonight."

"Make me proud. I'll be back in a few."

I turned to Rock, resting my hand on his big thick bicep. Damn. That was a big bicep. I flashed to an image of him throwing me around his hotel room like a little rag doll. *Oops.* "Rock," I said with newly flushed cheeks and a certain amount of regret. "I have an errand to run, but it was very nice to meet you."

He answered me by reaching into his suit jacket and extracting a room key. A hint of a smile rested on his lips — an invitation for mischief, and he gave me a questioning look with his dark blue-gray eyes, eyes that probably changed color depending on what shirt he decided to wear. God, I had been so good lately controlling myself on the job. Technically, though, this was a night off for me. I gave my head a mental shake. This had to be what chocolate cake looked like to a dieter. If this had happened last weekend before the case and before meeting Lorenzo, I probably would have raced him up to his room and let him violate me like a penal code, but here in Lorenzo's newly inherited casino, it felt wrong. Nonetheless, I opened up my clutch and let him drop his key inside.

"Two twenty."

"I can't promise," I said.

"I wouldn't want you to," he replied coolly. Oh, he was good.

I snapped my clutch shut, narrowly missing his fingers, and headed off into the crowd. There was one detour I wanted to make before I made my way to the VIP elevators. I scanned the crowd and spotted our tiny waitress by her tray, which, due to her diminutive stature, she was forced to balance above her head on her outstretched arm. I made my way over to the service bar and waited for her to punch in her order, which she did with lightning speed. I could tell she'd been slinging drinks for a good long while. When she was finished ordering I placed a twenty onto her tray. Her fingers closed on it instinctively, and she looked up at me with curious eyes.

"What's this for?" she asked.

"Just a little extra for taking such good care of our table tonight," I answered. She looked a tiny bit suspicious. "I'm a bartender over at Double Down," I said, "and I know you've been busting your tail tonight. You should come work over there. Some of our customers might actually get their drinks."

A smile broke out on the tiny waitress's face. Everyone, regardless of what they did for a living, liked to be validated.

"No problem. You guys were fun."

"Hey," I said, "I think one of our dancers is dating your manager Junior. Actually, I guess he's not your manager anymore, is he?"

"No, thank God! He was such an ass, always with such a

bad attitude."

She stopped short with a look of embarrassment on her face, realizing that she might have been insulting a friend of mine.

"Oh, don't worry," I said. "I'm not a fan of his, either. I'm worried about Amber, though. Nobody's seen her for days." I leaned in conspiratorially. "You wouldn't happen to remember what day Junior quit, would you?"

"Quit? He got his ass fired! Must have been Saturday or Sunday." She paused for a moment, thinking. "Yeah, it was definitely Sunday. I remember because I always hate working Sundays, they're always so dead. But when Junior got canned, he must have gone crazy or something, because security had to come and get him out of Lorenzo and Jimmy's office, and they dragged him down the service elevator, dragged his ass through the kitchen and threw him out the back door. I was having lunch back there, so I saw the whole thing."

She began loading her drinks onto her tray. "That was the best Sunday I ever had here." She hoisted her tray up over her head and gave me a smile. "Hope you find your friend, and thanks for the tip." And she disappeared into the crowd.

I rode the VIP elevator up, lost in thought. Jimmy Polonco fired and humiliated Junior Bloodgood. Two days later, Jimmy turns up dead. Apparently, they'd had a fight—an unfinished fight, thanks to Jimmy's security team. Had Junior decided to come over to Double Down and finish that fight by popping Jimmy in the forehead with a .38?

The elevator doors opened to the VIP foyer, and I was yanked from my thoughts by the familiar sounds of a belligerent drunk being denied access to the VIP lounge. That belligerent drunk just happened to be Candy. She threw one final scathing insult to the well-dressed woman behind the check-in desk, turned on her heel, and stormed into the elevator. One more drink in my system and I might not have had the reflexes to avoid a collision. Lord knows Candy's impaired reflexes were not to be relied upon. I let the doors shut us in and reached out to touch her shoulder.

"Are you okay?" I asked.

"Get your hands off me! And mind your own damn business," she barked. Her voice was unsteady, choking back tears. I wondered if she had heard the news about her friend.

"Candy?"

She turned big, dilated eyes to me, confusion clouding her already murky view of reality. "Do I know you?" she asked shakily.

"It's me, Brandi."

She stared at me, thinking, her brow furrowing with the unfamiliar exertion. There was zero recognition in her eyes, and I suddenly remembered that I was wearing a black wig.

"From the club...Double Down?" I said. "I'm wearing a wig tonight." I could see some of the fog lifting, so I continued. "I punched you last night. Remember?"

This seemed to strike a chord. "Brandi!" she cried, and threw her arms around my neck. Her body started to shake as she allowed the tears to fall. "I don't know what to do," she sobbed. I had gone from complete stranger to BFF in ten seconds. That must be a record somewhere.

The door to the elevator opened to a lobby full of people. "Piss off," I said by way of greeting, shielding Candy's face from the stunned onlookers. No one made a move to enter the elevator. Even in a slinky red dress and wildly impractical shoes, I had a cop voice that people automatically respected. I pressed a button and the doors shut us in again. Once we lifted off from the lobby I pressed the stop-car button and we jolted to a standstill. There was a brief ringing of an alarm, and then we were left in silence.

"Candy," I said pulling her away to arm's length, "why are you crying?"

"Because I still can't find Amber, and I can't find Steve, and I came to talk to Junior, like you said, but I just found out he doesn't work here anymore, and that stupid bitch up there wouldn't tell me why." Candy sniffled and wiped her nose with the back of her hand. "I know something's wrong but I don't know what to do."

What I was about to tell her was not going to make her feel any better. "Candy," I started softly, "they found Amber today."

The look of relief on Candy's face told me that she hadn't understood what I was trying to tell her. I shook my head slowly, letting her see that it hadn't been a happy discovery.

"I'm sorry, Candy. I really am. Her body was found early this afternoon."

Her face rumpled, and a fresh set of tears started rolling down her cheeks. But she was calmer now, the anger and frustration seemingly vanished, leaving just the pain of loss.

A disembodied voice over the elevator intercom interrupted the grieving session. "Ladies, is everything all right in there?"

I gave a thumbs-up to the security camera and pressed the button to start the elevator moving again. We traveled down in silence, Candy numb from the news and me lost in my own thoughts. I had so many puzzle pieces, but I couldn't figure out how they all fit together. In fact, I didn't even know for certain whether they all belonged to the same puzzle. When we reached the lobby, we slithered out past the team of maintenance men that had been rallied to remedy the problem with the elevator.

"Sorry 'bout that, gentlemen," I mumbled. "It seems to be working fine now."

I kept my arm around Candy's shoulder and steered her through the casino toward the blackjack area. I noticed that Rock was gone. He was probably upstairs in his room oiling up his big hunky body, waiting for me to arrive. Oh, well. Easy come, easy go. Bobbie was still holding court at our table and was leaning her head comfortably on the shoulder of her new friend. I knew just by looking at her that she would be fine with my request.

"Hey, girl, I'm going to help get Candy home. You mind cabbing it by yourself?"

She gave me a wink. "I think I'll be able to get a ride."

I didn't doubt it for a second. She might even make it home, too. It just probably wouldn't be tonight. I cast one last glance at my chip stack. It looked like I was up about five hundred bucks. If I wasn't scratching my itch, at least I was making some scratch.

"Don't forget to cash those babies in," I said, pointing at my neatly piled chips. "We can turn them into shoes tomorrow."

"Just like magic!" exclaimed Bobbie.

The cab was blessedly quiet after the noisy din of the casino, and sitting down felt like heaven. Shoes like the ones I was wearing always came with a side of regret. I remembered a line out of a Prince song: *The beautiful ones, they hurt you every time.* Everyone thinks he was talking about women, but I suspect he was actually talking about shoes. Prince is a short little guy; he wore high heels that would put some supermodels to shame. I'd bet a week's pay that he wrote that song while he was massaging his bunions.

I looked over to Candy, who was staring sullenly out the window at the Polonco Casino sign, where she and Amber had presumably taken their last photo together. This evening hadn't gone the way either of us had planned. Tonight Candy had found out that her only friend was dead, and I hadn't gotten to spy on anyone on my hit list. Sure, I was making some good money tonight thanks to Bobbie's blackjack prowess, but what I had really wanted tonight was to get some answers.

"Where to?" asked our driver.

Candy, numb from shock, remained quiet, so I gave her shoulder a gentle shake. "Where do you live?"

She mumbled her address to the driver, and we pulled away. We sat in silence for a while, each of us lost in our own thoughts.

"Hey, Candy," I said finally. "When was the last time you saw Amber?"

"We worked together on Tuesday night."

"The night Jimmy was killed."

"Yeah, I guess so."

"So everything seemed fine that night?"

Candy nodded her head yes.

"No fights with anyone? Any of her customers?"

Candy shook her head no.

"And did she go home with anyone? Did Junior come to get her?"

Candy paused for a moment then shook her head no. I took a deep breath, trying my hardest not to let my exasperation show. Questioning Candy was like questioning a child.

"Did she go home alone?"

"I don't know," answered Candy. She squinted at the darkness outside her window, doing a mental rewind of her night. "I got a customer and kind of lost track of her. Then when it came time to leave she was already gone." I waited for her to continue. "I thought she was going to come stay with me that night, so I thought it was weird that she was gone."

"Did you call her?" I asked.

"Yeah, of course I did, but her phone was off. It never rang. Just went through to her voicemail."

"Was that weird?"

"Yeah. No. Kinda, I guess. We always turn our phones off at work, 'cause we keep them in our lockers, and we don't want to wear down our batteries."

"Okay…"

"There's no cell reception down there, so if you leave your phone on, it just keeps roaming for a signal, and your battery dies."

"Okay," I said, redirecting her thought process. "Did anyone see Amber leave the club?"

Candy shook her head. "I asked the bouncers, but they said that they didn't see her leave."

That didn't strike me as being too unusual since most of the dancers would probably leave through the employee entrance in the kitchen, bypassing the bouncers.

"Did you ask Roger?"

This question was rewarded with a blank stare. "Who's Roger?"

Apparently Roger wasn't cooking special meals for Candy. "Never mind. So the last time you saw or heard from Amber was at work on Tuesday night." I thought for a second. "Did you check her locker?"

Candy knitted her brows together again. "How could I? It's locked."

"So her locker is still locked?"

"Yes!" she hissed, exasperated.

"So she never emptied her locker at the end of the night?"

"No! For God's sake. That's what I said!"

"So she just left. Didn't take her purse or her phone?"

Candy stared at me, dumbfounded, the penny only just starting to drop.

"You didn't think that was weird?"

"Oh my God," whispered Candy. "I didn't think."

No surprise there. I tapped on the dividing window to get our driver's attention. "Change of plans, sir. Can you take us to Double Down?"

It was just after midnight, and the Double Down parking lot was still fairly full. I guess every day is a good day to see naked strangers when you're a lonely guy. At my request, the driver circled around to the back door and let us out. Even though we weren't working, no good would come of going in through the front door. From my getup, I was sure some people would assume that I was looking for a second chance in the strip trade, and Candy would probably run into a customer, snort a pound of white powder up her nose, and flit off to a dark corner. I passed the driver a twenty and asked if he would wait for us. He pulled out a sandwich bag and a thermos and told us he would.

The kitchen was already closed down for the night, and the overhead lights were dimmed. It felt so strange to be sneaking into the club like this. It reminded me of going on sleepovers when I was a kid. We'd inevitably end up sneaking into the kitchen looking for cookies. Cookies were always better when they tasted like danger. I wouldn't have minded a cookie right now or a piece of Roger's chocolate cake, but I had other things to worry about.

We moved through the kitchen out into the dark little hallway and down to the dressing room, which, to our good fortune, was empty. I caught a glimpse of myself in the mirror and for a moment didn't recognize myself with my dark hair. I looked tired, though, and made a mental note to get more sleep.

"Show me which one is hers," I said to Candy as we made our way to the lockers.

"It's this one." She pointed to a locker that had been decorated with sparkly pink heart stickers that had faded over time and acquired a patina of grime. It made me feel a little sad, as if some poor sot had left those little hearts as a reminder of what could be lost in a place like this.

The lock on Amber's locker would open with a key, not a combination. Another lucky break, since I didn't happen to have a set of bolt cutters in my evening bag. I reached up into my wig and pulled out a long hairpin. There were approximately twenty-five more pins up there holding everything in place, so I wasn't worried about losing my black tresses. I slipped the pin into the lock and shut my eyes. It was an exercise in concentration, and the only two senses of any use in this endeavor were touch and hearing. I imagined myself inside the locking mechanism and felt for the release. A small click let me know I had found the sweet spot and I carefully turned the pin, releasing the lock arm. I gave a yank on the lock, and it opened.

"Bingo!" I said victoriously as I whipped off the lock. Candy's eyes were wide with shock. There was no way to explain this skill set to her, so I smiled and shrugged. Luckily, she possessed the attention span of a fruit fly, so I was fairly confident she'd forget about my criminal behavior in mere moments.

I was right. When I opened the locker, she shrieked, "My sweater! I've been wondering where that was." And she grabbed it, hugging it to her chest.

I shook my head in mild disbelief. Here we were investigating her friend's murder and breaking into a locker, and she was worried about a thirty-dollar sweater. I'm not sure why I was surprised.

I reached into Amber's locker and pulled out her bright red vinyl monstrosity of a purse. Sure enough, her Blackberry was still in there, along with her wallet and car keys.

There was no doubt in my mind that Amber had been taken against her will that Tuesday night. Not one woman on this planet, me included, would ever willingly leave work without her purse. At some point, you'd need your car keys, your cell phone, or your wallet, and you'd realize that you'd left them behind.

I pressed the power button on her phone and waited for it to come to life. Candy, meanwhile, busied herself with the rest of the contents of Amber's locker. She pulled out a pair of stilettos, a curling iron, a cosmetics case, a package of condoms, cigarettes, and a chocolate bar. My stomach gave an involuntary growl at the sight of the chocolate bar. I shoved everything minus the KitKat and Amber's cheap sweater into Amber's oversized bag and got to my feet.

"Let's get out of here," I said, pulling Candy to her feet and dragging her to the door.

"Where are we going?"

"We're gonna get you home."

"What about Amber's stuff?" she asked.

"I'll take it to the police tomorrow," I answered, swinging open the door.

We almost plowed right into Gary, who was on his way in for another inspection, I assumed. I looked down, not meeting his eyes. For some reason I didn't want to be seen in there. Ridiculous since I worked there, but true all the same.

"What's up, Gary?" Candy said, and we kept walking down the long corridor. I was proud of Candy for keeping her cool until I realized that she probably didn't think we'd actually done anything wrong. How liberating it must be to live in her world, I thought to myself. We reached the door to the kitchen, and I threw a brief glance back in Gary's direction. He was watching us, doing some kind of math in his head. Bad sign. I pushed into the kitchen and broke into a run, dragging Candy behind me, just as I could hear Gary yelling, "Hey! Get back here!"

We busted out the door into the parking lot and hopped into the waiting taxi.

"Go!" I yelled as Gary burst out the door.

Our driver was a peach. Completely nonplussed, he slammed on the gas, launching us backward into our seats, and we sped out of the parking lot. He'd probably seen just about everything in the back of his cab over the years and was well beyond the point of asking questions. Except, "Where to, ladies?"

Candy gave him her address again and I threw a look over my shoulder to where Gary was still standing out in the parking lot watching us drive away. I looked down at the huge bright red vinyl purse in my lap and felt a cold chill run through my body. Had he recognized Amber's purse and tried to stop us from stealing it? I chastised myself. It was stupid to bring the whole damn bag when all I really needed was the phone. I wondered if Gary had recognized me. I sure hoped not.

"Candy, if Gary asks who was with you tonight, I need you to tell him it was…I don't know, Amber's cousin, okay?"

"Okay."

I didn't feel reassured, but what else could I do? I pulled out Amber's phone and scrolled to her date book. She was either a detail-oriented person or a woman who forgot things easily, because her calendar was full of the most mundane things, from manicure appointments to work dates to when she needed to do laundry or go to the bank, or even pick up milk. She kept track of when she stayed at Candy's place and what nights she dated Junior—and Kevin. Hmm. She was dating a guy named Kevin at the same time she was dating Junior. I wonder if Junior knew about that.

I scrolled to the date that she went missing, Tuesday. She'd gone to the bank in the morning, picked up a sandwich for lunch, had her highlights done in the early afternoon and had been picked up for work by Candy at six that same day. She had been planning on staying at Candy's place that night, as Candy had already mentioned. There was another entry for that evening at one a.m. *MEET DADDIO.*

"Who's Daddio?" I asked Candy.

"What?"

I pointed at Amber's date book. "Daddio. Who is he?"

"Just some old dude."

I rolled my eyes. "Can you be more specific?"

"He's some old guy that comes into the club. He's her customer."

"Why would she put him in her appointment book?"

She rolled her eyes. "So she'd remember he was coming?"

I gave a sigh. "What did he look like?" Nothing. "Was he handsome?"

She screwed up her face into a look that said, "Ew," and turned her attention to the driver. "Old guys are gross." Our driver gave her a look in the rearview mirror. "No offense," she said. She wasn't smart enough to realize how offensive she was.

That was as good as I was going to get from Candy. Some gross old dude who was more "ew" than handsome. It was better than nothing, I guess.

We turned into the horseshoe driveway of one of the

city's new high-rise apartment buildings, and Candy started rummaging weakly through her purse for money.

"I got it," I said, waving her out.

"Thanks," she mumbled and got out of the car. She stumbled her way over the cobbled brick to the door, rummaged through her purse for her keys, and let herself in. I sank back into the seat and gave the driver my address. He wasn't that old, I thought to myself, probably not even fifty. I put all my thoughts of Candy out of my head, unwrapped Amber's KitKat bar, and sank back gratefully into the leather seat. Soon I'd be in my comfy bed. Sleep was going to feel amazing tonight.

Chapter Eleven

I woke feeling tired and parched, like I'd been running in my sleep, and my head felt like it had been stuffed with newspaper. That was the problem with margaritas—too much sugar. Yeah, sugar, that was the problem. I reached over and grabbed my glass of water from the night table and drained it, then flopped back down onto my pillow, closing my eyes against the morning sun. I wanted to recapture the wisp of dream that was still floating in the back of my mind. I caught a corner of it, a muscular fireman, naked but for his helmet, handing me a kitten, then felt it slip away again as the memories of last night jumbled into my brain. My case was a mess.

I swung my legs out of bed, willing the rest of my body to follow. Everything would be better once I brushed my teeth. I looked at myself in the mirror. Okay, maybe everything would be better once I took a shower.

Twenty minutes later I made my way, pink and clean,

down to the kitchen, put on the coffee, poured myself some Raisin Bran, and stood over the sink looking out the window. I was such a creature of habit sometimes. When the coffee machine had stopped its sputtering I poured myself a gigantic mug full and took it, along with Amber's Blackberry, outside to the front porch.

The coffee helped lift the fog brought on by the previous night's activities. Next time, I promised myself, I would remember to drink more water. Now that I was sober, and alone, and not on the lam, I decided to scroll through Amber's calendar again, starting with the day before her murder and working backward.

Monday—10 a.m. yoga, 12:30 p.m. lunch with Candy, 1:30 p.m. shoe shopping with Candy, 7 p.m. work, 2 a.m. break up with JB.

Wow. What a Monday. JB, I assumed was short for Junior Bloodgood. Made sense unless she had two boyfriends with those initials. Poor Junior, getting canned on Sunday and dumped on Monday. Not that I was surprised he got dumped. After all, he was no prize, but what crappy timing for the poor guy. Maybe getting dumped had been the final straw for Junior, two massive blows to his ego in too short a time period. He wouldn't be the first guy to take permanent action against a temporary problem.

The timing made sense, too. He probably would have spent the rest of Monday night begging Amber to take him back. She would have refused. He would have spent the next day working himself into a rage and been ready for revenge by that night. Junior would have known that Amber was working and he probably also knew she'd step outside periodically for a cigarette. He could have killed Amber in the parking lot on a smoke break, put her in his car, and then sneaked back in to shoot Jimmy. He could have dumped Amber's dead body in the river on his way home without even having to make a detour. Easy peasy.

I felt energized now that I had a theory to work with. I'd have to ask around to see whether anyone had seen Junior Bloodgood entering the club on Tuesday evening, although from my B&E adventure last night, I knew it wasn't too hard to sneak into Double Down unseen late at night. He could have waited for the kitchen to close, then gone in with his gun since there were no detectors back there. It would have been hard to get past the big burly bouncers who guarded the entrance to the VIP floor, though. Maybe he had come in through the emergency exit by the office. I mentally kicked myself for not trying that door when I'd first discovered it on Friday night. I'd have to go to Double Down and check it out.

My mind was racing. We definitely had a solid suspect with motives for the two murders. I glanced at the time. It was still early, but I desperately wanted to get this information to Chief Thompson. The faster you moved on a murder suspect, the less chance he had to take off or set up an alibi, and the better chance you had of bringing him in. Plus, I might have just solved a very important high-profile murder case, and dammit, I wouldn't say no to a well-deserved pat on the back. Then, I thought to myself, I'd be able to reveal my true identity to Lorenzo, and he would marvel at how brave I was and fall immediately and irretrievably in love with me. But first things first…

I dialed the chief's number, wondering to myself what kind of woman scheduled a breakup in her day planner. A cold one, I guess. Not surprisingly, the chief picked up on the first ring. He had a sort of military precision that probably snapped him out of bed at oh six hundred hours with his bed made and a spit shine on his boots.

"Chief!" he barked.

"Hey, Chief, it's Jones. Sorry to bother you so early, but I've got some information I think we're going to want to move on. Can I meet you at the station?"

"I don't go in on Sundays if I can help it. Why don't you meet me in half an hour at the Great Griddle out on Highway 5? You know where it is?"

"I do. See you there," I said and hung up. My mother would have been mortified that I didn't say good-bye, but Chief Thompson had already established precedence in that department, and somehow it felt strangely liberating to buck such an age-old tradition. Plus, I had shaved approximately three seconds off my talking time. Three valuable seconds that could be put to good use. Never mind that I had just wasted fifteen seconds thinking about how clever I was to have saved myself three.

Even though it was shaping up to be another scorcher, I threw on a pair of jeans, a red T-shirt, and a pair of motor-cycle boots. Somehow a sundress seemed inappropriate for a private audience with the chief. I gathered my hair into a loose ponytail and dashed out the door.

I arrived at the Great Griddle five minutes early. The smell of fried onions and bacon greeted me in the parking lot, and my stomach started growling despite that fact that I'd already filled it with Raisin Bran and coffee. The Great Griddle was practically an institution in these parts. It hadn't changed much from when I was a kid. The floor was a cheery black-and-white-checkered pattern, and red vinyl booths with Formica tables lined the windowed wall, just as I remembered. Solitary diners could sit at the long counter and watch the frenetic action of the kitchen while they put back their omelets and pancakes.

I spotted the chief immediately. As I had expected, he was already there waiting for me, and he stood up as I approached the table, an oddly intimate gesture, I thought. But then again, he was of a different generation, where men always stood up when a woman came to the table. They opened car doors for you and held out your chair when you sat down, too. We avoided that awkward little tradition, thankfully, by slipping into a booth.

He was dressed more casually than I had ever seen him, in a pair of dark jeans, black hiking boots, and a long-sleeved navy T-shirt. The dark blue of his shirt made his closely cropped silver hair and ice-blue eyes stand out in stark contrast.

"Are you hungry?" he asked.

"No," I said, "maybe just some coffee."

He flagged the waitress down and ordered two coffees, then turned his attention back to me. We made small talk about the weather until the waitress delivered our drinks. Once she left the table, the small talk portion of the conversation was over, and he leaned in. "What have you found out?"

I told him what I had learned about Junior Bloodgood, that he had been fired and humiliated by Jimmy, then dumped shortly afterward by his girlfriend, Amber. Then I told him about Amber, how the last time anyone had seen or heard from her was on Tuesday night at the club, the night that Jimmy had been killed. I gave the chief the condensed version of what I found in Amber's Blackberry, glossing over the less than legal details of how Candy and I had actually found it.

"Did you turn the phone over to evidence?" he asked.

"We found it late last night. I'll do it this afternoon."

He nodded his approval. "Make sure you do." We sat in silence for a moment, hunched over our coffees in a conspiratorial huddle. He gave me a serious look. "You like Junior for this."

"Yeah, I do."

"You think he was the one behind the poisoning, too?"

"Well, we don't have any actual proof yet, but at the moment everything seems to point to Junior. He definitely had the motive, and probably the opportunity. I don't know what else to tell you," I said with a shrug. He nodded his head gravely. "We'll get the lab results back soon from the bottle wrapper and the gift card, so maybe that'll help fill in some pieces for us."

Chief Thompson nodded his head again. "You've done great work, Cassidy. As soon as we leave here, I'm going to put out an APB on Junior Bloodgood."

"You don't want to wait for the lab results?"

"Like you said, we need to move fast. We don't know how long it'll even take to find Junior. He could be anywhere by now. I'd just as soon get a head start."

"Okay," I said. I was a stickler for hard evidence, but I could see the chief's point.

"You'll be back on regular hours starting Monday then?"

"Actually, I think I should probably stay undercover until we find Junior. 'Cause if we're wrong about him…"

"All right then," he said gruffly, "check in with me to-morrow." He stood up and tucked some money under the saucer of his coffee cup. Meeting adjourned. Suddenly I was very happy I hadn't ordered food. How uncomfortable would another thirty minutes at that table have been? When we reached the door he held it open for me, and I scooted out past him and down the steps to my department-issue Camaro. Even though he had been the one to issue the gross thing to me, I was still embarrassed to be driving it.

"Too bad you couldn't have found me a crappier car," I said.

"I think they brought in a wood-panel station wagon last night," he replied. "You can come trade it out if you want."

This was as close to a joke as I was ever going to get out of the chief, so I gave him a chuckle and climbed into my car. I watched him back out and turn on to the highway. The meeting had been slightly awkward, but at least he was tak-ing me seriously. All in all, it felt like it had gone well.

My thoughts, as they often did these days, drifted to Lorenzo. If we had been *really* dating, it would be consid-ered an enormous taboo to make the first move after a first date. But, as I had already established in my brain, last night hadn't been a *real* date. Therefore, unencumbered by the asi-nine courting rituals of the Twitter generation, I thumbed a text. *Everything okay?*

He responded immediately. *Yes. Thank you. How was the rest of your night?*

The usual mayhem. Not a total lie.

I bet. Can I call you later?

I guess that wouldn't be horrible.

Ha! I'll take it. Have a good day, Brandi.

I started my car. The day was starting to look up.

I had left the Great Griddle without any pancakes in my belly, which was tantamount to sacrilege in my books, especially since I usually self-medicated with carbs on a hangover morning. I pulled out an old red mixing bowl that I inherited from my granny and set about putting together some pancake batter.

Enough time had passed for me to safely call Bobbie and quiz her about her evening, so I dialed her number and set the phone on speaker as I cooked. She picked up on the second ring, giving me a grunt by way of greeting.

"You hungover?" I was a master at interpreting Bobbie's grunts. She gave me another longer grunt—a groan, really. That meant yes. "Did you have fun last night?" There was a long pause. That meant no. "What happened?" I asked. "Was he hung like a light switch?" She made a mewling noise. That meant yes. "I'm sorry, Bob."

"Thanks, Chuck," she said, her voice raspy. "You're a good friend." We both laughed.

"You are, too," I said. "I'm making pancakes if you want some."

"I need pork products."

"Copy that. Talk to you later," and we hung up.

The growling in my stomach was starting to sound comical as I stacked three perfect pancakes onto my plate. You can't argue with hangover belly. I rooted around in the fridge for the maple syrup, doused my stack, and took my plate out to the deck. Ah, heaven. What could be better than a stack of pancakes and an entire Sunday in front of you with nothing to do but things of your own choosing? Actually, I did have one errand to run today. I had stupidly promised to turn Amber's phone in to the lab this afternoon. It seemed like such a treasure trove of information, though, that I hated to give it up. I guess with the modern marvels of technology I didn't really have to. Amber wasn't the only one with a Blackberry. Granted, hers was decorated with a pound of pink Swarovski crystals and mine was plain black, but nonetheless, I had all the necessary power cords and I would have no trouble downloading the contents of Amber's phone to my computer.

After printing out copies of Amber's address book and calendar, I went through her voicemail. There were ten new messages. Nine were sent postmortem from Candy. The other one was sent just hours before Amber was killed. It was from Junior Bloodgood, and it wasn't pretty. The sound of his angry voice spewing threats and profanities made me shiver. He sounded drunk and crazy. This was going to weigh heavily against Junior in court.

Next, I scrolled through Amber's texts and, as I suspected, there were a lot of them, with the conversations dating back months. Many of them were to and from Candy, about the mundane details of their day-to-day lives. The ones from Junior before the breakup were one-sidedly romantic—Junior professing his love for Amber, and Amber avoiding the subject as best she could by responding with little happy face semicolons and emoticons. For the most part, Amber's texts to Junior had been information oriented. Nothing weird, but weirdly nothing, I thought to myself. After the breakup on Monday, Junior had sent a few pleading texts to which Amber had not responded. If Amber hadn't been into Junior romantically, then why hadn't she dumped him sooner? Better yet, why had she gone out with him in the first place? I gave my head a shake. There were lots of women out there who dated men for reasons other than romance. Maybe Junior was Amber's sugar daddy, or one of them, at least.

Speaking of sugar daddies, there were texts to and from Daddio as well. These, too, were oddly devoid of emotion. You'd think a sugar daddy would demand at least some affection for his money. Or maybe this was all about discretion. Maybe Daddio was a married man and didn't want to leave clues behind. All of his secret rendezvous with Amber sounded very businesslike.

The texts from the mystery boyfriend, Kevin, however, were decidedly...romantic, if porn did indeed fall under that mystical umbrella of romance. It would seem that the mystery boyfriend Kevin was the only guy she was bedding nonprofessionally.

I was curious as to what Kevin the magnificent looked like, so I scrolled to the photo album on her Blackberry and downloaded every image onto my computer. This was just too easy. With two presses of a button, I pulled up a picture of Kevin, the mystery boyfriend. (I deduced this from a certain jewelry installment on his penis that Amber had mentioned in one of her texts.) He looked young, maybe twenty-one, and short. His head was shaved and he had tattoos on much of his body. I noticed a familiar-looking bright turquoise crown tattoo on his chest nestled in among the various dragons and skulls. The crown looked identical to the one that Amber had tattooed above her heart, along with the words "Fit for a King." Kevin, it would appear, was Amber's idea of royalty.

I wondered if Kevin had known about Amber's extra-curricular activities. Would it have made him angry enough to strangle her and dump her body in the river? Maybe he had come to the club to pick up Amber after work that fate-ful night and had interrupted her "meeting" with Daddio. Maybe Amber's murder wasn't related to Jimmy Polonco's murder at all. Maybe it was just a crime of passion, and there were *two* murderers out there on the loose.

In lieu of screaming, I folded my arms on the table and dropped my forehead onto them. Yeah, I had a great suspect for the two murders, but there were so many loose ends, and loose ends in a murder investigation made me nervous. I needed to talk to Kevin.

Further investigation into the depths of Amber's Black-berry revealed that Amber had frequently met with Kevin at a place called the Den. I plugged the name into my com-puter and came up with a blank. Maybe Candy would know something about it, although, come to think of it, it was strange that Candy hadn't mentioned Kevin before.

I punched Candy's number into my phone and waited for her to pick up. After five rings, I was rewarded with a groggy "Hello?" I glanced at the clock. It was almost two p.m.

"Hey, Candy, it's Brandi." Silence. I started to think that she had hung up the phone, until I heard the flick of a lighter and a deep intake of breath. She was lighting up a cigarette. "You remember? Brandi?" I repeated. "From the club?"

"I know who you are. I'm not stupid, Brandi."

I was feeling generous, so I let it slide.

"What's up?" she murmured.

"I have a few questions I wanted to ask, if you don't mind." She didn't object, so I plowed on. "Did you know that Amber was also seeing a guy named Kevin?"

"Yeah, of course. We double-dated every now and then. He's super nice. Super cute, too."

"Why didn't you tell me about him?"

"Uh…'cause you didn't ask." Although the "duh" was silent, it was heavily implied by her tone, and it made me cringe. I took a deep steadying breath, summoning whatever patience I could muster. I had forgotten how impossibly specific I needed to be with Candy.

"Did Kevin know that Amber was dating Junior Bloodgood?" I asked.

"I think so. Every now and then Junior's name would come up and Kevin would roll his eyes and get real quiet." She paused, thinking. "He probably didn't like it, huh?" I couldn't imagine that Kevin would be real thrilled that his girlfriend was dating another guy, but I'm a traditionalist that way. What did I know?

"What about Junior, then? Did Junior know that Amber was dating Kevin, too?"

"Oh, God no," said Candy. "No, Junior thought he was gonna marry Amber. What a loser. Every time they were together he was so pathetic, always fawning all over her. It was so funny."

As much as I disliked Junior, I didn't really find the humor in putting someone's heart in a blender. I could hear Candy yawning over the phone. "Late night?" I asked. I couldn't imagine she would have gone out after I had dropped her off, but there was a chance that her recreational pharmaceuticals had kicked in, putting her into a party mood.

"Yeah, I didn't get much sleep," she answered. "After I got home, I called Steve and left him a message. I thought he'd want to know about Amber since he knew her and all."

"Uh-huh…" I said with trepidation. I hated that Jay had an in with her. I didn't want him learning my business through Candy's warped filter.

"Anyway, he finally called me back, but it was late, and we had a really good talk." She sounded almost giddy with excitement.

I felt a knot tightening in my stomach. "Did you tell him anything? You know, about what we did?"

"Oh, yeah! For sure! I mean, it was so cool," she said. "It was like a James Bond movie! I told him about how you picked the lock and how you found her phone and how I found my sweater that she borrowed from me." She seemed to catch herself finally, realizing that she had been talking with zeal about the personal effects of her now-dead best friend. "Steve wanted to borrow her phone for a bit," she said in her best sober voice, "but I told him that you took it home."

I could feel my heart thudding in my chest. What the hell would Jay want with Amber's phone? Was there information in there that related to him? I didn't think there was, or maybe I simply hadn't run across anything yet. Maybe I was missing something. Was he connected to Junior or Daddio in some way? Now my mind was really reeling. Instead of tying up loose ends, I only seemed to be creating more.

Candy gave a loud sigh on her end. "So is that it?" she

asked.

"Excuse me?"

"Is that the reason you called me?"

I racked my brain trying to remember why I had called Candy in the first place. The Den. "Have you ever heard of a place called the Den? I think Amber and Kevin used to meet up there a lot."

Candy giggled. "Oh, yeah. Kevin works there. It's a sex club, down in the old chocolate factory. You should check it out. It's lots of fun."

I bet. "What kind of sex club?" I asked.

"Oh, you know. It's a typical fetish club," she said.

Funny, I hadn't realized there was such a thing as a "typical" fetish club. I would have mentioned the oxymoron to Candy, but that probably would have ended poorly. "And it's real private," she said. "You can only get in if you know somebody. We knew Kevin, so we could always get in. Only he goes by the name Taurus there. I don't know why, but that's what they call him." That was one I actually could figure out, having seen Kevin's dangly bits.

"Well, thanks, Candy," I said. "Maybe I'll check it out. Do you know if he works Sundays?"

"Yeah, I think so. Listen, I gotta go. That's Steve calling on the other line." And the line went dead.

Great. I cursed Jay—Steve—silently and called Bobbie. She answered with another grunt, and I almost felt bad for asking, but I needed a wingman. "Do you still have those assless chaps? Because we're going out tonight." Silence. "Bobbie? I'm kidding...sort of." Yes, she had hung up on me, but I knew that I could count on her. She loved any opportunity to wear those damn chaps. I texted the time and place for our rendezvous at the Den tonight, and signed off with a smiley-face emoticon and a turd sticker.

I had hours to kill before I hit the Den, and I was feeling antsy, so I did what I always did when I had energy to burn. I put on my runners and hit the road.

I took my usual jogging route through the reservation. It was slower going today on account of the heat and the stack of pancakes sitting in the pit of my stomach, but somehow it felt invigorating to be outside doing what no other sane person would be doing today. In the back of my mind I could hear Bobbie lecturing me about heatstroke and dead people. Within minutes, I was slick with sweat and breathing hard. Bobbie definitely would not approve of this, but I was feeling more and more relaxed with every stride.

After a couple of miles, I approached the swimming hole on the reservation, and unseen forces (probably forces of self-preservation) slowed my pace down to a walk. I made a detour over to the water fountain and took a long drink, letting the water run down my chin. It was the water I grew up with—hard well water—and it was ten times more refreshing than the soft treated water in the city. As I stood looking out over the pretty little water park, I could see where some of the flowers had been trampled by the emergency crews, and there was a slightly worn path on the grass from the parking lot to the tree under which Amber's body had been placed after it had been pulled from the water. But aside from that, there were no traces of the brutal murder that had been discovered here yesterday. The bright yellow crime-scene tape was gone; there were no news reporters speaking somber messages into their news cameras. The park was alive again with the squeals and splashing of young children. It was hard to believe that only twenty-four hours ago a dead body had been fished out of this very river. Life had already returned to normal, the murder all but forgotten. Perhaps if Amber had been one of their own there might have been more fuss made, some kind of acknowledgment that something horrible had happened to another human being right there under their noses. Or maybe not. Who knows? I was constantly surprised at the callous nature of our species.

I wandered down to the boat launch, took off my shoes and socks, and sank my feet into the water. It felt like heaven. As a kid I had always loved coming down to the swimming hole, especially in August. By the time August rolled around the sun had warmed the water to an almost bathtub-like temperature, just cool enough to be refreshing but warm enough to make you want to stay in all day long.

I watched the kids splashing around and playing games, and smiled to myself as a couple of grinning teenagers resurfaced from under the dock, their faces flushed with excitement. When Bobbie and I were teenagers we'd come down here and make out with boys under that same dock. It was buoyed up on barrels, leaving just enough headroom underneath to sneak a few kisses, unseen from prying eyes. There was a certain amount of comfort to be found in the fact that some things never changed.

I scanned the little faces of the playing children trying to figure out if any of them had been part of the group that had stumbled upon Amber's body yesterday, but it was next to impossible to tell. Children all looked the same to me, especially when they were wet. I knew that Rosemary's daughters had been there, though. Maybe it was time for a visit.

Rosemary's house wasn't hard to find. She had lived on the reservation her entire life, so all I had to do was ask at the convenience store. That was the beauty—and the horror, I suppose—of small-town living. Not only had the clerk given me Rosemary's address but she also walked me out of the store and pointed me in the right direction. Then, after giving me a parcel to deliver that had arrived for Rosemary that morning, she sent me on my way. I could only hope that the sweet little old clerk would have been more discriminating had I shown up with a machete and an ax to grind.

Rosemary, Reggie, and their seven kids lived in a double-wide trailer that had been converted into a house with the addition of a small porch and an awning. How nine people managed to live in there was beyond me. I guess eventually you got used to living with no privacy. They do in prison. Yep, nine people in a double-wide. That sounded like hard time to me.

Their yard was littered with toys and bikes, but if you could see through the detritus you could tell that the house was maintained with love and care. Two of Rosemary's girls were out front building a castle-inspired object in a tiny red plastic sandbox. Now that they were dry, I could see that they were twins. I mean, they were wearing matching jumpers. Why else would she do that to her kids? When they saw me, they dropped their various tools, scrambled out of the sandbox, and rushed me like a couple of linebackers, squealing that high-pitched dog-summoning squeal that only five-year-olds can achieve. "Auntie Cassidy! Auntie Cassidy!"

I had only a moment to wonder how I had achieved auntie status before they were wrapped around my legs like little spider monkeys.

"Girls! Don't get Auntie Cassidy dirty!" yelled Rosemary from the door.

Mystery solved. "Don't worry, Rosemary. I've been out running. There's not a clean spot on me!"

Rosemary managed to pry the kids off my legs then gave me an equally enthusiastic hug. "Twice in two days. What a great surprise! I wish Reg was back from the lake, though. He'd love to see you."

"When's he back? I haven't seen that man in ages!"

"They'll be back in a couple of days. Hopefully they won't have eaten all the fish they caught." She gathered up some festive beach towels that had been slung over the swing set to dry and beckoned me to follow her up the steps into the shade. "So what's up?"

"Well, I was wondering if I could ask the girls a few questions about yesterday."

Rosemary looked at her little brood with a worried look on her face. "Really? Because they already questioned us," she said, a sliver of apprehension creeping into her voice.

"I know, but I have a few more questions, if you don't mind. I wouldn't ask if it wasn't important, Rosemary."

We settled into a couple of lawn chairs on the small front porch with Rosemary's daughters arranged at our feet like a flock of baby birds. She had given them all Popsicles, so I figured I had approximately four minutes of their semi-undivided attention before they lost the plot.

"Thanks for talking to me," I said. "I bet yesterday was scary, huh?" The girls nodded. Rosemary had trained them well, I thought to myself.

"How old are you guys?" One of the twins held up four fingers. The other held up five. One of us was wrong in our calculations, but I wasn't ready to concede that I was the one in error.

The eldest girl piped up. "I'm ten, and Nicole's nine," she said pointing to her tawny sister. I made a mental note…so that's what a nine- and ten year-old looked like. I was getting a real education about tiny humans in the last two days. They weren't entirely horrible. Who knew?

"Did any of you see the body?" I asked. All four of them raised their hands. "Okay, do you know who found the body?" They all looked at each other with wide eyes, then the oldest one raised her hand.

"I found it," she whispered.

"Okay. I'm sorry, what's your name, sweetie?"

"April."

"Okay, April, can you tell me where you found it?"

"Under the dock."

"Can you tell me what happened?"

She looked at her mother and, receiving her nod of approval, began relating the story. "We were playing Marco Polo."

"That's a great game," I said. "What happened when you were playing Marco Polo?"

"Well…Tyler was it, so me and Donnalee decided to hide under the dock. That's when we found her."

"That must have been scary, huh?"

She bobbed her head up and down, not noticing that her Popsicle was melting down her fingers. "It's dark under there."

"I know it is. I used to swim there with your mom. Can you tell me what happened?" I asked gently.

"Um… We were hiding under the dock, and I felt a hand on my head and I thought it was Donnalee fooling around, trying to scare me, so I pushed her hand away." I gave her an encouraging nod. "But she kept touching my head, so I pulled on her arm and tried to dunk her."

Her last words caught in her throat, and she took a ragged little breath. Tears would come next. She flitted her eyes over to her mother, looking ashamed of her behavior. "Hey," I said, bringing her attention back to me. "I would have done the same thing, sweetie. I dunked your mama on more than one occasion." I gave Rosemary a wink.

"I got you a couple of times, too, my friend," added Rosemary, playing along.

"Yeah, you did." I gave April a comforting pat on the knee. "See? Your mom and I played that same game when we were your age." Relief flooded her tiny features, and she even managed a crooked smile. "Can you tell me what happened after you tried to dunk Donnalee?" I asked.

"Um…then I heard a noise, and she started to sink. And then I heard Donnalee's voice on the other side of me telling me to shut up, so I knew it wasn't her."

"What was the noise you heard?"

"I don't know. It sounded kinda like a rip. But it was dark so I couldn't see what happened, but I think she was stuck there until I pulled on her." There was a silence while we all envisioned what had gone down.

"Did you tell the police officers this?" She shook her head no, turning her attention back to her cherry Popsicle. "Why didn't you tell them?"

She shrugged her tiny shoulders. "They didn't ask."

I had a lot to think about on my jog home. I thought back to yesterday afternoon, and Amber's body. Her blouse had been completely torn up the back and was barely covering the front of her body. Someone, presumably Junior, had trussed her up underneath the dock in an effort to keep her body from being discovered.

I jumped straight into the shower when I got home. Still, no amount of scrubbing could rid me of the creepy feeling that hung over me. I had grown up with Junior, played with his sisters. Had he assembled the building blocks of that murder scenario in his head when we were kids all playing down at the swimming hole together? Imagined what it would be like to truss someone up out of sight, left for dead? It wasn't a thought I cared to dwell on, and as luck would have it, the phone rang at just the right time to provide a diversion.

I streaked out of the shower, trying to trail as little water as possible into the bedroom, and grabbed my phone from the nightstand. I smiled. "Hello, Lorenzo."

"You sound out of breath. Did I catch you at a bad time?"

"No. I just…you just caught me in the shower."

"Oh, God," he groaned. "You're naked, aren't you?"

"Yep."

"You're still wet?"

"Yes, I am. And talking to you is probably going to make it worse."

"Oh, sweet Jesus! You're killing me."

"Something tells me you could handle it," I said, laughing. "Now, did you call to get me all hot and bothered, or is there something I can do for you?"

I could hear him chuckling softly on the other end of the line. "Brandi, I can think of about one hundred different things you could do for me right now, but I'll start with the one and only item on my list that involves you putting clothes on that gorgeous body of yours." He gave a theatrical sigh. "Did you hear about Amber?"

"I did. It's so awful."

"It really is." He paused for a moment, wondering, I imagine, how to segue from that to asking for a favor. "Listen, I hate to ask, but I really need you to bartend tonight… if you could. Our weekend girl freaked out and quit when she heard about Amber." All the humor had leaked out of his voice, and he sounded tired. "When Jimmy was killed, everybody just thought it was…you know, because he'd pissed off the wrong person. But with what happened to Amber, some of the staff is starting to get a little nervous about the club."

"Wow." What else do you say to that?

"What about you?" he asked quietly. "Are you afraid? Because I'd understand if you wanted to steer clear for a while."

"Me? Are you kidding? I live for danger. You should see the car I drive."

"Fast?"

"Not even a little bit," I said with mock sadness.

He chuckled.

"Are you going to be there tonight?" I asked, hoping to bring a smile back to his voice.

"Yes, I am."

"Are you going to kiss me again?"

"Definitely."

"I'll be there, then."

"Thanks, I owe you one. Oh, and Brandi?"

"Yes, Lorenzo?"

"Wear the wig." And he hung up.

I stared at the phone, my mouth suddenly dry. *Shit.* How much did he know about last night? Had he seen me at the casino somehow? I had kept an eagle eye out for any sign of him, so I didn't see how that was possible. He must have found out about our caper at Double Down. I could only imagine what the hell Gary told him. Ever since my bar brawl with Jay, I was on Gary's shit list. Apparently Brandi was going to have some fast-talking to do this evening. This was shaping up to be an interesting night. Seven uneasy hours at a strip club, followed by a visit to a fetish bar. What else could a girl ask for?

My new work schedule was going to conflict with our date at the Den, so I called Bobbie and left a message informing her of our new and not-so-improved rendezvous time. Two thirty in the freaking morning—Bobbie was going to love that. She had to be at work bright and early the next day. I was going to owe her big-time, not that I hadn't accumulated more than enough favor credits from Bobbie over the years.

One look at the clock on my nightstand told me there

wasn't enough time to both get ready for work and run Amber's phone into the lab, but I didn't feel too guilty about it. After all, it wasn't like I was slacking. I was on the case, and there was no way anyone would start processing a new job this late on a Sunday anyway. Besides, Amber's Blackberry might come in handy tonight at the Den. I would turn it in bright and early Monday morning.

As I toweled my hair, I realized that I was smiling. I was going to see Lorenzo tonight.

Chapter Twelve

The murders might have had a negative effect on staff attendance, but they didn't seem to have had a correlating effect on the patrons. I guess when forced to choose between the possibility of an untimely death and Roger's rack o' ribs dinner special, most red-blooded males would err on the side of meat. And boobs.

The parking lot, even around the back, was filling up fast. I climbed out of the hideous Camaro into the warm, moist evening air, savoring a few moments of heat before the air-conditioning of the club. Dressing like a tramp was definitely easier in the summer. I would have had to seriously rethink this assignment had Jimmy's murder happened in January.

I stepped into the kitchen just as Roger stepped out of the walk-in freezer. He stopped dead in his tracks when he saw me and clutched at his heart with both hands, as if to keep it from jumping out of his chest. "Lord Jesus!" he yelled.

"Roger, are you okay?" I was used to a lot of reactions when I play dress-up, but fear and horror weren't the ones I usually got. I would have gone to him, but the look of panic on his face told me it would be better to stay put.

The door shut behind me, sealing out the late afternoon rays of sun, and after a few seconds of staring at me, he loosened his grip on his chest and rubbed his hands nervously up and down his shirt. "Girl, I almost couldn't tell that was you."

"Sorry, Roger, I didn't mean to scare you," I said softly.

"No, don't be silly," he said, relief flooding over his features. "I can tell it's you now, but for a second with the sun coming in like that, and I couldn't see, you looked just like…" He ran his hand over his eyes as if trying to erase the image.

"Looked like who?"

"I'm sorry, Brandi. For a second you just looked like Amber. I don't know if you heard, but they found that poor girl dead yesterday, and then when I looked up and saw you in that…wig, I thought I'd seen a ghost."

"Oh, no! I'm so sorry, Roger. I had no idea I looked like her in this thing," I said, touching my black wig. "I never met Amber."

He gave an embarrassed chuckle. "Don't you mind me, I'm a silly old fool. You get on upstairs and get to work and I'll bring you a plate later."

I didn't know what else to say, so I gave him a quick hug and left him to his thoughts in the kitchen. Roger had been so sidelined by my wig that he hadn't had a chance to be shocked by my outfit. The same couldn't be said for Lorenzo, though, who was silently following me up the stairs to the VIP section.

"Are you trying to kill me?" he asked with a laugh when we were alone, halfway up the dark stairway.

A surprised squeal escaped my lips, and I spun around, my heart beating like crazy. "God, Lorenzo! You scared me. You can't sneak up on a girl like that." I let him catch up to me then gave him a playful swat on the shoulder.

"And you, sweetheart, can't wear an outfit like that and not expect everyone in the bar to want to attack you."

I looked down at my outfit. I was wearing a tiny pair of black short shorts over black fishnets, black leather thigh-high boots, and a black leather bustier. Point taken. I had dressed more for my second stop tonight at the fetish bar than for my bartending shift at Double Down. I gave him a sheepish grin. "Are you saying that you want to attack me?"

He leaned in, trapping me up against the wall with the length of his body, and I lazily relinquished control, letting him pin my hands as he ran his fingers up the length of my thigh. One word from me and he would have released me, but it was so bloody hot to imagine being manhandled by him. And he knew it. He had my number. The top buttons of his light linen shirt were undone, and I could see the lean muscles of his chest barely working to hold me there in place. I imagined him with his shirt off, those long strong muscles and that smooth buttery-caramel skin. I took in a deep breath, trying to soak in the scent of him. God, he smelled so good, like a man, and soap, and fresh laundry, and expensive cologne. His breath was warm and tingly on my temple as he answered my question. "Yes, I'm afraid I do want to attack you and do terrible things to you. But I have to admit I'm feeling a little conflicted about it."

"Really?" I asked him. "Why is that?"

"Well…" He traced his fingers up the length of my stomach, stopping when he reached the underwire of my bustier.

I opened my mouth to stop him, but he silenced any coming protest with a shush and started rubbing his thumbs back and forth over my nipples. A little jolt of heat ran through me, responding to his touch. "You see, I met this really great blond woman last week, a Canadian, if you can believe it, and I haven't been able to stop thinking about her. Then last night this beautiful brunette walks into my casino and turns all my blackjack dealers into pudding, and I haven't been able to stop thinking about her, either." He ran his fingers along my collarbone then down until they met the lace of my bustier. "What do you think I should do?" He watched my face intently as he pulled the lacy fabric down over my breasts, lightly stroking them. I caught my breath, the feeling of the cool air and his warm fingers on my bare skin tightening other lower places. I watched him as he looked down to see me for the first time, and a small murmur escaped his lips. He was pleased.

"How did you know I was there?" I whispered, my breath catching in my throat. "I didn't see you."

"I have my ways. Did you go there because you wanted to see me?"

His breath was hot against my neck, his lips so close that my skin tingled. "Of course not," I said, lying. His grip tightened on my wrists, a slow smile pulling at the corners of his mouth.

"I don't believe you," he murmured low and sexy in my ear. He grazed my earlobe with his teeth, making me shiver with anticipation.

"Don't flatter yourself—" I started to say, but the last half of the sentence was lost in his mouth, lost on his tongue, as he pressed me into the wall. I fumbled with the buttons on his shirt, dying to feel his bare chest against my skin, but I couldn't work them fast enough. He lowered himself a step and bent his head down, teasing me with his tongue over the soft flesh of my breast, licking, sucking. He softly bit down around my nipple, making me cry out, and as he worked his tongue lightly over the tip, I could feel it tightening in his mouth.

"Excuse me, folks."

I was so lost in the moment that it took me a minute to actually register another presence in the stairway. It wasn't until I saw the balding man make his way past us, his head bowed discreetly, that I realized we'd been putting on a bit of a show. Customers at Double Down were likely accustomed to seeing public displays of affection all the time, but I was more than a little embarrassed. The last time I'd acted like this in public had been back in college, and needless to say, there had been more than a little alcohol involved. Tonight, however, I was stone-cold sober and suffering from nothing other than a complete lack of self-control. Even so, if a second customer hadn't stepped through the heavy curtain and up the stairs at that moment, I probably would have had my top off and my panties down around my ankles with very little convincing.

"I'd better get to work," I whispered, my senses slowly returning to me.

Lorenzo gently rearranged the bits of fabric back into place, then tipped my chin up so that he could look into my eyes. "Can we pick this up later?"

Everything in my body wanted to say yes, but I needed to get to the Den. "How about tomorrow night?" I said.

"Sure," said Lorenzo. There was a tiny hint of disappointment in his eyes, but he bent down and kissed me softly. "I want to see you again, outside this place." And he loped up the stairs, leaving me to my thoughts.

It had been a pretty busy night until two local news vans arrived and stationed themselves outside the joint looking for sound bite reactions on the murders. Most guys wanted a certain level of anonymity when they came to look at strangers' boobies, and the thought of being spotted by their families and employers outside a peeler bar had limited appeal for anyone other than the frat boy set. So by one o'clock the place was pretty much deserted. I had already cleaned up the bar, run all the glasses through the washer, and cut the limes for the day bartender. It was time to do some poking around.

I made my way down the long dark hallway toward the bathrooms and Lorenzo's office. The faint smell of cigarette smoke greeted me and grew stronger as I went along. I peeked into the ladies' room—empty—and the men's room was the same. I continued down the hallway, my feet silent on the dark carpeting, and stopped dead in my tracks. The emergency exit door was set slightly askew, not properly shut. If I hadn't been snooping, I probably wouldn't have noticed. I crept up to the door. A matchbook cover had been folded over and wedged between the door and the doorjamb, preventing the door from locking. I heard low murmurs coming from outside the door.

Here goes nothing, I thought and gave the door a push, hoping I wasn't about to interrupt anything dangerous, messy, or awkward. I didn't. Three of the VIP dancers were out there smoking on the steps. One of them flicked her cigarette over the railing, and another ground her butt under her shoe, giving me a guilty little smile. I got the feeling they weren't supposed to be out here.

"Oh, hey, ladies," I said with a smile that let them know I was on their side, as opposed to the side of establishment.

"What's up, Brandi?" one of the girls answered. The girls upstairs were very nice to me, mainly because I was nice to them, I suppose.

"I was just looking for Sandy." A lie. "But I see she's not out here, so I'm going to go cash out. See you guys tomorrow."

"Later, girl," said the dancer who was on the highest step.

She reached back with one hand to keep the door from closing and picked up the matchbook cover in order to reset it.

I gave the door the once-over before I pulled my head back inside. There was no door handle on the outside, which explained why they had propped the door open. It could only be opened from the inside.

There was still no sign of life in the hallway, so I backtracked a few feet to the supply room. It was unlocked. I flicked on the light, stepped inside, and shut the door quietly behind me.

It was a little on the messy side—to be expected, I suppose. There were shelves of every type of liquor and mix that the bar carried, along with the CO_2 cartridges for the fountain drinks, napkins, straws, paper towels, and toilet paper. The usual. There was a tiny bistro table in the corner, along with two folding chairs. A little strange, I thought to myself. I couldn't imagine who would feel the need to take a breather in here, but what did I know. There was a coatrack nailed into the wall beside the door, for aprons to be hung on, perhaps. I wasn't sure, but one thing I was sure of was the rusty splotch of color on the center hook. Blood. There was a tiny cluster of black hairs wrapped around the hook as well. I couldn't be 100 percent sure, but I was 99.9 percent sure that I had found Amber's murder scene.

My heart started to pound, fueled into overdrive by my oldest and dearest friend, adrenaline. In my head I worked to piece together what might have happened in this room the night Amber and Jimmy died. She had definitely struggled with her attacker (Junior, we were assuming). Her missing fingernails and the bruises and abrasions covering her body had already told us that. It wasn't inconceivable to imagine that she could have lost her balance during the fight and fallen back onto the hook, accidentally braining herself, but the more likely scenario, based on the ligature marks that had been found on her neck, was that someone had rammed her into that hook intentionally. Dumping Amber's body in the swimming hole had merely been the final indignity. If the struggle had indeed happened here, it stood to reason that those missing fingernails might still be in this very room.

I dropped down to my knees, thanking my lucky stars for Lorenzo's incompetent cleaning staff, and scanned the floor. They were pink, I remembered from the swimming hole. Pink acrylic fingernails. I felt a pang of sorrow for this girl that I would never meet. I was sure she never imagined when she sat down for her last manicure that they were gluing the puzzle pieces to her own murder onto the ends of her fingers.

My eye caught a hint of pink wedged up against a metal CO_2 container, and I scurried over on my hands and knees, ignoring the fact that the concrete floor would leave me some lovely bruises by morning. It looked incongruous suddenly, a shock of pink against all the gray metal and concrete and dirt. It reminded me of a tiny flower pushing its way up through the sidewalk cracks on a neglected street, demanding to be seen.

I grabbed a cocktail napkin from the metal shelf above me and used it to gingerly pluck the lonely fingernail from its nest of dust. It was crusted and filthy, but with any luck some of that filth would translate into her attacker's DNA. The lab had their work cut out for them, that was for sure. Before I could find something suitable to put the fingernail in, I heard a noise at the door.

I whipped my head around, watching the knob turn. Shit. I jammed the fingernail into the tiny pocket on the outside of my boot and reached instinctively for the comfort of my tiny Arms Guardian gun. Lorenzo came through the door, and we locked eyes for what seemed like an eternity. He looked confused to see me there. I guess I couldn't blame him. I was on all fours, in a dirty storage room, in what amounted to an S&M Halloween costume. What was odd about that?

"Brandi?" he asked tentatively. "Are you okay?"

"I don't know," I replied slowly, buying myself a moment to think. I rubbed my head and painted a confused expression on my face. "I think I fainted." A classic, no-fail diversion technique that always yielded the desired effect.

Lorenzo rushed to my side and gently brushed the hair out of my eyes. "Are you okay? Did you hit your head?" he asked.

I let him lift me to my feet and inspect me for damage, bless his heart. Even though I told the world that I didn't like playing the damsel in distress, I had to admit that it felt nice to have someone make a fuss over my health and welfare. I searched his face for even the tiniest hint that he wasn't being sincere, but his deep chocolate eyes held nothing but concern. He looked truly worried about me—not worried that I was snooping around the storage room, but worried about my health. I decided to trust him.

I leaned into him, knowing that he would fold his strong arms around me, and pointed at the coat hook. He looked to where I was pointing and back to me, confusion clouding his face. "I think I found where Amber was murdered," I said quietly.

"What are you talking about, Brandi? They found Amber in the river, down on the reservation."

Shit. I realized that I had no idea what information had been made available to the public. I could only hope he hadn't been tracking the investigation under a microscope. "No, didn't you hear?" I asked with what I hoped sounded like the guileless enthusiasm of a rambling gossip. "They said her body had only been dumped there...that they think she was killed someplace else." I tried to muster up a face full of sincerity and wide-eyed innocence, not really my forte. "Look," I said, pulling him over to the coat rack. "I think that's blood. And black hair." He was staring at the evidence, trying to do some mental math. "The last place anybody saw Amber alive was here at the club, Lorenzo."

He gave a long exhale and raked his hand through his hair. "Shit," he said.

"Yeah." It was his move now, and I was more than a little curious to see if he'd take the high road or the low road.

He dropped his head, and his shoulders sagged a little under the weight of the situation. "We'd better call the cops."

Despite the dire circumstances, I let my heart feel a moment of lightness. Someone with Lorenzo's pedigree might not want to involve the police, but this stood as a grand gesture to me, a sign that he truly was trying to walk the straight and narrow.

"I can call them if you want, Lorenzo. I know you have to cash the girls out."

"Really?"

I nodded.

"Thanks, Brandi."

He smoothed my hair again, placed a protective kiss on my forehead, and gently escorted me from the storage room. He pulled a set of keys from his trouser pocket and locked the door behind us.

"Are you sure you're okay to call?"

"I'm fine." I gave him a reassuring smile. "Really."

He pulled his lips into a grim smile and crossed the hall to let the gaggle of girls into his office. I watched him settle wearily into his leather chair and headed out to the bar to dig my phone out of my purse.

Chief Thompson picked up on the fourth ring. That had to be a record for him. I hoped I hadn't caught him in the middle of something, like a romantic interlude with Mrs. Chief. His businesslike demeanor made me dismiss that notion immediately.

"Chief," he barked. "This better be good."

"This is better than good, Chief. We may have just found the lead we've been looking for. Amber was killed here at the club. I think I found the murder scene."

"Are you absolutely certain?"

"Sure as I've ever been, Chief."

I could almost feel his excitement thrumming through the line. This was the break we'd been looking for.

"I'll get down there with a team right away."

I was waiting for the line to go dead, but instead he said, "Cassidy…good work." Then the line went dead.

I'd never admit it aloud, but I had been waiting for that validation for a very long time. Solving this crime would give me a new place at the station. Hopefully, Andrea would be the one on duty from the coroner's office. She had been the one to inspect Amber's body down by the river, so she would know exactly what she was looking at.

I jolted back to reality and looked at the time on my phone. Shit! I had fifteen minutes to get to the Den to meet Bobbie. For so many reasons, I did not want Bobbie to be left to her own devices outside a sex club.

I pulled my cash drawer and hustled down the dark hallway to Lorenzo's office. The last girl was just leaving as I walked in, and Lorenzo looked up at me with tired eyes. "Did you call the police?"

"Yeah, I did. They're sending a team out right away."

"Good," he said, raking his hand through his hair again. It was a nervous gesture I hadn't noticed before tonight, but then again, we hadn't found ourselves in a sticky situation like this before. "If you don't mind waiting till Bertrand gets here, I can drive you home."

I hadn't expected such a sweet invitation, so I didn't have an answer ready for him, but obviously I couldn't take him up on his offer. For one, I had to get my tired ass over to the Den, and for another, I couldn't let Lorenzo know where I lived. Hard-up-for-cash illegal alien waitresses didn't live in beautiful country houses on the outskirts of town. Nope, just didn't happen. They lived in crappy studio apartments next to strip malls and Taco Bells. It would take him five minutes to do a title search on my property and figure out my real identity. He took my silence for shock, I think, because he rounded the desk and folded me into his arms again.

"It's okay," I muffled into his expensive shirt. "I'm feeling better."

He pulled back, holding me at arm's length, and fixed me with a tender look of concern. "Listen, you already fainted once tonight. What happens if you faint when you're on the road? Let me take you home."

"It's okay. I really am feeling better." He didn't look convinced. "It was probably just the blood. The sight of it always makes me queasy. And besides, I have a…uh…a thing…that I have to do." I winced. That sounded lame, even to me.

He raised his eyebrows just a hint, and I could tell that he was thinking the worst. I was dressed like a complete skank and it was quarter past two in the morning. What kind of *thing* could I possibly have planned that didn't involve crawling into bed with some other guy? "It's not what you think," I said. "And you wouldn't believe me if I tried to explain it to you, so I'll just say that I would ten times rather stay here with you and have you drive me home, and leave it at that."

Now that was the God's honest truth.

Chapter Thirteen

I rolled up to the Den five minutes past our scheduled meeting time. It was located in the old abandoned chocolate factory in the industrial part of the city. The chocolate factory had been a magnificent stand-alone building, built out of stone and dark brick back in the 1940s. Back then it would have been the only structure around for miles, a shining beacon of prosperity in a tiny but growing frontier town. Now it sat wedged in among rows and rows of nondescript, innocuous aluminum-sided beige buildings, the chocolate makers having long since moved to another city.

It was actually kind of a genius spot for a debauched sex club. First…chocolate? Yeah. Second, the industrial park was empty at night, so there were no neighbors nearby to offend, not to mention there was plenty of parking, acres, in fact, if you had the nerve to leave your car unattended and the courage to walk from your car to the building in the dark. Lucky for me I was driving arguably the crappiest car in North America and I was carrying a weapon. What could possibly go wrong?

Bobbie was waiting for me at the front door, talking to a tall, well-built gentleman. It never took her long to make friends, especially in the kind of outfit she was wearing. She had poured herself into a short black vinyl trench coat and finished off the look with cherry-red stiletto heels. I was betting there wasn't much, if anything, underneath her coat. Her lips were painted a dark red, and her long dark hair was twisted into two schoolgirl braids, which hung down over her shoulders, her nod to yin and yang. The man next to her was muscular and tanned, wearing tight black leather pants, a...harness, I guess would be the best word for it, over his bare torso, and a leather hood that covered his face down to his generous lips. All in all, a look that says, "I'm into pain, but I like to party." Who said men didn't know how to accessorize?

When Bobbie saw me coming, she gave a little wave, and they both made their way down the steps to greet me. Apparently, they were together. As I got closer, I could see her friend's mouth turn up at the corners.

"Nice getup, Cassidy," he said. "I don't think I would have recognized you in that wig."

I recognized the voice—my partner Ken. I looked over at Bobbie with what I could only imagine was disbelief, then turned my eyes back to Ken. For the first time in a very, very long time, I was momentarily speechless.

"I can say the same to you," I replied when my voice returned to me. "Cute harness."

"She likes to be called Brandi when she comes here, though, Kenny," said Bobbie, slipping her arm through his.

Maybe this was payback, my punishment, compliments of the universe, for dragging Bobbie out to a fetish bar so late on a school night. "When did this happen?" I asked, wagging my finger back and forth between the two of them.

"What?" Bobbie asked innocently.

"This. You two together?"

Now it was Ken's turn to look uncomfortable. He looked to Bobbie then back to me. "Promise you won't tell anyone?" he asked nervously. I gave him a curt nod. "I um...I work here. On the door," he added hurriedly.

My jaw dropped, slack-jawed, I believe is the term. "What?" Of all the things that could have come out of sweet, pretty, conservative Ken's mouth, working at a fetish club was not one of them.

"Look, Cass—sorry, Brandi—this is how I put myself through school, and now I work here a couple nights a week to make extra cash. My school loans are killing me." It was a lot to absorb. I had no idea that my pink plastic Ken doll had a dark leather side. "Promise you won't tell anyone at the station? I could lose my job."

I hoped Ken knew he could count on me, hoped he knew there was no way in hell I would ever sell out my partner, short of him performing some super-heinous crime. To underscore my loyalty and cement our bond, I turned around and pointed at my ass cleavage. "Do I look like the kind of girl to throw stones, Ken?" A tiny smile played on his lips. "Whaddya say we both pretend that neither one of us was here tonight, cool?"

Ken let out a relieved chuckle. "You got it...Brandi."

This was actually a great turn of events for me—lemons into lemonade, and all that crap. Ken would be our instant access into the deep dark Den. "Listen," I said, getting down to business. "I'm looking for a guy who goes by the name Taurus. Any idea where we can find him?"

Ken's shoulders stiffened into their defensive posture again. "Taurus?" He paused a moment, trying to decide how to proceed. "You need to see Taurus…specifically?"

"I do."

He hesitated again, pursing his lips in disapproval.

"Oh, for God's sake, Ken!" I hissed. "It's about my case!"

Again, his shoulders relaxed. "Oh, thank God," he said. "I was worried that you wanted to…never mind."

"What in the hell are you blithering about, Ken?"

"You know what? Nothing. Let me give you these," he said, pulling two thin white leather cuffs off his wrist. "These will give you access to anywhere you want to go in there without having to…uh…participate." He wrapped one of the cuffs around Bobbie's wrist. It had the word "Voyeur" spelled out in small silver letters. "This lets you watch."

As he strapped an identical voyeur cuff around my wrist, I saw that he had many other cuffs in his possession for distribution—dominant, masochist, sadist, submissive, slave. Whatever kink you wanted, apparently you could get it here. Not a bad idea to wear your kink on your sleeve, I suppose. It could eliminate a lot of potentially embarrassing scenarios. You'd never have to worry about getting slapped when all you wanted was a tickle. And if you really thought about it, a similar system could be employed at regular mainstream bars. The doormen could hand out wristbands to all the patrons—single, married, just want to talk, horny, one-night stand, gay, lonely, whatever.

"So where can we find Taurus?" I asked Ken again.

Ken pointed toward the building, resigned. "Once you get in, you're going to head straight down the stairs and turn right. Walk to the end of the hall and turn left. It's either the third or the fourth door down." He paused, showing his distaste. "You're looking for the Plow Room."

My eyes widened. Bobbie choked on her gum. Ken didn't blink. I couldn't even imagine what delights the Plow Room had to offer. "Well, that sounds horticultural. Thanks, Ken."

"Moose," he corrected.

"Moose," I repeated.

"Sweet Jesus," whispered Bobbie. "Is there a reason?"

"Okay, kids!" I said. No need to get in the middle of that conversation. Although I had to admit, he had my attention. "Let's get this done."

"Hey," he called out as we started to move off.

"Yes...Moose?"

He hesitated, embarrassed maybe. "Nothing. Just be careful." And he walked us up the steps, opening the front door for us.

It took a good thirty seconds for our eyes to adjust to the darkness, and when they finally cooperated with the low light I could see that the old factory had been fixed up to look like the inside of an old castle. The foyer, where Bobbie and I stood getting acclimated, was grand and imposing, lit with nothing but black alchemy candles that were scented with, if it's possible, the smell of sex, somewhere in the realm of leather and tobacco meets bourbon and men's cologne.

A woman wearing a beautiful corseted gown stood death still behind an ornately carved bone desk, waiting for us to collect ourselves. "What's your pleasure, ladies?" she asked demurely. "Heaven?" she purred, pointing to the plush velvet-covered stairs leading upward, "or Hell?" Her voice slid off into a low growl as she pointed to the cold stone stairwell leading down into what was essentially the basement.

Ken had told us to go downstairs. Really? There was no Plow Room in heaven? "Hell," I answered, my mouth suddenly dry.

"As you wish." She drew a small sheet of paper and a quill pen from out of her desk and looked at us expectantly. "I'm afraid I'll need you to sign this."

It was a waiver absolving the Den from any responsibility for injury to body, mind, or spirit. Sweet Jesus! What the hell. I gave Bobbie an apologetic look and signed my name Brandi Hammer. Bobbie signed in next as Trixie Davenport, and gave me an impish grin. She had finally been given an opportunity to use her fantasy stripper name. We were even.

The hostess, satisfied their asses were covered (not literally), invited us to descend into the bowels of the building with a graceful sweep of her arm. The stairs were wide and shallow and the sound of our spiky heels ricocheted off the stone to mingle with the groans and creaks of the building's old pipes. The handrails, forged of industrial-grade iron, were bolted into the walls with massive rusted studs. The lighting, although still dark and moody, was different here than in the lobby. Low-wattage dirty bulbs glowed dim and yellow behind their rusty metal cages, casting spidery shadows around the stairwell. On the facing wall at the bottom of the stairs was a fun-house mirror that stretched your reflection into giant proportions as you descended. Then, somehow, when you reached the bottom step, your reflection stared back at you, completely normal, but upside down. An interesting choice, I thought.

There was a hallway to the left and another one to the right. Both looked the same, like the starting point of an ancient maze in the dungeon of an ancient castle. We turned right as instructed by Moose and continued along. The hallway started to narrow as we got farther along, and whether it was my imagination or not, I could swear the temperature began to change. The lobby had been comfortable, but it was downright hot and humid down here in Hell. How apropos.

I could make out a muffled stomping and scuttling sound coming toward us from around the next corner. Bobbie and I traded a look. We came face-to-face-to-crotch with a master and slave combo. The master, a big construction worker–sized guy, with a shiny smooth cue ball head, was decked out in enough black leather to cover a corner booth at the Great Griddle. The slave who was being dragged along behind him, on the other hand, could have benefited from a few more square inches of fabric. She was a pudgy, pale, ordinary-looking woman, wearing nothing but a dog collar, a G-string, and a pair of knee pads. In jeans and a T-shirt, she could have been anyone's mom.

When he saw us, he pulled up on her leash, yanking her back awkwardly onto her haunches. My hand went up to my own neck reflexively. That couldn't have felt good, but she didn't complain.

"What have we got here?" he growled. Maybe if we pretended not to see him…nope. That lame plan never worked.

He dropped the leash onto the floor and crossed the last few feet toward us on his own, his outfit creaking and squeaking as he moved. I downgraded his leather outfit to vinyl. Leather just doesn't sound like that.

He was a big man, probably pushing two fifty, and he managed to block out a great deal of the light in the hallway as he encroached on our personal space. He reached out with a big, callused hand and clamped onto my wrist, pulling me in close. His breath was hot and foul, and the heat radiating from his vinyl cocoon told me that a sweaty, stinky mess was lurking just beneath. "You look good enough to eat," he said. He yanked my hand up to his face to look at my cuff—white for voyeur, and he growled again. I noticed he was wearing three cuffs. A black one for sadist, a red one for dominant, and a blue one for master. No control issues there.

He didn't quite seem ready to let me go, and I wasn't quite up to speed on rejection protocol, so I pointed at my cuff with my free hand and said, "Sorry, Igor, white for 'just watching you weird fucks go at it.' Guess you'll have to take your lunch to go." I nodded over to the poor woman he'd left in a heap and flashed him a big grin.

He let me go with a growl, cast a look over at Bobbie's matching white cuff, and stomped back to his chew toy. She cowered, whether for effect or for preservation I'm not sure, and waited for an order. He snapped his fingers and pointed to the leash on the ground. She bent her head down to the floor, picked up the end of her leash with her teeth, and handed it to him, Lassie style. He fired us one last scathing look, which I rewarded with a sincere eye roll, and yanked his pet into motion. *Good call on the knee pads*, I thought as she skittered after him. Crawling around after some douche bag must be murder on the knees.

Bobbie gave a nervous giggle. "Wow. You really know how to show a girl a good time."

"Yeah. Don't say I never take you anyplace nice."

She grabbed onto my pinkie finger. "I'm picking next time, though."

When we got to the end of the hallway, we turned left as directed. This hallway was pulsing with men and women in varying states of dress and undress. There was more skin to be seen than fabric, some of it good and some of it not so much. Although there was a fair amount of groping and petting being done, most of the attention was fixed on what was going on behind a series of tinted windows.

"What do you think everybody's looking at?" whispered Bobbie.

"I'll give you three guesses," I answered. "But I'd say the Plow Room isn't the only attraction down here in good ol' Hades."

Bobbie and I inched up to the first window, careful not to obstruct anyone's view, and even more careful not to make any inadvertent flesh-to-flesh contact with any of the other patrons. The iron-etched wall plaque told me that this attraction was called the Rack. The room looked for all the world like an old-fashioned torture chamber. A man and a woman, both completely naked except for blindfolds, were trussed up and splayed out like game hens. Their hands were shackled over their heads with leather cuffs, while spreader bars wrenched their legs apart like wishbones. Don't ask me why all of this made me think of food. Whatever.

An expensively turned-out dominatrix was holding court with her whip and cat-o'-nine-tails, ordering a small team of barely dressed slaves to do her bidding. As Bobbie and I passed by the window, the dominatrix gave an impressive snap of her whip, sending the slaves scurrying over to the hog-tied pair. It became a writhing blur of tongues and fingers, and I turned away, my face turning bright red. I didn't need that visual haunting me night after night. It was bad enough that I was having Neanderthal cop wet dreams.

Bobbie, however, was having a hard time looking away. "I had no idea…"

"Well, now you do," I said, trying to sound businesslike. "Come on, let's find the Plow Room." Bobbie didn't move. "Or you can stay here. Maybe our new friend Igor and his pet will come back and keep you company." That worked. Bobbie shook her head, refocused her eyes, and followed my lead through the crowd.

We continued on past the Iron Cross Room, which looked decidedly less religious than the name would imply, and the Doll House, which contained a lot more PVC than actual human flesh. How someone could have sex with an inflatable pool toy, in public, no less, was well and truly beyond me. The next window looked into the Plow Room. It looked as though an act, if that's what you would call it, was just finishing, because the crowd had mostly turned away from the window and begun to take interest in one another. I pulled Bobbie up to the glass and looked inside.

Two big men were beginning to extract a small, mostly naked woman from the plow machine. She was shackled on her hands and knees, legs apart, her neck tethered by a chain from the floor. A blindfold and ball gag completed the ensemble. Taurus was leaning back against the wall, naked, drinking a Gatorade. He was bigger than I had imagined from the photos on Amber's phone. Wiry, I suppose. He looked spent. And sticky. Apparently he'd been working hard, or more appropriately, hard at work.

"What should I do?" I asked Bobbie.

"Knock, I guess."

"Here goes nothing." I rapped on the glass, pointing at Taurus. The two fellas who were busy unshackling the woman whipped their heads around at the sound and marched over to the door with dark, ugly looks on their faces. One of them flung open the door and grabbed Bobbie, who was closest. The other one reached out and grabbed me. They heaved us inside the room and slammed us up against the window.

My head bounced off the glass.

"Are you fucking blind?" he said. "Can't you fucking read?"

I made a choking sound through my constricted airway, hoping he might get the hint and loosen his grip on it. He did minutely, allowing me to squeak out an, "Excuse me?"

"The sign out there. Says no touching the glass." A little spittle flew out of his mouth and landed on my cheek. I tried my hardest to ignore it.

"I'm sorry," I said. "It's our first time here." He didn't look impressed. I flicked my eyes over to Bobbie. Her eyes were wide with surprise, and she was trying fruitlessly to pry her goon's fingers off her neck.

Ordinarily when I get into a bind, I flash my badge and tell people to fuck off, and when someone lays their hands on me uninvited, I break their thumbs. Neither of those approaches was going to work here, so I opted for honesty yet again. "I need to talk to Taurus," I said, loud enough to get his attention. He looked over as he capped his Gatorade.

"Get in line," my goon growled at me, unimpressed.

"It's about Amber," I said.

That got Taurus's attention. "Let her go, Bubba," he said. Bubba was nothing if not obedient. He released his death grip on my throat, and I gave it a little rub. If I found paw-print bruises on my neck in the morning, I would track Bubba down and give him a matching set.

"You want I should let this one go, too, Taurus?" asked the other goon.

"Yeah, yeah, for Christ's sake. Let her go." Taurus grabbed a pair of black gym shorts and managed to slip them on gracefully as he walked over to us. "So you've seen Amber?"

I looked at Bobbie as she tried to rub some circulation back into her neck. She had a grim expression on her face. "Yeah. We saw her," I answered.

"Did she say why she took off? Is she pissed at me or something?" He had an abandoned-puppy-dog look on his face that didn't quite fit with the chip on his shoulder.

"Why, did you guys have a fight?" I asked.

"No, man. She just blew me off." He dropped his bad-boy facade in an instant, as if the effort of holding it in place was suddenly overwhelming. "It's been killing me, man." He looked like a man nursing a broken heart, and call me crazy, but I just couldn't see Taurus killing Amber. Tying her up and screwing her unconscious, yeah, but killing, no.

"I don't know how to tell you this," I said slowly, trying to find the right words, "but Amber's dead. Her body was found on Saturday."

I watched him process this information, confusion and disbelief settling onto his face. "Is this some kind of sick joke?" It was a rhetorical question, but he wanted an answer anyway, and I could see anger building up behind his eyes, fast, like a forest fire. He lunged for me, grabbing both of my arms, and gave me a joint-popping shake. "Is this some kind of sick fucking joke?" he screamed this time, his wild eyes searching my face for answers.

I locked onto his eyes and slowly shook my head no. "I'm sorry."

Whatever he saw in my face stopped him in his tracks, and he froze, his anger evaporating instantly, converting to shock. Anyone who has been delivered bad news by a cop knows the look, can testify to its analgesic effect. Even decked out in my S&M ensemble, he could see that I was telling the truth. Deep down he probably even knew I was a cop. But right now he was just working to stay upright. His fingers went slack, as if someone had pressed a release button, and his arms fell limply down to his sides.

"But...how?" The question died on his lips as his face started to crumple, tears filling his eyes. "What happened?"

Before I could answer him, two slender arms wrapped themselves around his chest. "It's okay, Taurus."

I recognized the voice, and a familiar drug-addled face peeked out from behind him, her arms still clasped around his chest. "It's okay," she slurred again, resting her head on his back. Taurus gave her hand a pat, accepting the small comfort.

"Candy?" I hadn't recognized her when we first came in, between the blindfold, the ball gag, and all the other accoutrements. But sure enough, it had been Candy getting plowed here in the Plow Room. By Taurus. I don't know how it was possible after everything I'd seen tonight, but I was shocked. "You didn't tell him, Candy?"

Candy's eyes went wide like saucers, the realization that she'd messed up only now dawning on her. "I…I didn't want to bother him at work."

"What?" Taurus yanked her hands off his chest and swung her around to face him. "You knew? You fucking bitch! You fucking knew?"

Candy's bottom lip started to shake. Tears, her only defense, wouldn't be far behind. Taurus dug his fingers into Candy's shoulders, leaving white pressure patches on her skin, and shook her hard enough to rattle her teeth. "Are you fucking kidding me? Why the hell didn't you tell me? You little bitch!" He took a ragged breath. "You just come in here and let me do that to you"—he gestured to the device—"all the while you know my girlfriend is dead?" He rattled her again. "What the hell is wrong with you?"

"That's enough," I said putting my hand on Taurus's shoulder. He didn't respond, so I pulled on his arm and yelled, "That's enough!" He let go of Candy long enough to backhand me into the plow machine and kept on with his assault.

"A little help!" I yelled to the two baboons that were supposed to be in charge of security. "He's going to hurt her!"

"Sorry, lady," said one of them, "we're here to protect Taurus."

"How's an assault charge going to help Taurus, you morons?" I scrambled to my feet, ignoring the trickle of blood that was now running down my back, and wrenched on Taurus's arm. "Taurus!" I screamed at the top of my lungs, and gave him an open-handed slug across the face.

"Get a hold of yourself!"

Tweedledee and Tweedledum lurched toward me, and I spun on them like a hellcat.

"Touch me again, you Cro-Magnon assholes, and you'll pull back a bloody stump! You got it?" They stopped in their tracks, wide-eyed.

"I think you're wearing the wrong wristband, lady," muttered the goon who had been restraining Bobbie.

"I don't need a wristband to kick your ass! You remember that." I turned back to Taurus. He didn't look happy, and he was rubbing his cheek, but at least he wasn't mauling Candy anymore.

"You okay?" I asked.

Before he could respond there was a wild thumping on the glass and the two goons leaped into action again, snarling and swearing. They must have taken a blood oath to protect that window. Bubba whipped open the door, but before his goon buddy could grab the offender, a man dressed all in black stormed into the room and grabbed my arm. It was Detective Coleman.

"I need that phone!" he hissed into my face.

I did a wrist sweep, freeing my arm from his grip, and backhanded his nose with my knuckles. Before he could step away, I slammed both of his ears with my palms as if I were banging cymbals. His head would be ringing for hours. He reached up instinctively to protect his ears from further abuse, and I took the opportunity to relieve him of his handcuffs. I captured his right wrist first, then whipped both of his hands down behind his back and cuffed his left. When I was done, I spun him around and slammed him into the glass. "First of all, you piece of shit...don't you ever grab me like that again." I got up into his face even more. "Second of all, that phone is going straight into evidence, and whatever secret you're trying to hide, well, you can just consider yourself fucked."

His eyes were burning angry. "This is going to cost you your job, you stupid bitch."

I put my weight into a gut punch. "Guess what," I hissed. "I'm not interested in your career counseling." I turned to Bubba and his friend. "A little help here, guys?" Whether it was the fact that they were perhaps just a wee bit afraid of me, or that they were really used to taking orders, the goons actually lumbered over to offer their assistance.

"Hold him, will ya?" They each grabbed an arm and Jay started to protest, so I grabbed Candy's ball gag and shoved it into his mouth. I was pretty sure they had shared more than just saliva in the past, so I didn't have any qualms about it. "Do you have any scissors?" I asked the goons. Blank looks. "Of course not. A knife then?"

Bubba unclasped a switchblade from his belt and offered it to me. "Thanks." I slit the fabric on Coleman's right shoulder and ripped the sleeve off his long-sleeved shirt, then did the same on the left side. Next, I poked a hole into the cotton just below his nipples, and ripped the fabric away there, too. I hacked away at the seams until the entire bottom half of his T-shirt was gone, leaving his muscular torso exposed. I stood back and studied the view. Not quite right. I split the fabric at the neck and ripped it apart down the middle, making a vest. Better.

Next, I undid his belt buckle and the buttons on his pants and pulled his jeans down around his knees, trapping his legs. "Hold him, guys," I said and pulled his boots off. I couldn't help but notice that Jay had pitched a tent in his Calvin Kleins and was straining to poke my eye out with it. God bless him. Once I had his pants off, I put his boots back on, then his belt—very Village People. I looked around and spotted Candy's collar, and put that on him, too.

"Hey, Bubba, do you have any wristbands on you?" I pointed to my white cuff. "Different ones than this?" He reached into the pocket of his cargo pants and pulled out a handful. I selected a pink one, a yellow one, and a purple one—submissive, masochist, and slave. Perfect. I put all three onto his wrist. "Lipstick?" I called out to the room.

Bobbie pulled a tube from her trench coat pocket and handed it to me. I turned Jay around and wrote a message on his back. "Leash!" Bobbie passed me Candy's tether, and I hooked it to Jay's collar.

As an afterthought, I grabbed the remnants of Jay's T-shirt, ripped the fabric in half, and tied the strips of fabric around his knees for extra padding. After all, I'm not a monster. Then I swept his legs, dropping him to the floor, and dragged him out of the room. Nobody even looked twice as I marched down the hall with Jay scrambling after me, handcuffed, on his knees. I stopped at the hitching post outside the Iron Cross Room and tied him up with the other slaves. I looked down at him as he looked up at me, pure hate in his eyes. "You have a LICK ME sign on your back," I said and left.

Bobbie caught up to me on the sidewalk and silently fell into stride. That was the hallmark of a good friend. They knew when you went too far, but they also knew when you knew that you'd gone too far.

We made our way to the now nearly empty parking lot and didn't speak until I reached my Camaro. As luck would have it, my crappy night was just getting crappier. "Shit."

Bobbie looked from me to my car. "Shit," she echoed. The driver's side window had been smashed. There were shards of glass on the ground, but most of it had landed inside the car on the seat. "I think it looks better, Cass." I looked at Bobbie. "Seriously, it couldn't have gotten any worse." She had a point, I suppose. And at least now I had some form of air-conditioning.

I stuck my key in the rusted lock and opened the door. I had left nothing of value inside, and the parts on this car would have been worth approximately nothing. Nobody would have broken into a rusted-out, twenty-five-year old Camaro unless they were looking for something specific. It had to have been someone who knew that I was going to be here, which narrowed the field considerably. The only people who knew were Bobbie, Ken, Candy, and Detective Coleman.

The only person who wanted something I had in my possession was Detective Coleman.

The only person who had physically assaulted me this evening was Detective Coleman...and Taurus...and his meatheads...but only Coleman's attack had been personal.

I was putting my money on Detective Coleman for this. And I knew what he was looking for. He obviously hadn't managed to get into the trunk. Like everything else on this car, the trunk release was broken and could only be opened with my car key. I walked to the back, popped the trunk, peeled back the rug, and pulled out Amber's bejeweled phone. *What are you hiding?*

A car growled to life across the parking lot, its headlights bathing the derelict industrial park in an unnatural halogen glow. I watched its progress, feeling suddenly uneasy. "Let's get out of here," I said. Instead of turning onto the road, the car adjusted its course and headed in our direction.

"Bobbie, get down!" I yelled, pulling her down to the ground behind the car. I reached into my boot for my tiny Arms Guardian, released the safety, and peered over the hood at the oncoming headlights. I would have done anything to have my Glock right now. "Bobbie, I'm sorry I got you mixed up in this."

Bobbie was busy making signs of the cross. Her eyes were as wide as saucers. "What happens if we die and get fished out of the river in these getups? Can you imagine what our parents will say?"

I hadn't thought about it, but she had a point. "We're not going to die, Bobbie."

The car approached shooting distance, and we waited for the inevitable hail of bullets, but instead, it stopped about twenty feet away, and I heard a car door open.

"Brandi? Are you okay?" I peeked around the front bumper to see a man emerge from the vehicle. I couldn't make out the face because he was backlit like an angel from the headlights of his car. But I knew the voice. "Brandi?" he called out again.

I stood up slowly. "Lorenzo? What are you doing here?"

"I wanted to make sure you were okay. You were pretty shaken up when you left."

"What about the police? I thought you had to wait for them."

Lorenzo started walking toward me. "Bertrand's handling it. He got to the club right when you were leaving, so I followed you." He paused, looking down at his feet, thinking

God knows what, then at a volume that was almost too quiet to hear said, "I was worried about you."

I had a moment to appreciate the sweet gesture until I realized how bad this had to look. He had probably already called Bertrand and told him just how shaken up I was. *Yeah, I'm glad I went after her. She was so distraught that she decided to work out her anxiety at a skanky sex club. Should I wait for her to polish someone's knob, or go in after her?* I was silently mortified.

"Are you okay?" He must have asked the question a couple of times, because he had closed the distance between us and was looking at me with concern.

I snapped out of my stupor. "Um, yeah. I'm okay. My car's seen better days, though."

We both looked at the car. If it hadn't been such an uncomfortable situation, we probably would have laughed. It hadn't seen a better day since the early eighties.

There was nothing I could say to dispel the awkwardness, so I switched to cop mode. "Did you see who did this?" I asked. "I mean, if you were following me, you must have seen something."

"I saw a guy running from your car when I pulled into the parking lot. I would have chased him down, but I thought you might be hurt. Obviously you had already gone in." He gave me a bewildered look. He was waiting for an explanation, but there wasn't one that I could give him.

"This isn't what you think it is," I said lamely.

"And what do I think it is?"

"I don't know, but whatever you're thinking, it's not that. In fact, whatever you're thinking, think about the opposite of that and you might be in the right ballpark."

This night wasn't turning out the way I thought it would. I dropped my head into my hands and prayed for the night to be over. I was tired. My eyes were burning, my mouth was dry, and my feet were suddenly killing me—an adrenaline hangover. All I wanted was to go home and crawl into bed.

There was a groan from behind the car. "Can I get up now?" Bobbie was still in her tuck-and-roll position. "My legs are starting to cramp, and right now I'm willing to risk getting gunned down over lying in a pile of glass in a dirty parking lot."

"Shit. Sorry, Bobbie." I rounded the car and pulled her to her feet. "Bobbie, this is Lorenzo, my…boss."

Bobbie slipped back into her charm and extended a hand. "Nice to meet you."

"Likewise," said Lorenzo, then turned his attention back to me. "Let me drive you home?"

"Actually, I'm more worried about Bobbie." I shot her a pleading look. "She had a lot to drink in there." Bobbie obliged me with a shoulder shrug and a giggle, bless her heart. "Could you take her home? I'm so beat."

"Pretty please?" Bobbie was doing the prayer thing with her hands, which, I knew from previous experience, was damn near irresistible to the male of the species.

Lorenzo looked conflicted. On one hand, there was a damsel in distress who was asking for his help, wearing a shockingly tiny trench coat and a killer smile. On the other hand, the woman he had actually come to rescue, who at the moment was nervously clutching a tiny pink gun, looking like a demented trick-or-treater, was blowing him off. I tipped the scales for him.

"That would be great if you could take care of Bobbie,

Lorenzo. I'm fine. I just need to go home and get some sleep."

"That's what you want?" Lorenzo's expression gutted me. I had dismissed him, was sending him away with my gorgeous friend, as if I didn't care. He was giving me a chance to fix it, but I couldn't. I was getting closer and closer to uncovering the truth, and I couldn't let my feelings, no matter how quickly they were evolving, get in the way of that.

Lorenzo slipped off his coat and used it to clear the glass from my car seat, then said coolly, "Call me when you get home so I know you made it there safely." As I began to protest, he cut me off. "Just do it, okay?"

I gave him a nod, feeling the sting. It was the first time I had seen his harder edge, and I deserved it. I watched him lead Bobbie away through the parking lot. I felt numb. For the first time in my life, I hated my job.

By the time I made it back to my house, I was dead on my feet. These late nights were killing me, and the high heels... well, they weren't helping. Disappointing Lorenzo, though, that was the worst part of all. I keyed open the door, locked it again behind me, and flung my purse into the corner. It was all I could do to peel the long leather boots off my legs and crawl barefoot up the stairs. My mind was focused on one thing...sleep.

I was having the most delicious dream, literally—my semi-recurring Gordon Ramsay/*Hell's Kitchen* go-to. As usual, Gordon, the bad boy that he is, had abandoned his restaurant set, told his producers to sod off, and come to my house to cook me dinner. Needless to say, I was immeasurably flattered.

The kitchen was full of fresh flowers and candles, an expensive bottle of red wine open on the counter. He leaned in for a tender kiss, which became more passionate with every passing second. When he pulled back to speak, though, it was Lorenzo's face.

"You've been a very bad girl," he whispered in his raspy English brogue. Lorenzo's face with Gordon's accent...Lord help me. He reached down and ripped my blouse open, scattering buttons everywhere. "That's for scrubbing your nonstick pans with an abrasive sponge, you naughty, naughty girl." This was actually a new turn of events, too. I tried to tell him I was sorry about the pans, but he ran his lips down my neck and gave me a little nip at the base of my throat as he tore at the buttons on his crisp white chef's jacket. I caught my breath and tried to apologize again, when the kitchen timer went off and he pulled away. "Sorry 'bout that, darlin'. Just give me a sec." He ran to the stove and opened the screen door. What a silly oven, I mused. What kind of oven has a screen door? What the hell?

Great. I was awake. I lay there sweating in the pitch black of my room in that limbo state between dreaming and consciousness, feeling groggily frustrated. My oven had a screen door, and I'd been about to be double-teamed by Gordon and Lorenzo. Pretty sure that would that never happen again. And I didn't get to apologize, either...about the pans, which had seemed weirdly important somehow. Damn screen door. Nothing made sense. I pulled the sheet around me tightly and willed myself back into the kitchen with Lorenzo and Gordon.

Then I heard it—a tiny noise. Not the familiar settling

noises an old house makes, or the creaking sound of old pipes, or the gentle whirring of my ceiling fan. No, this was the distinctive squeak of the seventh step on my staircase. Someone was in my house. I sat bolt upright, my heart racing, willing every one of my senses into overdrive.

Nine-one-one. I needed to call nine-one-one.

I reached over to my bedside table for my cell phone and realized at once that I had left it in my purse, which was lying in a heap halfway across the kitchen floor. Shit! I had been so tired when I got home that I'd eschewed every one of my nighttime rituals. I hadn't plugged in my phone or set the alarm system. I did remember locking the front door, though, before shedding my boots, dragging myself up the stairs, peeling off my bits of clothing, and crawling into bed naked. My service weapon was safely—and uselessly—stowed in my gun safe, and my tiny pink Arms Guardian was tucked into my leather boot, somewhere between the front door and the foot of the stairs. Awesome.

I could hear the faint creak of the guest bedroom door opening. Someone was looking for me. I gingerly slithered out of bed to the side farthest away from the door and felt along the wall for the security panel of my alarm system. It was too dark to be precise, so I covered the keypad with my palm and pressed every button at the same time. This would summon not only the police, but the fire department and an ambulance as well. Unfortunately, my call had also set off the alarm and the mechanized voice rundown of all the doors and windows in the house. Yes, I'd managed to call the cavalry, but I'd also announced my presence in a very loud way. As the alarm blared and the serene robot voice announced, "Front door open," I crouched down beside the bed and reached out for the familiar curves of my Louis-ville Slugger. *Thank you, Dad.* I wrapped my fingers tightly around the taped handle and drew it silently out of its hold-er, then crawled on my hands and knees to the foot of the bed and waited.

It took every ounce of my self-control not to storm into the hall and confront my would-be attacker. I hated more than anything else in this world to feel like a victim. And cowering naked in my bedroom while someone hunted me made me crazy.

I trained my eyes on the door and saw a man's shape slowly inch his way into the room. I could make out the shape of his hands, feeling in front of him for obstacles. I strained my eyes to try to make out any detail, but it was impossible to see anything other than his shape. One arm looked to be longer than the other—a weapon. He continued forward, hitting his shin on the wooden bed frame, and he momen-tarily lowered his hands for balance. My window of oppor-tunity. I leaped up, brought the bat back and threw my entire weight into my swing, connecting hard with some part of his body—his back, I think. The impact dropped him forward onto the bed, and whatever he'd been holding flew out of his hands and skittered across the hardwood. He bounced back fast, striking out wildly with a closed fist, and connect-ed with the side of my head, staggering me for a moment. I regained my balance and took aim at where I thought his head should have been. I connected with something softer, though, an arm, maybe. Somehow he'd managed to block my swing, and he closed the space between us, grabbing at the bat. He was strong, and he pulled me off balance, but there was no way I was letting him have that bat. That would be a death sentence. I drew my leg up and threw a side kick into his upper thigh. If I had connected with his groin, the fight would have been over, but I'd missed, and he held onto the bat, using it to jerk me into his chest.

I felt his muscles tense and his body shift, and realized too late what was coming. His fist connected with my temple, snapping my head back. The next hit launched me backward into the wall, and I felt a stabbing pain as my bare shoulder blade impacted the light switch. I could feel my knees start to buckle and my head start to swim from the impact of the blow to my head. I willed my legs to work again, but they were turning to rubber.

If I were going to die tonight, it would not be from some anonymous attack in the dark. I wanted to see who had my number. I pressed my weight into the wall, turning the light switch on with my shoulder. The sudden light was blinding. I tried to focus my eyesight, but everything was blurry and slow and my vision became tunneled as I started to slip down the wall into unconsciousness. I was going to die naked and alone in my own bedroom.

"Who the hell…" was the last thing I heard before I hit the floor.

Chapter Fourteen

"Miss? Miss? Can you hear me?"

Someone was shaking me. If I could have, I would have told them to stop. Every movement felt like a knitting needle being jabbed into my brain. I opened my eyes a sliver and saw a pair of heavy black boots two inches from my face. I felt someone cover me with a blanket, a furry brown one like the one that I kept on my bed. As the fog started to lift, I realized that I was on the floor in my bedroom. And I was alive.

"Miss? Can you hear me?" a woman's voice repeated.

I tried to open my mouth to speak, but it was sore and as dry as a bone, the aftereffects of adrenaline and a severe beating. "Yeah," I said.

I could hear more action in the hallway, men's voices. "Where is she? Is she stable?" Paramedics, I thought. Good. There were more inquiries about my ability to hear, and finally I was positioned on a backboard and hoisted onto the stretcher. I could finally see who was in my bedroom. Lisa Miller, the only other female cop at the station, was peering into my face, a deep look of concern in her eyes.

"Can you tell me your name?" she asked.

"Lisa," I whispered. "It's Cassidy."

She looked confused for a moment, and suddenly her eyes widened with recognition. "Officer down!" she yelled into her walkie. "Officer down!" A buzz went through the room and people started moving double time. They hadn't recognized me. "It's Officer Jones," she yelled. Why hadn't they recognized me? Through the corner of my eye I could see a fringe of black hair framing my face. I was still wearing my wig. They hadn't recognized me because of my wig.

The next time I regained consciousness, I was in a hospital room hooked up to a bunch of wires. The blinds were drawn, creating a cozy cocoon in the room, but sunlight was squeaking in around the edges. The sun always managed to find me. Lisa was slumped down in an old pastel-blue vinyl armchair beside my bed with her chin on her chest, sleeping. My mouth felt like it had been stuffed with cotton, and my head like it had been stuffed with sandpaper. As I took inventory of my injuries, I felt sure that nothing was broken. I wiggled my fingers and toes. All good. I turned my head to the left and felt a sharp ping shoot through my neck and on down into my back. Not good. My peripheral vision was partially obscured by a fleshy outcropping, which would turn out to be my eyelid, swollen partially shut. I must look like a real treat right now, I thought to myself. The pain wasn't awful, more like flags of throbbing dullness thrown down onto the landscape that was my body. Ah, Percocet…or was it Vicodin? Whatever. It was probably morphine, I thought as I drifted off.

When I woke up again, the room was dark except for the blue light of the TV screen. My eyes drifted to the chair. Lisa was still sitting there, awake this time, watching some soap opera on mute. "Hi," I tried to say, but nothing came out. My mouth was as dry as the bottom of an ashtray—tasted like one, too—and didn't seem to want to open up to form words. I willed my right hand to lift from the bed. Lisa jumped, clutching her chest in surprise.

"Oh, thank God you're awake," she said, hustling to the door. As she flung it open, light flooded into my room, but all I could do was close my eyes. My head still didn't want to turn. "Can I get a doctor in here?" she hollered. It was a voice that people would heed.

Within seconds, a doctor hurried into the room with Chief Thompson and Officer Miller quick on his heels.

"How are you feeling, Cassidy?" the doctor asked as he lifted my left eyelid and shone a light into my eye.

"Like shit on a stick," I whispered as he repeated the procedure on the right side.

"I'm not surprised. Can you follow my finger with your eyes, please?" He traced a figure-eight pattern in the air with his finger, and I dutifully followed it with my eyes.

"Just don't make me pull it. I don't feel like laughing." The doctor smiled, and apparently satisfied that I wasn't going to die this very minute, he stepped aside and nodded to the chief.

The chief took a couple of tentative steps forward, his bright blue eyes full of worry. "Hey there, Jones, are you okay?"

I forced the working corner of my mouth up into a smile

and gave him a thumbs-up. He let out an audible breath, relaxing his shoulders, and relief flooded onto his face. Part of me felt good that someone other than me cared about my well-being, but the cop in me was more than a tad bit ashamed. I'd been given my big break, given a chance to prove my worth, and all I'd managed to do was get myself beaten to a pulp. I felt my smile slide into a little puddle as a tear worked its way out of the corner of my eye — the final indignity.

Chief Thompson pulled a chair up close to the bed and sat down. "Hey, Cassidy, no tears. You did it, kid. You were right." He smiled and gave my arm a gentle squeeze. "It was Junior Bloodgood, and we've got him dead to rights thanks to you."

I swiped at the rogue tear. "Really?"

"Really. I got the lab results back from the scotch bottle wrapper that you managed to recover from the club. They found one of Junior's fingerprints on the inside, just like you were hoping. That was some bloody amazing detective work finding that, by the way. And when we scoured the storage room at Double Down we found Junior's wallet, if you can believe it, under one of the shelves. He must have lost it during the struggle with that poor girl."

"Wow," I said, giving him a weak smile. I was happy we'd caught the killer, but there was still a part of me that was weirded out by the fact that one of my childhood playmates had brutally murdered two people. I glanced up to Lisa's face, but it was unreadable. I guess I didn't know what kind of reaction I expected from her, anyway.

"We're guessing he came after you when he found out you'd been the one investigating, but we'll know more when the lab results come back. Our guys swept every inch of your place for prints."

Muddled as my thoughts felt, I did have the presence of mind to cringe at the fact that I was giving the lab a substantial number of fingerprints to process. There had been a certain amount of…traffic in the master bedroom. Oh, well. Hopefully it would be Bobbie doing the processing. She would understand.

The chief gave me another pat on the shoulder and stood up. "Giving you that promotion was the smartest thing I've done in a very long time, Cassidy. You've made me look like a smart man. I wouldn't be surprised if the mayor gave you a commendation. I'm going to let the doctors tend to you now, but I just thought you should know…good job."

As the door shut behind him, I felt my heart swell inside my chest. I would have settled for the chief not thinking I was a liability to the police force. Being given credit for solving two murders—one of them a really high-profile murder— was more than the icing on the cake; it was the whole damn cake, the start of me being taken seriously at the station.

"I'll be outside," Lisa mumbled, turning to go.

"Hey, wait. Did they bring Junior in yet?"

"No, not yet. We can't find him. He probably skipped town or something." She swept open the door to leave, and I caught a glimpse of Detective Coleman standing out in the hallway. *Shit.* The last I'd seen of Jay, he'd been hog-tied and nearly naked in the basement of a sex club. At my doing. I wasn't ready to spar with him again, and a tingle of something akin to panic set my skin tingling all the way to the tips of my fingers.

"Lisa, wait!" I called out again, working to keep the fear

out of my voice. She let the door close again, underlining her irritation with a heavy sigh. "Please don't let him in here."

Lisa appraised me silently for a moment, then asked, "Who?"

With my eyes I pointed to Detective Coleman through the tiny window. "Please," I said again.

To Lisa's credit, she didn't ask any questions. She just nodded. "I'll take care of it." And she was gone.

I closed my eyes, trying to bring order to my jumbled stew of thoughts. When was the last time anyone had seen Junior? Had anyone seen him since Amber's murder? When was the last time I ate? Was my house locked? How many cops had seen me naked and unconscious last night? Had Bobbie and Lorenzo made a love connection last night on the drive home? I hadn't had the chance to call dibs. I moaned, imagining the very worst, and covered my eyes with my hand.

The doctor looked up from his chart. "Everything okay?" he asked. He was cute in a nerdy kind of way. His light brown hair was wavy and slightly unkempt. He had really nice blue eyes and a nose that was just the tiniest bit crooked, suggesting he'd endured either a rowdy adolescence or a car accident. I was voting on a rowdy adolescence, but only because I was a firm believer that everyone should have one.

I peeked at him through my fingers. "Not really," I answered. "I was just wondering how many cops saw me naked last night."

He leaned against the bed and fixed me with an amused smile. "Well, I know I did, but I'm not a cop, so I suppose that's okay, huh?"

"Usually I at least get dinner out of it," I mumbled, trying not to smile.

"How 'bout a drink instead?" he asked, pouring me a glass of water from the jug on my night table.

"God, yes!" I answered.

He unwrapped a long straw and dipped it into the water glass before handing it to me. "I guess I should introduce myself, seeing as how I've already seen you naked. I'm Dr. Massey. We actually did meet last night, but I doubt you remember."

"Yeah, I was a little busy being unconscious."

"You gave everyone a scare, you know."

"Is it bad?" I asked, reaching up to feel the lumpy contours of my face. "Bet I look pretty sexy right now, huh?"

"The good news is that nothing's broken. We were worried about your orbital bone. It looks like hell right now, but it's intact."

This little tidbit of honesty made me smile. "Gee, thanks. Your bedside manner's awesome."

Dr. Massey laughed. "Sorry. I thought you were a straight shooter. If you want me to, I can sugarcoat the rest."

I gave him a grim chuckle. "Why start now?"

"All right," he said. "You have a concussion, but you probably already figured that one out, and you've strained a couple of ligaments in your neck—whiplash, basically—but it could have been a lot worse."

"Awesome," I said.

"Yeah, but the coup de grâce…we found a blush on your CT scan, which is a—"

"A bleed in my brain?" I interrupted. He gave a slight nod. "That's not good, right? Do you need to shave my head and drill a hole into my skull and drain it or something?"

"I don't think so," he answered. "Believe it or not, that wig you were wearing last night probably saved you." He nodded his head toward the tangled mass of black hair on the far side table and turned back to me with a smirk. "Probably gave you some extra cushioning. And judging from how you're talking and responding now, I think everything will be okay, but I want to keep you here another night to monitor you. We'll do another scan in the morning, and if it comes out clear like I'm expecting, we'll send you on your merry way. Deal?"

I smiled. "Deal."

"All right, then. I'll leave you, but try not to get into any more fights today, okay?" He flashed me another brilliant smile and opened the door in time for a pudgy, no-nonsense nurse to bustle into the room carrying a tray of food. "Ah, look," he said with a satisfied smile, "your dinner—and a drink. I guess we're even. I don't like to disappoint the ladies." He shrugged off a disapproving look from the nurse and slipped out the door.

I propped myself up in bed, suddenly ravenous at the thought of food. The tray looked a little sparse, though, and I quickly tried to manage my expectations in order to avoid disappointment. I'd been using that technique for years with men. There was no reason to believe it wouldn't work here.

"Here you go," said the nurse, setting the tray down on the table and rolling it into position over the bed.

It was even worse than I'd imagined. The tray held a brown plastic cup filled halfway to the brim with a clear-looking liquid, a single-serving package of soda crackers, a spoon, and a napkin. I bent over the tray and inhaled, my nose working to glean information but coming up empty. "What is it?" I asked.

"Soup and crackers," she answered.

I picked up the tiny brown plastic cup and waved it under my nose. It smelled like a plastic cup. "Where's the soup?" I asked, genuinely confused. The nurse used her chubby finger to push the paper napkin aside, revealing a tiny yellow packet that read "chicken bouillon." "Really?" I asked. "This is the reward I get for surviving a vicious home invasion?"

"No," she answered. "Your reward is being alive. This is my reward for not going on to medical school. Now, you gonna eat it, or do you want me to take it away?" She had her hands on her hips in a gesture of defiance.

"No, no. Leave it. It looks lovely," I said, lying. "You obviously went to a lot of trouble putting this together." The nurse stared at me for a beat. "Thank you?" I added tentatively.

She pursed her lips, gave me a sour "mmm-hmm" and left the room.

What the hell was wrong with me, I wondered to myself. I really must have sustained a head injury. Everyone knew that there was a list of people you shouldn't piss off, and the nurse who was in charge of your well-being while you were incapacitated was one of those people. I was an idiot.

I tore open the bouillon packet, dumped it into the cup, and watched sadly as the powder floated in clumps on the surface of the water. I stuck my finger into the water. It was barely even lukewarm. I looked at my call button and dismissed the thought immediately. Nurse Ratched would probably be only too happy to bring me a cup of hot water, fortified with a huge loogie. So much for the soup, I thought sadly, feeling my stomach start to churn. I ripped open the packet of crackers and chewed them gratefully. This wasn't going to work for me. I wasn't the type of girl to skip a meal, and crackers weren't going to cut it. I was going to starve in this place.

Stomach still growling, I decided to call Bobbie on the big beige hospital phone. She was going to freak out when she found out that I was in the hospital. Better to hear it from me, though. Bobbie picked up after four rings and gave a tentative, "Hello?"

"Hey, Bob, it's me."

"What's up, Chuck? Call display says you're calling from County General. You owe me two hundred bucks, by the way. My truck got towed."

"Shit. I'm sorry, Bobbie."

"Don't sweat it. Wait. Why are you calling from County General?"

"Well…let's just say I had a rough night last night."

"Are you all right? What happened?" She'd gone from zero to panic in approximately three seconds.

"I'm okay. I've got a concussion and a rearranged face, but other than that, I'm doing okay. Oh, yeah, and a possible brain hemorrhage, but other than that, it's all good."

"Oh my God, Cassidy! What happened? I'm coming over right now!"

"Wait, Bobbie! Finish up at work. I'm not going anywhere till tomorrow morning. But maybe you could swing by my house and grab me some clothes and my toothbrush. And my purse. And if you could bring some real food, that would be great. I think they're trying to kill me here. Nothing too chewy though, okay? My face hurts like hell."

"Okay, but I'm coming over the minute I'm done with work." There was a pause. "Hey, Cass, does Lorenzo know? 'Cause he's gonna freak out. He was really worried about you. Said you fainted at work and hit your head? He probably thinks you're gonna file a workman's comp claim."

"Shit. I'd better call him. I'm scheduled to work tonight, but that ain't gonna happen. I'd scare away all the customers the way I look right now."

"I'm sure it's not that bad," she said comfortingly. "You need me to call him for you?"

"Nah. I can do it, but thanks. See you tonight?"

"As soon as I'm done. Try to stay out of trouble in the meantime, though, okay?"

"Why does everybody keep saying that to me?" I snorted, hanging up.

I looked down at the big beige phone in my lap and took a deep breath, trying to quell the surge of giddiness I felt at the thought of hearing Lorenzo's buttery voice. I chastised myself internally for making a ceremony out of a simple phone call, but dammit, I was lying in the hospital in a paper gown with a swollen face and a possible brain hemorrhage, potentially dying of starvation. Wasn't I deserving of at least a little comfort? So what if I was a tough-ass cop. I was also a woman, a woman who'd had the crap kicked out of her, and I steadfastly refused to feel bad about wanting to hear a friendly voice. A sexy, buttery voice, oozing with sympathy and innuendo.

With renewed zeal, I dialed information for the number to Double Down and waited to be connected. As the phone rang, I wondered if anyone had told Lorenzo yet about

Junior. Surely by now someone would have told him they'd found his brother's killer, but maybe not. Maybe they were keeping things under wraps until they'd actually apprehended Junior. That would make sense with mobsters involved. It would reflect poorly on the police department if their main suspect got whacked before they'd even had the chance to convict him.

Lorenzo picked up the phone with a businesslike "Hello," and I felt my heart flip-flop. Even a concussion couldn't seem to dampen the hormonal effect he had on me, and I smiled, ignoring the dull pain in my jaw.

"What are you wearing?" I asked in a teasing voice.

There was silence on the other end of the line for what seemed like a lifetime and then, "Who is this?"

"Lorenzo? It's…it's Brandi." Silence. "How are you doing?"

I could hear him get out of his leather chair, cross to the door, and slam it shut. "Well, Detective Jones," he said slowly and deliberately. "I'm feeling like an idiot at the moment, but I'll be fine."

My forehead started to prickle with sweat, and I could feel adrenaline starting to pulse its way into my system. He knew my real name! Somehow he'd found out who I was, that I was a cop. I had known the truth was going to come out eventually, but I had wanted to be the one to tell him everything, to explain. And in my dreams, I'd pictured it going down in a very different, very sexy, heroic way. Not like this. The moment of silence was stretching into an eternity of awkwardness. I had to say something to try to explain, but all that came out was, "How did you…?"

"Your boss told me last night when he was finished

processing Amber's…whatever. You know what? It doesn't matter. Your job's done. Congratulations on getting your murderer. Hope you enjoyed making me feel like a complete chump."

I closed my eyes as a wave of nausea washed over me. "Lorenzo," I got out before he cut me off.

"Do you even realize how humiliating this feels?" Before I could collect my thoughts to explain, he spat out an angry laugh. "Oh my God," he whispered. "Remember at the ball field? You must have thought it was hilarious when I told you that you were *just so real*. What a joke! How did you not choke on the fucking irony? How did you even keep a straight face?"

I started to protest, but Lorenzo wouldn't hear it.

"What were you thinking when you kissed me all those times?"

He sounded so angry, and my brain wasn't working as fast as it was supposed to. "What do you mean?"

"I mean, God, Brandi! Or whatever the hell your name is! How far would you have gone to keep up your little charade? Would you have had sex with me? Or were you planning to stop just short of prostitution?"

I yelled, "Lorenzo!" and regretted it immediately, the sound thunderous in my own head. "Lorenzo," I pleaded over the ringing in my ears. "Please let me explain." But it was too late. The line was dead.

I let the receiver slide down my cheek and onto the ratty blue acrylic blanket that covered my lap. It was spackled with bits of dried-up food from a previous tenant. Suddenly I felt dirty and very alone. The thought of crying was so tempting, but I knew it wouldn't help. I had to fix this. I wrestled with the thought of calling him back, but he obviously wasn't in the mood to hear what I had to say, and to be honest I didn't blame him for being mad. I had lied to him, not that I'd had a choice, and now he thought the only reason I'd gotten close to him was just to spy on him. Shit!

I let out a loud groan of frustration. What he must be thinking about me! The problem was that he was probably half right on a lot of things. Yes, I had suspected him, but only for a heartbeat. And yes, it had been the cop in me that got close to him on our first encounter, but it was definitely the girl in me who couldn't keep my hands or my mind off him after that. He had no way of knowing that, though. Big surprise—the girl in me was getting the shaft (not literally, though) again.

I must have drifted off into a restless sleep, because Bobbie woke me when she pushed through the door into my room. "Pancakes, anyone?" she whispered.

I pressed the light button on the side of my bed, activating a sickly green overhead reading light. Bobbie looked like an angel of mercy standing there with a gym bag, my purse, and a takeout bag from the International House of Pancakes. When she caught sight of my face, she stopped dead in her tracks, her smile slipping for a fraction of a second.

"That bad?" I asked.

"No! No. I just. I forgot…never mind. You'll be back to your old self in no time."

"You don't need to lie to me. I know I look like hell," I said, working sleep out of my good eye. "Hand me my purse, will ya? I want to check something."

Bobbie handed it over and I rummaged through. My Blackberry was still in there, but the only thing that remained of Amber's Blackberry was a collection of pink crystals from her bedazzled phone case. "Junior, you son of a bitch," I muttered under my breath. He'd been willing to almost kill me in order to get his hands on that phone...and he'd seen me naked. I wasn't sure what bothered me more.

"You heard, huh?" Bobbie asked as she set up two containers of pancakes on either side of the little table.

"Yeah. It's so weird," I said, accepting a plastic fork from Bobbie. "I mean, I know he was a suspect and he's one of the creepiest dudes I know, but something inside me always believed we'd find him innocent." I ripped the plastic off a container of maple syrup and doused my stack. "Guess I'm not a very good judge of character, huh?"

"Not necessarily," said Bobbie. "You never liked the guy and our dads never let us play with him, not that we ever wanted to. So, it's not like he was some prince or something. There was always something off about him."

I stuffed a forkful of pancake into my mouth. "Oh my God! These taste like magic!" I moaned, not caring that my mouth was full. And they did, too. I couldn't remember ever tasting anything so amazing, but then again, it had been almost twenty-four hours since I'd eaten anything more substantial than a soda cracker. I shoved another forkful into my mouth. "Thank you so much for bringing these."

"Slow down and chew, will ya? If you get sick, I'm on the shit list here," she said, snagging a container of syrup for herself. "Holy cow," she said, taking another look into the takeout bag. "I should have asked for more syrup."

"Sorry," I said with my mouth full. "I'm medicating."

"Your face hurt that bad?"

"Nah," I said, poking my straw through the foil of an orange juice container. "They gave me some pretty cool drugs." I gave her a look that only she would be able to interpret.

"A boy?" she asked knowingly. "What happened?"

"Well, long story short, the chief told Lorenzo my real identity and now he hates me. I'm not kidding, Bobbie. You should have heard the things he said to me. He all but called me a whore."

It was Bobbie's turn to hitch her eyebrows at me. "Why would he call you a whore?"

I focused my attention on my Styrofoam container and pushed a piece of pancake into a lake of syrup.

"Did you sleep with him?"

"No...almost, but no." I tossed my fork into the puddle of syrup, my appetite suddenly gone.

"You like him!" Bobbie shrieked.

"No," I said with a shocking lack of conviction. "I just... wanted to tell him myself."

"Because you like him!" she shrieked again. "Oh my God! When did this happen?"

I looked at Bobbie, trying to muster up a look of denial, but it was no use. We'd been best friends our entire lives, and I couldn't put anything past her, especially in the romance department. Instead, I shrugged my shoulders, resigned. "Doesn't matter," I muttered. "He hates me now. And anyway, how would it look? Falling for a gangster on the job? I'd be the laughingstock of the station."

"You told me he wasn't a gangster," Bobbie said.

"Let's just say he's gangster adjacent. You think any of those good ol' boys I work with would let that one slide?"

"Wow," said Bobbie, shaking her head slowly. "I can't believe I didn't see that one coming. I mean, I know we've been working kind of opposite hours these days, but I don't usually miss these things. I thought…" She stopped, weighing her words. "Never mind."

"Come on!" I balled up a napkin and hurled it at her. "You thought what?"

"Nothing. I'm obviously on crack," she said as she dumped her empty Styrofoam container back into the takeout bag.

"You can't do that! Tell me!"

"All right, all right," she said, giving in. "I actually thought you had a thing for Detective Coleman. I didn't see the Lorenzo thing coming at all."

"What?" I protested. "How could you think I like Coleman? I hate that guy!"

"I don't know…the lap dance, the dry humping, the attempted breaking and entering at his house… You do the math. Seriously, you did everything but dip his pigtails into the inkwell."

"That's ridiculous." I snorted.

"Sorry, Chuck. Remember the last guy you really liked? What was his name again? Brian McGregor! Remember him? You gave him a black eye and keyed his car."

"Oh, come on, Bobbie! That was high school! And by the way," I added as I swabbed the last drop of syrup out of the tiny container with my fingers, "you're a total shit head for bringing that up."

"Hey! I'm just pointing out…you know…that love

makes you act a little bonkers. You get a little cock crazy. Not gonna lie. It's weird."

I flopped back into my pillow. How could she be so off base? I despised Jay Coleman. "For the record, Bobbie, I don't like Detective Coleman. God, I actually thought he was the one behind the murder for a while!"

"Okay, I'm sorry."

"Seriously, though," I said, pushing myself up onto my elbows. "What the hell was Jay doing at the strip club? In a disguise? And why the hell was he at the fetish bar that night? And who else would have broken into my car? They can't all be coincidences!" I sank back into my pillow. "None of it adds up."

"I think you need to get some sleep," Bobbie said as she rearranged my pillows and tucked my blanket up under my chin. "Maybe things will look different tomorrow. I'll come back and spring you in the morning?"

"Thanks, Bobbie…for everything."

"You don't have to thank me. That's what family's for," she said and blew me a kiss as she backed out the door.

Chapter Fifteen

Bobbie had been wrong. It was morning, but nothing looked different to me, and as we pulled into my driveway in Bobbie's huge white Escalade, my sense of foreboding only deepened. I could see Bobbie watching me with concern out of the corner of my eye.

"You worried about being in your house again?" she asked. "'Cause I could take you to my house, you know. I've got tons of junk food there that'll speed up the healing process."

I gave her a grim smile. "No. I'm good. I'll snap out of it."

The look on Bobbie's face told me she wasn't convinced. "Cass, nobody would blame you for being afraid. God, if I was attacked in my own home…"

"I'm not scared! I'm pissed off. I'm pissed that I was too tired to bother setting the alarm and I'm pissed that I didn't beat the shit out of Junior when I had the chance to, and I'm pissed that…" I trailed off, lost in thought.

"What?" Bobbie prompted.

I closed my eyes. I was pissed at so many things, that I'd gracelessly bungled my way through a murder case, that even though we'd found the killer, it felt unresolved. And I was pissed that I'd let myself feel things for Lorenzo, a guy who obviously didn't even care enough about me to get my side of the story. But anger was so much better than sadness in my book, and I felt a crumb of gratitude for it. None of this I shared with Bobbie.

"Don't worry about it," I mumbled, weariness creeping into my voice. I opened the door and gingerly climbed down. My head had stopped throbbing when I was perfectly still, but any jarring movements made things feel precarious in my skull. I slowly picked my way up the front steps with Bobbie spotting me from behind. When I reached the door, I bent over and peered at the lock, feeling for scrapes with my fingers. "I could swear I locked the door that night. So how did he get in?"

Bobbie dug the keys out of my purse and opened the door. "Cassidy, you need to relax and stop worrying about everything. Remember what the doc said? No stress, lots of rest. Now, why don't I make you some breakfast while you go up and take a shower? Might make you feel better."

"I doubt it."

"Do it for me then. You're making my eyes water."

I smiled. Bobbie always knew how to cheer me up. I called her a smart-ass and shuffled up the stairs to my bedroom. Someone had obviously cleaned up. The bed had been made, my fuzzy blanket restored to its spot at the end of the bed, and my slutty club clothes had been stuffed into my hamper. My Louisville Slugger was back in its holder. I was happy not to have to deal with it. Any gratefulness I felt was cut short, though, when I saw my reflection in the bathroom mirror.

I looked past my matted mess of hair and inspected my face. The swelling around my right eye was starting to go down. It still looked like hell, though, and it was a deep purple, punctuated with a bright red bleed on the white part of my eyeball. *Sexy*, I thought to myself, *in a zombie apocalypse kind of way*. The rest of the right side of my face was just a colorful bruise, the damage being more ligament based than bone based. I had minimal swelling around my jaw, not that anyone would ever notice with my zombie eye to focus on. All in all, I looked pretty much how I expected — like shit. It was strangely and sadly appropriate.

I stripped off the sweats that Bobbie had picked out for me. My front looked fine, but there was a huge welt on my shoulder blade with a patch of peeled-off skin. I flashed back to the attack, remembering smashing into the light switch on the wall just before I lost consciousness. It could have been worse, I guess.

I heard the cheery sound of cartoons when I finally emerged, pink and clean from the bathroom. I slipped on a pair of ripped jeans and a white tank top and headed down. By the time I reached the top of the landing, I could hear the squeals and giggles of children. Odd. I couldn't imagine why there would be kids in my house — ever — yet apparently there were kids in my house today. I peeked into the living room to see Rosemary's girls cuddled up on the couch in front of the TV watching Bugs Bunny with rapt attention and backed away quietly, not wanting to draw their attention. I padded into the kitchen to see Rosemary at the stove manning a frying pan, and Bobbie sipping coffee from her spot at the kitchen table.

"I was wondering why you hadn't triggered the fire alarm," I said to Bobbie.

"Smart-ass," she shot at me with a grin, reaching for the coffee pot to pour me a cup.

"Oh, Cass…come here," clucked Rosemary in her mom voice. She set down her spatula, wiped her hands on the dish towel that was slung over her shoulder, and folded me into a comforting hug. "This is what you needed, isn't it?" she cooed. "Sometimes you just need a big ol' hug, especially when you've had the crap beat out of you."

I hugged her back, resting my head on the tea towel. She was right. It was exactly what I needed. "I can't believe Bobbie called you in to babysit me, Rose. I'm sorry."

"Don't you be silly," she said, pulling back to inspect my injuries, her eyebrows gathering in the middle of her forehead with concern. "I'm glad she called me. And I hope they caught the bastard who did this to you!" she said with the intensity of a mama bear.

"Mommy!" shrieked Rosemary's youngest.

I turned around slowly, trying not to disturb the equilibrium in my head. Rosemary's girls had either heard my voice or been drawn by the smell of bacon, and they were lined up like little puppies just inside the kitchen, waiting.

"Sorry, honey. Mommy said a bad word."

The little girl rushed toward me, ready for a hug, then skidded to a stop when she saw my face. "Auntie Cassidy," she whispered softly.

"It's okay, sweetie, come over here and give me a hug. It looks worse than it feels," I lied. She minced over softly and wrapped her arms around my waist, and before I knew it, the other girls had flocked over for hugs, too.

Rosemary broke up the love fest. "Okay, girls, let Auntie Cassidy catch her breath." She handed them each a piece of bacon. "Go watch your cartoons. And don't eat on the couch!" The girls scattered like mist and Rosemary chuckled. "You have to end these things while they're still sweet. It can go from a Hallmark movie to *The Gong Show* in the blink of an eye."

I laughed, enjoying the moment and grateful for the company. Bobbie set the table while Rosemary doled out bacon, eggs, and toast. "I hope you like it," she said handing me a napkin.

The food smelled like magic and tasted even better. "My God, Rosemary! Where did you learn to cook?" I got out between mouthfuls. "I swear if Reg hadn't scooped you up first I would have married you myself!"

Rosemary basked in the compliment for a moment then turned to me and said, "I would have said yes, too. I bet you wouldn't leave your dirty socks and underwear all over the bedroom floor."

"Nah, you wouldn't have, Rose," Bobbie chimed in. "Cass would have put out on the first date and you'd have lost respect for her."

"You're one to talk!" I said laughing. "At least I might have lasted till after dinner!"

Rosemary giggled, looking around to make sure the kids weren't within earshot, then whispered, "Reg and I slept together on our first date."

"What?" I roared. "You were like fourteen!"

"We were sixteen!" she protested.

Bobbie dropped her knife and fork onto the plate. "You

little hussy! We all thought you were the innocent one! Turns out you beat all of us."

I dabbed my lips with a napkin and lifted my eyebrows at Bobbie. "Um…not all of us, Bobbie," I said.

"What? Me? With who?"

"That skinny kid. What was his name, Rose? The guy with the twin brother who wasn't really his twin?"

Rosemary slapped the table, trying to remember. "That's right!" she squealed. "With the curly blond hair. Justin!"

"That doesn't count. He tricked me," muttered Bobbie, and Rosemary and I stopped laughing.

"Did he…rape you?" I asked.

"Oh, God no! That's not what I meant! I meant he tricked me like…oh, brother." She paused, hoping we would drop the subject. Seeing that wasn't going to happen, she flushed pink, and covered her face with her hands. "I thought we were playing 'just the tip.'" She peeked at us through her fingers, shaking her head with embarrassment. "Turns out that was all he had to offer." She pushed her plate aside and rested her forehead on the table, choosing a view of breakfast crumbs over our laughing faces.

"So let me get this straight," I said, giggling. "He was hung like a light switch so you figured it didn't count?"

"It's not something you can just take back with a receipt," roared Rosemary. "I mean, sure, you can take it out of the package, even play with it for a bit, but once you get it wet… no returns, refunds, or store credits!" Tears were streaming down Rosemary's face from laughing so hard, and I would have been laughing harder, too, if it didn't hurt so bad.

"What about you?" Bobbie said, pointing her finger at me. "You weren't Little Miss Innocent yourself!"

"Yeah, but I never claimed to be. And besides, we can't talk about this today. I have a brain injury. Didn't you listen to my doctor? If I get agitated, my brain might explode."

"Fine. I'm leaving then," she said faking a pout. "See you after work, okay?"

"I'm fine, Bobbie."

"I know you are. I'll see you later." She scooped up her purse, gave us each a kiss on the cheek, hollered a good-bye at the kids, and swept out the screen door, letting it slam shut behind her.

"Now you just sit there," Rosemary said getting up and shaking out the place mats. "I'm gonna tidy up and you're gonna sit on that chair like a blob and tell me what's been going on. Do they have any leads on who did this to you?"

I put down my coffee. "Wait, Bobbie didn't tell you?" Her blank look was answer enough. "It was Junior Bloodgood, Rose. I can't believe Bobbie didn't tell you."

"Junior Bloodgood?" she asked, her face draining of color.

"I know. It's creepy, right? We've known him since we were kids."

"There's no way," Rosemary whispered. "It's not possible."

"I know it's hard to believe. They got him for both murders—Jimmy Polonco and Junior's girlfriend, Amber. I guess I should count myself lucky that I didn't end up with a toe tag."

Rosemary's face was as white as her T-shirt, and she shuffled over to the table, letting her tea towel drop as her knees buckled her into a chair. "No, Cass. I mean there's no way he could have done it."

"What is it, Rosemary?"

"Crap, this is crazy," she whispered. She took a deep

breath and looked at me with big nervous brown eyes. "You know Reg has been away on a fishing trip with the boys, right?"

I nodded.

"Well, Junior went with them. They're still out at the lake. I talked to Reg this morning."

"What?" My scalp started to tingle. "What?" I repeated, this time under my breath as I slumped forward, assuming the crash position. My face felt numb and my hands felt cold, and I wondered if I was going to faint. Shock, I thought to myself. I didn't have time to fall apart, though. If Junior didn't do it, then my attacker was still out there. Falling apart was a luxury I couldn't afford. I felt Rosemary's hands on my shoulders. She was trying to help me into the upright position.

"I'm okay, Rosemary," I said, only half lying. "I can do it." Rosemary's eyes were brimming with concern. I faked a smile for her and said, "I'm okay. I'm not going to fall apart on you. It's just…" I paused, trying to do the math in my head. "When exactly did Reg and Junior leave on their fishing trip?"

Rosemary counted back the days in her head. "Tuesday afternoon."

"Are you sure, Rose? The time is really important."

"I'm positive. I remember we were having lunch, and then all of a sudden Junior pulls up. And he was a mess, drunk as a skunk, going on and on about how his girlfriend had dumped him and how he'd done something stupid and needed to get out of town for a few days."

"Did he say what the stupid thing was that he did?" I asked.

Rosemary shook her head. "No, but it must have been bad, he was freaking out. Anyway, Reg had already planned to take the boys out to the lake for their yearly fishing trip, so he asked Junior if he wanted to tag along. Junior didn't even go home to pack. He just jumped around waiting for Reg to load up the car. I remember wishing they'd just leave already 'cause he was starting to freak me out." She stopped her rambling and looked at me. "What do you think he did, Cassidy?"

"Do you promise not to tell anyone?" Rosemary gave a tiny nod. "'Cause I'd be stacked in three feet of shit if anyone knew that I was talking about an open investigation."

"I promise, Cass," said Rosemary.

"Okay…shit, I can't believe I'm telling you this." I raked my fingers through my hair and drew a steadying breath. "Jimmy Polonco was killed by a gun, everyone knows that from the news. But the info they didn't release was that before Jimmy was shot, he'd actually been poisoned. Someone sent him a really expensive bottle of scotch that had been laced with cyanide. They found Junior Bloodgood's fingerprint on the inside of the bottle's security wrapper. You only get your fingerprints on the inside if you've tampered with the contents."

Rosemary looked sick. "I can't believe it. He actually tried to kill Jimmy Polonco?"

"Afraid so," I answered. "But if you're telling me he's been out of town since Tuesday afternoon, then there's no way he could have shot Jimmy or killed Amber." I paused, hating that I was going to ask. "You're sure you're telling me the truth, right, Rosemary?"

"I swear on the lives of my kids, Cassidy. He's been with Reg the whole time, and I swear I had no idea that he was a suspect in those murders." Her face darkened with anger. "I never would have let him within a hundred feet of my kids if I'd known he was capable of this!"

"I know, Rose. I'm sorry, and I do believe you. I just had to be sure, 'cause if Junior didn't kill those people then somebody else did. And whoever broke into my house…" I stopped, a knot forming in the pit of my stomach.

Rosemary sat back in her chair, casting a look toward her girls in front of the television. "Do you think he'll come back here?" she asked, panic beginning to spread over her features.

"I doubt it. Not when he thinks Junior's taking the rap for everything, but I don't like you and the girls being here if there's even a remote chance that he might."

Rosemary made a weak gesture of protest for my sake, but I could see that she was aching to grab her girls and get as far away from me as possible. I couldn't blame her, either.

"Rose, I think you and the girls should go, just to be on the safe side." She started to object, but I stopped her before she could get a word out. "And would you please stop worrying about me? I'm feeling a hundred times better now, and Bobbie's coming back to check on me after work. I'll even lock all the doors and turn on the alarm."

"Are you sure? I don't mind staying," she said, even as she collected her purse.

"I know, and I love you for it, but I'm fine. You guys go. And if you talk to Reg… Shit. I don't know if he should warn Junior or not. I mean, he did still try to kill Jimmy." Rosemary's eyes were pleading. She didn't want to get in the middle of it. "Just do what you think you ought to do, okay?"

"Okay, honey. Call me if you need anything." She gave me a quick hug and left with the girls. I waved from the porch as they backed down the driveway and sped away toward the reservation, watching them until they became nothing but a cloud of dust in the distance, indistinguishable from the hazy cloud of heat that hung like a giant blanket over the horizon. Suddenly I felt very alone. At least it was a feeling I was used to.

I locked and bolted the door, armed the security alarm, and headed upstairs. I fished my holster from my underwear drawer, strapped it over my tank top, loaded my Glock, and slipped it into its leather casing. "Locked and loaded, motherfucker," I mumbled to myself then smiled at my own bravado. I wasn't going to be taken by surprise again. For good measure, I grabbed my baseball bat, tested its weight in my hands, and headed back down the stairs. Daddy would be proud of his girl.

First things first, I had some phone calls to make. I pulled out my phone, took a deep breath, and dialed the number for Double Down. I doubted very much that Lorenzo would take my call, but I felt duty bound to tell him that his brother's killer was still on the loose. If he was going to act like a big baby, so be it. After five rings the machine picked up. "Lorenzo, it's me…Cassidy…Detective Jones. Listen, I know I'm not your favorite person right now. I get it, but I need to talk to you about something, and it's important." I was pressing the phone too tightly to the injured side of my head, and the sudden jolt of pain shot through me like lightning. I contemplated hanging up for a fraction of a second then thought better of it.

"So if you'd just put aside your stupid pride for a fucking minute and stop acting like a stupid teenage girl and call me back, that'd be great. Oh, and by the way? Brandi Hammer, for God's sake? Did you really think that was the name on my birth certificate?" And I hung up.

That felt good, I thought to myself as I dialed Bobbie. As I expected, she was less than pleased with the fact that the killer, my attacker, was still on the loose, and it took all my power of persuasion to convince her not to rush back and babysit me.

I hung up and pressed another number on my speed dial. I was looking forward to this next call the least of all. Chief Thompson. He'd been ecstatic when he thought we were going to be able to close the case. This new development wasn't going to reflect well on him or the department, and most especially, me. I listened to the sound of the phone ringing with dread. I was about to go from hero to zero in less than a minute.

"Chief," he barked.

"Hey, Chief. It's Jones."

"Detective Jones! How's our local hero doing today?"

"Yeah…about that. Listen, I need to tell you something really important." Silence. "About the case."

"What is it, Jones? We've got a press conference about it in ten, so it better be important."

Shit, he was going to the press already. This wasn't going to end well. "Ah, you might want to hold off on that."

"No can do," he said cutting me off. "Everybody's already assembled in the conference room. It's a done deal. You're going to be a household name by dinnertime."

Yeah, I thought to myself, *the cop who bungled up the highest-profile murder case in the city's history.* Perfect. Couldn't wait to bear that dubious distinction.

"Sir, you can't do that." I winced. "I think we got the wrong guy." There was nothing but dead silence on the other end of the phone, and I checked to see if my battery had run out.

"That's impossible," he said firmly. "We found his print on the bottle wrapper and his wallet at the second crime scene. Whatever new information you've found, it's obviously not true." He paused for a second, and I could hear him closing a door. "What did you find?" he asked.

"Well, apparently Junior wasn't even in town when the two murders happened. He's been out at the lake with my friend Rosemary's husband since the afternoon before the murder. And they're still there, so there's no way he could have killed either one of them...or attacked me."

"This Rosemary person, you say she's a friend of yours?"

"Yes, she is. We grew up together. She still lives on the reservation."

"So she's Indian," he said, cutting me off.

"Well, yeah. She is."

"And her husband, too? You know, it would be just like them to protect their own. Especially the son of their chief. They'd owe him a certain amount of their loyalty. They probably consider it their duty to protect him."

"I don't know, sir," I said. "I don't think Rosemary feels like she owes him anything. She never liked Junior." There was another long pause.

"Maybe she didn't care for Junior, but everyone loves Junior's father, Chief Bloodgood. Something like this—the chief's son being a double murderer—would bring shame to everyone on the reservation. It wouldn't be the first time their people banded together to protect their tribe."

"But sir..."

"I hate to say it, Jones," he interrupted softly, "but I think they're using your friendship as a way to beat a murder rap. There's just too much evidence against him. We're closing this today. The town needs to know that they're safe from all this madness. And your little theory wouldn't serve the department very well at all. Do we understand each other?"

I felt sick. "Yeah, I get it."

"Good. Now maybe you should take a few days off to recover. You're going to be a hero. This town could really use a hero right now." And he hung up.

I felt numb. In a million years I hadn't imagined that the chief wouldn't believe me. Now I was stuck. In my heart, I really did believe Rosemary. She'd been too shaken up to be faking ignorance. And I knew for a fact that she would never put her boys in danger by sending them on a fishing trip with a man capable of poisoning another human being. But what was I supposed to do? I sure as hell couldn't let Junior get away with his murder attempt on Jimmy Polonco, but I also couldn't let him go down for a bunch of crimes that he didn't commit. There was also the frightening fact that the real killer was out there free.

Free to kill again.

Free to kill me.

I wandered through the house feeling rudderless. It wasn't in my genetic makeup to lie down and convalesce like a normal head injury patient. I needed purpose to get me through the day. The whole relaxing thing that everyone raved about just made me feel nervous. And the fact that my attacker was still out there on the loose didn't help on the relaxation front, either.

I threw in a load of laundry, finding an atom of comfort at least in performing a mindless task. I threw out the fishnet hosiery that I'd worn to the Den. Crawling around on my hands and knees in the parking lot had torn gaping holes in them, rendering them unusable. I would go from slightly slutty to total rough trade in a heartbeat if I gave them another wearing. I picked up my tall leather boots. They had come out a little worse for wear in the parking lot debacle, too. They were dusty and scuffed, and one of the buckles had come off—nothing that a little TLC from my creepy shoe repair guy couldn't fix. I'd probably never look at them with the same adoration again, though—they'd been silent witness to too much crazy shit. Still, a good polish and a new buckle would go a long way to erasing some of those memories.

I wandered back down the stairs with my boots, feeling more and more like a caged animal. Usually when I felt like this I'd go for a run, but the pounding in my head told me that was off the table. Groceries, though—a run to the grocery store would be a low-impact/low-risk endeavor. And a girl had to eat, right? My creepy shoe repair guy had his booth in the same strip mall. I could kill two birds with one stone.

I rooted around in my purse for my car keys and came up with the key to the Camaro. There was no point in driving the rust bucket anymore if Brandi Hammer had been retired. I'd go to the station, pick up my beautiful black Jeep from the police impound, turn in the poor Camaro, go drop off my boots and hit the grocery store. Having something on my to-do list other than "wait around in vain for justice to be served" made me feel better immediately.

Chapter Sixteen

The parking lot at the station was a zoo when I arrived, with news vans taking up the premium spaces in front of the building. I'd have to go in the side entrance through booking if I wanted to avoid that spectacle, and today, the way I was looking, I really did want to avoid that spectacle.

The booking room was a study in despair. It had the air of a subway station you might find in the worst part of town. People only ever passed through here, some on their way to prison, some off to the holding tank to await bail, the only common denominator being that the destination was someplace sad. It wasn't a part of the station that needed to impress, so it didn't.

The stark overhead fluorescents bounced light off the stained, hospital-blue walls to cast a sickly pallor on everything and everyone in the room. The desks were cheap and chipping, made of beige melamine that was slowly but surely accumulating a patina of grime and sleaze. The only people to look up at my arrival were a urine-stained homeless man who was absently fondling his genitals and a tired office clerk. I flashed my badge at them both as I crossed through the room and out into the station. Neither one seemed impressed.

The hallway was empty, for which I was enormously grateful. Down the hall to the right, I could make out the din of excited voices in the lobby. The press conference must have just ended. Soon bodies would spill into the hallway and I'd be forced to talk to people, an idea that filled me with dread. I turned left toward impound, walking as quietly as I could in the hallway. I was being silly, of course, sneaking around my own station, but I wanted to get in and out with no drama. My happiness at being alone quickly evaporated, though, when I heard footsteps approaching from around the corner. I was dreading the inevitable "What happened to your face?" Maybe I'd get lucky. Maybe it was just an accountant from payroll. They never made eye contact.

I should have known, given my track record of late, that I would not be so lucky. Of all the corners in all the world, Detective Coleman had to round this one. He paused for a fraction of a second while his brain did the math. I wasn't dressed like a cop today. He'd also never seen me with a rearranged face before, either. As he fell back into step and continued toward me, he looked over his shoulder. I did the same. We were alone. I stopped in my tracks, trying to slow the sudden thudding in my chest, and with a certain amount of shock I realized I was nervous. Or was it afraid? The adrenaline coursing through my body made it impossible to tell. The last time I had seen Jay he was eyeballing me through the door in the hospital. Aside from that, our last interaction had been contentious, to say the least. If the situation were reversed, I'd want revenge. Big-time. I would have come at him swinging, but Jay didn't do that. His face was unreadable.

"Jones," he said, stopping at arm's length.

"Detective," I answered, hoping that my voice sounded stronger than I felt.

"Looks like you're a big hero now," he said quietly. His gaze was steady as he looked at me, his smoky green eyes studying my face. I could feel my cheeks flush pink, which made me feel foolish. I hated that he could make me feel that way. The problem was he'd seen me pretty much naked, sat there obediently while I'd rubbed myself up and down his entire body. Then again, my last memory of Jay was of him bound, gagged, and defenseless in the basement of a sweaty sex club, wearing a leash and a LICK ME sign. Perhaps we were even in the public humiliation department.

"I'm not in the mood to deal with you today, Jay."

I stepped to the side, hoping to avoid any more confrontation, but he moved with me, blocking my way. "I need to talk to you."

He had just pressed the wrong button, and I could feel my anger flare, rising from my gut like a wounded animal. "Get the fuck out of my way," I spat out, low and angry. "Or I'll tie you to that bench over there with another LICK ME sign on your back."

Before I could react, he snatched my arm and jerked me tight to his chest, his fingers digging into my flesh. "You better hope you got the right guy," he hissed. "Next time you might not get off so lucky." Before I could say anything he pushed me away, almost knocking me to the ground, then stalked off. He threw one last look over his shoulder. His face was devoid of emotion. I'm sure mine wasn't. His words had shaken me even more than his physical treatment of me.

Jay Coleman had just declared war.

I looked down at my arm. His handprint stood out red against my tanned skin, a bruise in the making. You'd think I'd be used to it by now. I wasn't.

Things were quiet in impound. Things were always quiet in impound. Impound was in the basement of the building, far from the hubbub of the rest of the station. If you worked in impound, it usually meant that you'd either done something wrong and were being punished for it, or you were injured and were therefore a liability on the street. Whichever way you sliced it, it was a shitty piece of pie that was painful to eat. I suppose it should have come as no surprise when the beautiful Officer Ken answered the call button. There was no way Ken was ever going to win over the meatheads at this station, not until a woman took over as captain, and it would be a cold day in hell when that happened.

Ken stepped up to the window and gave me a concerned smile. "Hey, Cass, what are you doing here? You okay? Are you supposed to be out of bed?"

"You kidding me? You can't get rid of me that easy," I answered with false bravado.

Ken smiled. "Glad to hear it. And I'm proud of you for catching our murderer. You showed those assholes." His smile dimmed. "I'm glad you got the chance to actually do something."

"Hey, you'll get your shot, Ken," I said.

"Yeah, I suppose…if I ever get out of here." He gestured with his thumb to the cavernous space behind him.

"What happened?" I asked. "Why'd they stick you down here in impound?"

"Your guess is as good as mine." He snorted. "But now that you've made detective, it seems Captain Rye has a new punching bag."

"Shit, Ken. I'm sorry. Is there anything I can do?"

Ken smiled. "Can you build me a time machine so I can go back and take my parents' advice about dental school?"

"You would have hated being a dentist. Too boring."

"I guess," he answered. "'Cause this is a thrill a minute."

I made a split-second decision. If there was anyone I could trust at the station it was Ken. I leaned forward over the counter and gestured for Ken to get closer. "You want thrills?" He gave me the nod to continue. "I think they've pinned the murders on the wrong guy."

Ken's eyes went wide. "Are you sure?"

"Yeah, pretty damn sure," I answered. "My friend Rosemary says Junior Bloodgood has an airtight alibi. She says he's been out of town with her husband the whole time."

"No shit," he said with disbelief.

"No shit," I said. "And, Ken, here's the thing…I believe her. I really do. There's no way Junior could have committed either murder, and there's no way he could have attacked me." I thought for a moment. "And you know what else, now that I think about it? Whoever attacked me was strong and he knew how to fight. Junior's a big pussy. There's no way he would have had the balls to do it. Or the skill."

Ken stood up, absorbing the information and let out a

big breath. "Shit, Cass. What are ya gonna do? Did you tell the captain?"

"I did, but he didn't want to hear it. He's gung-ho to close this thing. I mean, the pressure on him to solve this must be crazy. The mayor's probably three miles up his ass. He wants to put a shiny face on the department, so he's closing the case. I've got a really bad feeling about this."

Ken leaned back in. "What are you gonna do?"

"I'm going to find the son of a bitch who did it, and I think I know where to start."

I collected my thoughts for a moment, knowing that I was about to open up a giant ugly can of worms. "Ken, what time did Detective Coleman leave the Den that night?"

Ken looked at me with surprise then checked over his shoulder. "Do you think he did it?"

I lifted my shoulders a fraction. "I don't know if he did or not. I just know that he's not clean of it. There's something going on, and I feel like he's dirty. I mean, I know he's had it in for me since I got here, but…" I paused. "Can you promise this stays between me and you? For real, if word gets out and I'm wrong, I'm done."

"Of course, Cass. We're partners…"

"So what time did he leave the club? I kind of tied him up and left him there, and hey, if he was there for hours, then there's no way he could have attacked me. No harm, no foul, but—"

"Shit, Cass!" Ken hissed, cutting me off. "This is fucked up. He came storming out of there like five minutes after you left, wearing nothing but a towel around his waist and a pair of boots. Some weird chick with spiky blond hair was hanging off him, crying and acting all crazy, but he left her there.

He looked like he was in a hurry. And he looked pissed."

"Shit," I whispered. I hadn't wanted it to be true, and there was still a chance that I was wrong, but I could feel my stomach turn. This was going to get messy.

Ken put his hands on my shoulders and gave me a steadying squeeze. "How can I help you?" he asked.

I looked into his big doe eyes. People underestimated him every day, but he was a good partner and a good friend. "I'm not sure yet," I told him, "but I think I'm definitely going to need your help when I figure out my next move. Thank you."

Ken smiled. "Just say the word."

I knew at least someone at the station had my back. It felt good.

"Shit, my Jeep," I said, remembering why I'd come to impound. "Sorry, Ken, I spaced. I actually came down here to get my Jeep out." I unfolded my impound slip and handed it to Ken, then fished the Camaro keys out of my pocket and set them on the counter.

"No problem, Cassidy," he said. "Give me a sec and I'll find your keys for you." He walked over to the key cupboard and unlocked it. Even in my dark mood I was still able to appreciate the view, not that I was interested.

"Hey, Cass," he called out. "Can you come here?"

He pointed at the number on my claim slip, then to the matching numbered cubbyhole. It was empty.

"Do you see your keys in here anywhere? Someone must have filed them away wrong. It happens, I guess."

"That's weird," I said. "Look for a key chain with a World Series of Poker chip on it." It was a souvenir from one of my many trips to Vegas, a good luck charm. The key could be replaced, but I'd be bummed out if I lost my poker chip.

"This it?" he asked, fishing a key out of a pile at the bottom of the cupboard.

"Yes!" Relief washed over me. If I'd had to spend the rest of my day hunting down another key to my Jeep, I might have lost it. I was keenly aware of the fact that I had a horrifyingly tenuous grip on my emotions today.

"Just sign here then," he said, handing me a pen. "If I screw up impound duty, who knows where I'll end up next. Probably out emptying the parking meters."

"We can't have that," I said, and scrawled a quick signature on his form.

"Remember what I said, Cassidy. Anything you need, you call."

"Thanks, Ken. It means a lot." I slipped my finger through the loop of my key chain and gave it a twirl. I looked down at the keys in my hand. Something was missing. I had goose bumps. My house key was gone.

"You okay?" I looked up to see Ken eyeing at me with concern. "Cassidy, what's wrong?"

"Holy fuck, Ken," I whispered. "My house key's gone." We both stood there staring down at the keys in my hand. "My house key…"

"Are you sure?" he asked. "You didn't take it with you when you traded vehicles?"

"For Christ's sake, Ken, no! I didn't take my house key with me. I forgot it. I had to bum my spare key off Bobbie."

"Okay, calm down. There's got to be a good reason for this," said Ken.

"There is," I said, feeling worse and worse with every passing second. "Coleman. That's how he got into my house."

I was starting to panic. "I *knew* I had locked the door that night! I *knew* I wasn't that out of it."

Ken grabbed me by the shoulders and steadied me. "We're going to figure this out, Cass. I promise you."

I took a deep breath. "I'm missing something, Ken. I know I am. I've got to find a way to connect him to those murders."

"Well, we know he's connected to the strip club, right?"

I shot him a look. "How did you know about that?"

Ken had the decency to look contrite. "Bobbie might have mentioned something about it. Sorry."

I made a mental note to talk to Bobbie. I'd asked her to keep her mouth shut about the whole Coleman/stripping fiasco. Not cool. But now wasn't the time to worry about it.

"Okay," I said, getting down to business. "We know that Detective Coleman was hanging around the club. We know he'd been wearing a disguise there, and that the girls knew him. We know he made friends with Candy, who was Amber's best friend. But why would he want to kill Amber?" I felt my frustration building again. "Why the hell would he want to kill Jimmy Polonco, for that matter?"

"All right, let's think about this," said Ken. "Cops and mobsters are always gonna butt heads. Maybe Coleman had some dirt on Polonco and was offering him protection or something, and Polonco wasn't having it?"

"I don't know. According to Lorenzo, Jimmy's brother, they had severed ties with their family, like ten years ago. They were doing things legit. I don't know what kind of dirt Coleman could have found. And what about Amber? Why would he do that to her?"

Ken shrugged his shoulders. "Maybe she saw something

she shouldn't have."

None of it was getting any clearer. I'd been batting all of these theories around in my head ever since I got put on the case.

"You can't ignore the evidence, though," said Ken. "I mean, you did find Junior's wallet at Amber's crime scene."

"What are you talking about? I wasn't the one who found it."

Ken's eyes grew wide. "How hard did you hit your head? I read the report. It says you found the wallet and called it in."

I was starting to understand why everyone was calling me a hero, but it was a title of which I was completely undeserving.

"I didn't find the wallet, Ken. I found... Shit!" I'd completely forgotten! I'd gone right from the crime scene to the Den, to my house, and then was attacked. In all the excitement, I'd forgotten about a piece of evidence. Amber's fingernail was still in the tiny side pocket of my tall black leather boots, which were still in the passenger seat of the shitty Camaro in the parking lot. DNA is a cop's best friend, and I really needed a friend right now.

"Ken, I gotta go take some evidence to the lab. Thank you!" I was almost out of the building when I remembered something else that I needed. I spun around, instantly regretting the action as my head desperately tried to recalibrate. Fuck it, I thought to myself. I wasn't going to let a headache stop me. I ran down the hall until I reached the bullpen. It was a hive of activity, but I was looking for one man in particular. I could hear voices calling my name and feel the odd pat on my shoulder. Part of my brain registered that I was getting the royal welcome, but this was not the time.

"Where's Coleman?" I yelled. I could hear the voices around me stop. "Where the fuck is Detective Coleman?" I repeated.

Lisa got up from her desk and walked over to me. "What's going on?" she asked.

I looked at her. She looked sincere. That was new. "I need to find Detective Coleman. Do you know where he is?"

"He's left for a crime scene. You want me to call him?"

"No. Thanks, Lisa." I turned on my heel, avoiding the prying eyes around me. Lisa followed me for a few steps.

"Hey, Jones," she said stopping me with a gentle hand on my shoulder. "You don't look so good. I think you should take it easy."

"I will, Lisa. There's just something I have to do first."

She dropped her hand and shrugged her shoulders. No one could say she hadn't tried.

The boots were still in the car. If you ever wanted to hide something valuable, a twenty-five-year-old rust bucket was the perfect hiding spot. I was a little worried about what the heat and humidity might have done to my DNA sample, but there was nothing I could do about it now. I grabbed the boots and ran around the building to my Jeep. I was almost happy about the jagged pain that shot through my skull with every stride. It was like penance for being such a shitty detective. Now the only thing I needed was a sample from my friend Detective Coleman. If he had been at the station I would have grabbed a handful of hair, or raked off some skin with my car keys. But now I was going to have to go to plan B.

I squealed to a stop in front of Detective Coleman's house, grabbed the red paper–wrapped parcel from the passenger seat and hopped out. The house looked the same as before—lonely and empty. The plants on his front doorstep were nothing more than shriveled-up sticks by this point. I guess if he didn't have qualms about killing people, what was to prevent him from murdering his plants?

I walked directly into the backyard and tapped on the patio door. I heard a deep bark insulated by the walls of Jay's closet followed by the skittering of sharp claws on hardwood. Finally Jay's big German shepherd rounded the corner into the family room and pitched himself against the sliding glass doors. Instead of screaming this time, I unwrapped the parcel and pulled out a gorgeous dripping hunk of prime rib.

"Mmm…you want some of this, boy?" The dog stopped his barking. "I bet this is gonna taste good."

I fished my handy lock pick from my pocket and went to work on the door, all the while making idle chitchat with Jay's dog. He let out a loud whimper and put a big paw on the door.

"You're lonely, aren't you, buddy?" I cooed, sliding the door open with one hand, offering him the massive steak with the other. "Here ya go, buddy. A nice juicy steak. This should keep you busy for a while."

Jay's dog sniffed it, gave it a lick, then gently took it from my hand and settled down to feast in the middle of the living room carpet, not giving me a second look. I'd been expecting more resistance, and the relief I felt from not having to wrestle the dog outside made me feel almost euphoric. Still, I didn't know how much goodwill Jay's dog would be willing to extend once the steak was done.

I didn't want to linger. All I needed was a sample of Jay's DNA to cross with the DNA hopefully left on Amber's fingernail, and if I happened to find Amber's phone while I was at it, that would be the final nail in Jay's coffin. I'd call in the cavalry. I passed the dog, gave him a scratch behind the ears, and tiptoed into Jay's bedroom. There was a towel beside the bed. Charming. I could only imagine what kind of petri wonderland that was. I dumped it into my bag and headed for the bathroom. I grabbed a comb, a toothbrush, and a razor, dumping them into the bag with the towel. Overkill, maybe, but I was leaving nothing to chance.

I went back into the bedroom and checked the drawers of his night table and his dresser. Nothing. I walked past the dog again and into the kitchen. He looked at me curiously, but didn't protest. The only thing interesting in the kitchen was a lonely doughnut, which I ate. I opened up the fridge and guzzled milk from the carton. It was petty and highly caloric but I needed to violate him, perhaps not the way he'd violated me, but still…there would be no peace in my addled brain without some form of petty retribution.

I grabbed some Milk-Bones from a box on the counter and presented them to Jay's dog. The steak had left a bloody basketball-sized stain on Jay's beige shag carpet. Jay was going to blow a gasket when he saw that. I was probably doing him a favor, though, I reasoned to myself. Shag carpet was total vagina repellent. I left Jay's big dog to finish the cookies at his leisure. I hoped he wouldn't get punished for his less-than-stellar guarding. "'Bye, dog," I cooed. He rolled over on his back for a belly rub, and I obliged. Jay was an ass, but his dog was all right.

Bobbie was waiting for me at the front door of the building when I arrived. She shook her head as I handed her the new piece of evidence and my myriad samples of Jay's DNA. "You look like shit, Cass."

"I didn't realize this was the swimsuit round. Sorry," I shot back.

"This isn't how you're supposed to be recovering," she said. "Running around in the heat, breaking into houses, wrestling with guard dogs."

"I didn't exactly have to wrestle him, but I did feel a little sick paying twenty-five bucks for a piece of steak. That shit's expensive when you get it from the butcher!"

Bobbie rolled her eyes at me. "God, you're a stubborn one! I don't know why I even bother to worry about you. *You* don't even bother to worry about you." She put her annoyance away and gave me a hug. "If I promise to rush this job for you, do you promise to go home and lie down? You don't have to sleep, but just lie down." She waited. She wasn't going to take no for an answer.

"Yes, Mom, I promise."

"Good. I should have the results by tomorrow morning. Now go." I turned around and retraced my steps down the hall. "Straight home!" she added. I waved. She could interpret that however she wished.

I had no intention of going home. My first stop was to drop off my boots with the creepy shoe repair guy. His shop was a tiny hole in the wall that was recessed from the rest of the strip mall, making it very easy to miss. His customers could only be the result of good word of mouth, since nothing about the shop or the shopkeeper would inspire one to cross his threshold. He had his operation set up in such a way that he could watch the parking lot as he worked. He could see his customers approaching from a distance, giving him ample lead time to greet them at the door with an alarmingly affectionate smile and a lengthy sweaty embrace. Today was no exception. Some probably viewed the ritual as a sexual violation. I preferred to think of it as an exchange of currency—a tacit agreement whereby the creepy shoe guy would give me an inappropriate boob-smushing hug, followed by what I could only imagine would be a furious shoe-sniffing jerk-off session in the bathroom, in exchange for exquisite and prompt service at a very reasonable price. It was a fair trade in my estimation, although I had to admit that the events of the last few days made the transaction nearly unbearable today. Hug finished and boots proffered, I wearily accepted my claim ticket and backed out the door.

The next stop was the Pick and Save grocery store. My heart wasn't really into the task anymore, but I soldiered on, determined to finish the errands I'd set out to do. I slumped over my cart, willing my legs to navigate the aisles. I was dimly aware that people were staring at me. I felt like hell, and probably looked even worse. When one of the stock boys offered to push my cart, I decided that perhaps I'd had enough action for one day. I mumbled something that included the word "whippersnapper," steered my cart over to the frozen food aisle, and abandoned it in front of the frozen waffles.

The temperature change from the frozen food section to the humid parking lot was a huge jolt to my system. The black leather seats of my Jeep made it feel like I was sitting on a skillet, and I was suddenly, unmistakably exhausted. I had successfully thumbed my nose at the instructions given me by the medical professionals and ignored the well-meaning advice of all my friends and colleagues who loved and/or cared about me. *I guess I really showed them*, I thought to myself as I sat immobile in the parking lot, sweating and aching. A wave of nausea rolled over me thick and heavy like a night fog, forcing my head back onto the headrest. I closed my eyes, feeling miserable, but even the tears welling up behind my eyelids refused to fall, years of stubbornness having trained them to stay at bay. I was a fool, lying in a bed of my own making. Poets called it tilting at windmills. My dad called it pissing into the wind. Ever since I got out of the hospital I'd been fighting a war of attrition against myself. Nothing stung as much as that crystalline moment of clarity when you realized that your supposed bravery was nothing more than common stupidity, measured in units of defiance. It was time to go home.

I pulled up my long driveway and stared at the house that I'd admired since my early childhood. For the first time in a very long time, I saw my beautiful house with fresh eyes. Sitting all alone on a hill under the late-day sun, it looked suddenly ominous and isolated. My safe house seemed more like a plundered vault, and as much as I wanted to, and desperately needed to, I couldn't bring myself to go inside. I reached into my purse and pulled out my Glock and my phone. I scrolled through my contacts until I found the number of my dad's locksmith, and I waited.

John Brenner's truck pulled up the driveway and parked behind me. John was probably in his late sixties. He was tall and stocky, with gray hair and a gray mustache. I'd always thought he looked like the guy on the Orville Redenbacher popcorn box. He'd done the locks on my childhood house beside the reservation, and he'd done the locks on this house not too long ago. He was my dad's hire, so I knew without asking that he'd been security cleared to a level of about CIA status. I could trust John. I waited in the Jeep while he changed the locks and added dead bolts and tested the veracity of every damned window in the house. Only when he stood out on the porch and waved me in with his big callused paw did I leave the canned safety of my Jeep and limp my way up the steps.

"Everything's tight as a drum now, Cassidy," he said, giving the doorframe a gentle pat. "You're good to go." To preserve my pride, he had made it sound like he was talking about the windows and the doors. But his fatherly smile and look of concern told me that he'd looked under the bed for monsters and checked the closet for the bogeyman. I couldn't remember the last time I'd felt so grateful to another human being.

"Thanks, John," I mumbled. The tears that had been threatening to spill finally came, and I let him fold me into a gentle hug, tears rolling down my face and onto his crisp cotton shirt. I didn't care.

When my body finally stopped shuddering, I pulled back and smiled. "Sorry I got snot on your shirt."

He smiled at me in return. "Don't even think about it."

I pulled a wad of cash out of my purse and held it out to him. He selected a twenty-dollar bill and put the rest back in my hand. "That's not enough, John."

He smiled and pressed two keys into my hand. "Yes, it is." And he left, shutting the door behind him quietly.

I locked the door and threw the three dead bolts. Nobody was getting in this house without a key or an express invitation.

I was determined to be a good patient from here on in. My pain pills were still on the table where Bobbie had left them. I popped the lid and took two as per the doctor's orders, then swallowed a third to make up for my previous lack of compliance. I shuffled into the living room, wrapped myself in a throw blanket, curled up on the couch and closed my eyes, and I slept, that heavy dreamless sleep of the utterly exhausted and the overmedicated.

Chapter Seventeen

I was awakened by the sound of knocking. My eyelids felt heavy, as if they'd been weighed down by lead fishing sinkers. I blinked them open slowly, confused for a moment. The house was in pitch darkness, although as my eyes slowly adjusted, I found a sliver of light trickling in from the kitchen, the nightlight over the stove.

I shrugged off the cobwebs of sleep and took inventory. The pounding in my head had tapered off to a mild ache, and the various insults to the flesh thrummed with nerve action when I directed thought to them. I wasn't going to be entering an arm-wrestling contest any time soon, but I was definitely feeling better. Another knock at the door pulled me into the upright position. So far, so good. I stood, wrapping the blanket tightly around myself. It was probably Bobbie checking on me. I made my way through the living room and kitchen to the front door, turning lights on as I went. "Coming, Bobbie," I called out.

The voice on the other side of the door answered, "It's not Bobbie."

I stopped in my tracks. It definitely wasn't Bobbie. It was Lorenzo's voice. My first thought was that I looked like hell and didn't want him to see me. My second thought, the thought that won, was that Lorenzo was a jerk and I didn't care what he thought of me. If he was here to sulk or pick a fight, he could kiss my ass. I pulled open the door.

Lorenzo looked amazing, of course, which only served to irritate me more. He was wearing a pair of expensively faded jeans and a black linen shirt. When he saw me, his eyes widened in shock. "Shit," he whispered.

I must look like a real treat, I thought to myself. I put my hand up to my hair. It was a matted mess, I could tell. I peeked down at my T-shirt with its wrinkles pressed in from sweating in my sleep—not how Kevin Costner would have played it at all, but I was well and truly beyond caring. "How'd you find out where I live?" I asked.

"Bertrand followed you here from the station," he said quietly. "He told me you were hurt, but I didn't realize…" His words trailed off into nothing.

"Didn't realize what? That I got my face rearranged? That I got my ass handed to me?" I let the words hang there for a moment. "You know, you were the first person I called when I woke up in the hospital. I was worried about you."

Lorenzo looked stricken. If I'd wanted to make him feel terrible, I couldn't have chosen better words, and I was filled with a sick and inexplicable satisfaction. "Listen, don't worry about it," I went on, emptying my voice of emotion. "I'll be fine." I drew my arm out of my cozy blanket and reached for the door. Lorenzo took in the sight of my bare arm then pressed his eyes shut with his right hand. In the light of the kitchen, Jay's paw print stood out dark and purple, an ugly addition to the already impressive patchwork of bruises on my skin, further testimony to the indignities and violence I'd endured over the past two days. It was violence that I'd attracted to myself because of my involvement with Lorenzo, and from the anguished look on his face, I could tell he felt responsible. Making him feel guilty hadn't been my intention—at least I didn't think it had. After all, I was being paid for my involvement.

Granted, it was a meager pittance when you consider what I'd had to offer in return, but it was a contract that I'd entered into willingly, if not happily. Lorenzo hadn't asked for my help. In fact, it was his sister-in-law who had set the wheels in motion, unbeknownst to Lorenzo, leaving him entirely blameless. Still, a part of me, the twelve-year-old, immature, insecure, passive-aggressive part of me, was secretly happy to know I had affected him this way.

"Um...Roger wanted me to give you this," he said awkwardly, handing me a Styrofoam takeout container. I took it slowly and peeked under the lid. Spaghetti and meatballs. My mouth started watering. It smelled like magic, and I realized I was famished. I hadn't eaten since breakfast, and I'd left all my groceries in front of the waffle case at the Pick and Save. "This too," he added, popping the lid on a second container. "He thought some chocolate cake might make you feel better."

I let a tiny smile escape. It was a smile meant for Roger, though, not Lorenzo, so I aimed it at the cake. "He was right," I answered. There was an awkward pause. "Tell him I said thank you," I mumbled, and moved to close the door.

"Wait, Cassidy." For the first time since I'd met him, Lorenzo looked like he was miles out of his depth. "Listen, have I completely blown it with you?" he asked.

"What do you mean?"

"I mean..." He stopped, searching for words. "I mean that I like you...a lot...which is why I acted like such an ass yesterday. I handled things poorly. When I found out you were a police officer, I felt like everyone was in on this big secret but me, that I was the butt of a really bad joke. I should have let you talk when you called me, but I bulldozed through the conversation because I was embarrassed. You deserved better, and I really hope you can forgive me." He gently lifted my chin with his fingers. "I hope you'll give me another chance."

I was stunned. A million thoughts raced to the tip of my tongue, yet none of them seemed able to commit to sound. Lorenzo let his hand fall away, disappointment clouding his handsome features. "I really was an idiot," he whispered under his breath. It was my turn to feel confused. "You don't feel the same way at all, do you? This really was just a job for you." He turned to leave.

"Wait, Lorenzo." He stopped. "It's taking me a little longer to make sentences today. I'm a little stoned."

This earned me a smile.

"And besides, I wasn't expecting you to be nice to me, so I only had crappy things to say to you. You caught me a little off guard."

He chuckled. "So you accept my apology then?" he asked.

"Only if you hand over the cake." He looked down at the Styrofoam container still in his hand. "Seriously? You thought you'd get away with my cake? You don't know me very well, do you?" The irony of that question hung for a minute, and we locked eyes. We both had a lot to learn. "Would you like to come inside?"

I left Lorenzo to set up the food in the living room while I went upstairs to freshen up. I shook my head when I saw my reflection in the mirror. It wasn't pretty. On the upside, though, he'd seen me look my absolute worst and hadn't run for the hills. That had to count for something. I took a quick birdbath in the sink, wiped on some deodorant and lip balm, swiped a brush through my hair and brushed my teeth. It was as good as it was going to get.

When I finally made my way back downstairs, I found Lorenzo looking at the Polonco family tree I'd assembled the night I was assigned the case. The photos of Lorenzo and all his various supermodel giraffe companions were scattered front and center.

"You're very photogenic," I said, trying to lighten what could have been an awkward moment. He turned around and gave me a look that I couldn't quite interpret. "I'm sorry," I said, exhaustion creeping into my voice. "This is weird, isn't it?"

"Yes, I guess it is."

I settled on to the floor in front of the coffee table and picked up a fork. "Okay, how 'bout this," I said, spearing a meatball. "Let's work on this together. I'm sure between the two of us we can figure out who killed Jimmy."

Lorenzo raised his eyebrows. "Really? I'm not on your

suspect list?"

"Nope. I ruled you out the first night, during our little Caesar adventure." I grinned at him and got a warm smile in return.

"So all that stuff about being Canadian and a bartender..."

"Not Canadian, although I did do my fair share of drinking there. And yes, I did bartend once upon a time. It's how I put myself through college. And to answer your earlier accusation...no, my feelings for you were not related to the job. Not sleeping with you was because of the job, but everything else was me, not the job."

Lorenzo laughed. "Good to know." He brushed the hair away from my face, gently tucking it behind my ear. "How's the spaghetti?"

"God, it's so good," I moaned. "I love that man. Have some. He made me a ton."

"You eat. Roger already fed me."

Once I had put away most of the spaghetti, all of the cake, and two more yellow pills, Lorenzo and I sat down with my file. "Okay, so I'm just going to dive right in. That work for you?" Lorenzo nodded, so I plowed onward. "All right. So your brother was killed on Tuesday night. That's also the night that Amber was killed. Now, you know that Jimmy was popped in the forehead with a .38, but what you don't know is that the bottle of scotch he'd been drinking at the time had been laced with poison. He'd already started to feel the effects of it when he got shot."

Lorenzo looked stunned. "He was poisoned?"

"Yeah. We didn't release that information because we didn't know how it would affect the investigation. There were no usable prints on the bottle, but we found Junior's prints on the inside of the plastic security wrapper, which makes him the one who had to have tampered with that bottle." Lorenzo nodded his head, so I continued. "Junior had a motive. Jimmy had just fired him from the casino, and from what I gathered it was a pretty humiliating ordeal for the guy."

Lorenzo nodded again. "Yeah. I heard about that."

"Then Amber dumps him the next day, a pretty shitty run of luck, which he blames on Jimmy. So he orders up an expensive bottle of scotch, one he knows will catch Jimmy's eye, he adds the poison, carefully replaces the seal, wipes the bottle for prints and has it delivered to Jimmy with…" I rummaged through the pile and pulled out the gift card that I had found on Lorenzo's desk. "This."

A look of hurt flitted across Lorenzo's face, making me wince. "I'm sorry." I felt like a turd, like I'd violated his trust. "It's just I remembered you told me that you and Jimmy only ever called your father Enzo, not Dad, the way the gift note was signed. Made me think someone else had sent it. Anyway, when they discovered Junior had poisoned Jimmy's scotch, I guess they made the leap that Junior had pulled the trigger as well." I gave Lorenzo a moment to let the information sink in. "What do you think so far?" I asked.

"So far, it sounds like Junior is our guy," he said hesitantly.

"Yeah," I said, "but the only problem is Junior left town for the lake on Tuesday morning with my girlfriend's husband, and he's still there. So there's no way he could have shot Jimmy or murdered Amber that night or attacked me. See the problem?" Lorenzo nodded. "The chief just announced to the world that we got our double murderer, but I *know* we got the wrong guy."

"Damn," Lorenzo said quietly. "Can I ask you something?" I nodded. "How did you get put on the case?"

"The morning after your brother was killed, I was called into the chief's office. Jimmy's wife, Leora, was there. Poor thing, she was grief stricken. Anyway, she had gone to the chief in a panic. She was all scared that if we didn't find the killer, your family from Chicago would come and sort out the mess for us. She thought it might have been an inside job, and was quite adamant about wanting a cop to be put in undercover at the club. And, since there are only two female cops on the force, and the other chick looks like a male bodybuilder, they picked me."

Lorenzo took a long draw from his bottle of beer, mulling over the information I'd just shared with him. "And you say Leora was grief stricken? That's weird."

"Why?" I asked.

"'Cause Leora and Jimmy didn't exactly have a picture-book marriage. I'm actually surprised she's still in town. She was furious when Jimmy decided to move out here. She hated this place."

"Why didn't she divorce him?" I asked.

"It's a long story. You want to hear it?"

"I'm not going anywhere."

Lorenzo thought for a moment and shook his head. "I can't believe I'm gonna tell this story to the woman I want to go out with."

"Hey, don't sweat it, Lorenzo. I hit my head pretty hard. I probably won't even remember it tomorrow morning." I was aiming for nonchalant, but my heart swelled a little at his admission, and I looked down, hoping to hide the look of pleasure that was threatening to hijack my face.

Lorenzo smiled. "That makes me feel better. Okay," he said, back to business. "So Jimmy and Leora didn't exactly get married out of love." I nodded for him to continue. "Back then, there were two really powerful crime families in Chicago—ours, and Leora's. Our families had been feuding for years and years, and the whole thing was beginning to escalate out of control. My dad and Leora's dad were both trying to find a way to end the fighting, but neither wanted to be the side to call a truce. They figured the only way to do it was to tie the two families together. Their marriage was kind of like a peace treaty. It worked, too. Our families quit fighting with each other, and they figured out how to work together."

"That sounds good," I said tentatively.

"Yeah, but shortly after the wedding, Jimmy decided he wanted to go legit. That's when he first came out here and started talking about opening a casino. That would have been around ten years ago."

"And Leora didn't like the idea of going legit?"

"Not one bit. She liked her life in Chicago. She had money, power, status…"

"So why didn't they get a divorce?" I asked.

Lorenzo looked grim. "It would have been like a declaration of war. My father told Jimmy in no uncertain terms that he was not allowed to divorce Leora. I'm sure her father gave her the same warning."

"Wow," I said. "I can't imagine having to be married to someone you're not in love with."

"I know. Me either. At least in Chicago, Leora was able to keep herself busy. They kinda lived two separate lives and never really had to see each other. I think at first

Leora thought that Jimmy was going through a phase with the whole legitimate-business thing, and that she'd eventually be able to change his mind. She was pretty ruthless, too, not the best influence on someone who's trying to do things right."

"What do you mean?"

"Well, Leora is kind of the reason why the Indians got stiffed out of their own casino."

"What do you mean by that?" I asked.

Lorenzo took a deep breath. "When Jimmy made the deal with Chief Bloodgood to put up a casino on Indian land, everything was aboveboard. They agreed to split the expenses up front, and then share the profits once it opened. Leora is a greedy woman, though. She wanted the whole casino to be theirs, didn't want the Indians to have any part of it. So she convinced Jimmy to 'talk' to the city, got them to delay the permits, deny them liquor licenses, organize labor disputes, stuff like that. And she kept finding new ways to stall the development, hoping the Indians would run out of money. It took three years, but she finally got her wish. Chief Bloodgood went to Jimmy and told him that the casino had all but bankrupted their tribe."

"That's terrible!" I said.

Lorenzo had the decency to look ashamed. "I know," he said quietly. "Leora and Jimmy offered to buy back their half of the casino for pennies on the dollar. It was enough money to keep them from bankruptcy, but it was still a real raw deal."

I thought about the school on the reserve with its overgrown grass, and George Bloodgood's home with the FOR SALE sign on the lawn. It was starting to make sense. "I guess that would explain Junior Bloodgood's animosity toward Jimmy," I mused. "I'd probably want the guy dead, too." The words had slipped out unthinkingly. I had forgotten I was talking about Lorenzo's recently deceased brother until I saw the pained look on his face. "I'm sorry," I said quickly, "I didn't mean…"

"That's okay. I was pretty disappointed in my brother, too." He took another swig of his drink. "All that stuff happened right around the time that I came to town. I had a long talk with Jimmy. I told him that if he wanted me to stay and be his partner, we couldn't be screwing over everyone we did business with. That's how our dad did business. That's all he knew from the time he was a little kid. I reminded him that we were trying to be different."

I digested the news for a moment. "But that was, what, seven years ago," I said. "Why did it all come to a head now?"

Lorenzo shook his head. "I'm not quite sure. Actually…" He stopped speaking.

"What?" I prompted.

"It's probably nothing, but a couple of months ago, I heard Jimmy and Leora fighting up in the office. I didn't think anything of it since that's all they ever did. But… Jimmy yelled something about not needing 'some pig' on the payroll, and then Leora yelled something about how dropping dead would be the best thing he could do for business."

I felt all tingly. This felt like a lead. "Do you think Leora killed Jimmy?" I asked.

"I highly doubt it," he answered. "Don't get me wrong, she probably wanted him dead. She was a mean one, and manipulative, too, but I think she'd have been too scared to do anything like that, you know, with the whole family situation and everything?"

I did. I wouldn't even want to slap one of their family members with a parking ticket for fear of retribution, let alone kill one of them. Still, greed was a powerful motivator. "Why didn't you tell all this to the police?" I asked. "I don't think anyone even considered her to be a suspect."

"Because Leora said something about a pig on the payroll."

"Wait a minute. People still call cops pigs? What is it, the eighties?"

"Sorry to break the news to you," Lorenzo said with a chuckle. "And then when I found out you were a detective…I wondered…"

"If I was the dirty cop on the payroll."

"It was a fleeting thought at the most," he said sweetly. "Mostly I just had my feelings hurt."

"This is bad," I whispered. It really was. I'd been hoping beyond hope that I'd been wrong in thinking that there was a dirty cop behind this, and as much as I hated Detective Coleman, I had really been hoping that he was just a plain old pig, not a dirty cop. Now it seemed as though that was were very unlikely. I turned to Lorenzo. "I think I know who it is."

I had Lorenzo's attention. "Are you serious?" he asked.

"Unfortunately, I'm dead serious. You know that guy who attacked me at Double Down on my very first night? The one the bouncers kicked out?" Lorenzo nodded. "He's actually a detective. He had no idea that I was on the case, but he was there at the club, and the dancers all knew him."

"Maybe he just likes strip clubs," offered Lorenzo.

"I don't think so. He was close to Candy, you know, Amber's best friend? There has to be a reason why he got close to her. I know for a fact it wasn't her stimulating conversation, and Candy says they've never had sex. He was also there at the Den the night that I got beat up."

Lorenzo nodded his head slowly, remembering. "I needed to talk to Amber's *real* boyfriend," I said in answer to his silent question. "Turns out he works in the Plow Room." Lorenzo raised his eyebrows, and I said, "Don't ask." Lorenzo held up his hands as if he'd already heard too much information, and I laughed, feeling the tension ebb from my body. It felt so good to finally be able to confide in him.

"Anyway," I said. "Jay knew I was going to be there. I think he was the one who broke into my car looking for Amber's phone, and when he didn't find it, he came inside looking for me." Lorenzo was nodding thoughtfully, taking it all in. "We kind of got into a fight that night. I did something really awful to him at the Den and he was really pissed at me."

Lorenzo raised his eyebrows. "What happened?"

"I sort of tied him up almost naked in the dungeon with a LICK ME sign on his back." I looked up at Lorenzo, expecting to see a look of disapproval. Instead, he was holding back a laugh. I could only imagine what he thought of me now. "Anyway, like I said, he was really pissed off. Then a couple of hours later, someone broke into my house and beat me up. The kicker is, whoever broke in used my own house key, the one that had been on my key chain in the police impound." Lorenzo's eyes widened at the implication. "I know," I said, echoing his thoughts. "Whoever attacked me had to have been a cop. Nobody else would have had access to the impound." I shook my head. "I just found out about the key today. It's all starting to make sense."

Lorenzo put a comforting arm around me. "This is big," he said softly. "How are we going to prove that he did it?"

I liked hearing him say *we*. It felt nice to have him as an ally. "Actually, we should have our proof tomorrow morning. Bobbie has one last piece of evidence to process, and if she can match it to the DNA samples I collected of Jay, then we have him, for Amber's murder, at least." I put my head on Lorenzo's shoulder. His cashmere sweater felt like the softest thing I'd ever felt. Suddenly it was all I could do to keep my eyes open.

"Let's get you to bed, okay?"

I nodded my head sleepily. "Sorry I'm not better company," I murmured.

"You're great," he whispered, and helped me to my feet.

We were halfway up the stairs when I heard the gravel crunching under tires in my driveway. Suddenly all thoughts of sleep vanished. I looked at Lorenzo. He didn't look as worried as I felt. Of course, no one had attempted to kill him in the last few days. I padded down the stairs, took my Glock from my purse, and crept to the door.

There was pounding on the other side. "Open the door, Jones!" It was Detective Coleman. He sounded pissed. I shot a look to Lorenzo, letting him know that this was not a good development. "I know you're in there! Open the damn door!"

Before I could make up my mind what to do, Lorenzo strode to the door and whipped it open. "I would think long and hard about what you say next," he said to Detective Coleman.

Jay was not to be deterred, though. "Where the hell is

she?" he spat out.

I stepped out from behind Lorenzo so that I could see him. "What do you want?" I asked, keeping my voice rock solid steady.

"What do I want? Are you fucking kidding me? What do I want?" His lips were pulled back as he yelled, giving the impression of a vicious dog, and he was shaking from the effort of keeping his anger from seeking a physical outlet. "You broke into my house, you crazy bitch! You broke into my fucking house!"

"I guess it would have been easier if I'd had a key," I said.

Detective Coleman took a deep breath, suddenly eerily calm. "You're going to regret this."

"We'll see in the morning," I answered.

Coleman stepped back from the door, his green eyes full of hatred. He wasn't yelling anymore, but his calm manner was even more frightening. Despite the heat of the late summer evening, I felt a deep and unsettling chill.

I stepped back from the door, allowing Lorenzo to throw the dead bolts. It wasn't until I looked down at the gun in my hand that I realized I was trembling. Some tough cop I was turning out to be. "I'm staying here tonight, by the way," Lorenzo said. Anticipating an argument, he added, "I'll sleep down here on the couch, watch some TV, but I'm not leaving you alone tonight."

I nodded, grimly thankful. I actually hadn't been planning on arguing. I was tired and hurt, and though I would never speak the words out loud, I was also scared. I punched in the alarm code, accepted a gentle and comforting kiss from Lorenzo, and dragged myself upstairs for the night.

But I couldn't shake the image of Jay's angry green eyes, couldn't forget his words: "You're going to regret this." I knew I'd never be able to sleep waiting for the ax to fall, so I reached out for my phone, punched in the chief's number, and told him everything, right up to the scary visit that Detective Coleman had just paid me.

Chief Thompson let out a low whistle. "This is some serious business, Cassidy, and I know you wouldn't be telling me this unless you were sure." He paused, searching for the right words. "But we can't tell anyone, and we can't move on this until we have absolute proof, you understand?"

"I know, Chief," I said. "Bobbie said she'd have the results for me in the morning. We'll have everything we need then."

"Good," he said. "Why don't we meet in the morning, the diner at nine? I don't want to get his suspicions up if he sees us together at the station. Then when we get the word we can make our move."

"That sounds good, Chief. I'll see you in the morning."

"Get some sleep, Cassidy. Tomorrow's going to be a big day."

I hung up feeling like a giant weight had been lifted from my shoulders.

Chapter Eighteen

Whether it was the drugs or the rebound effect from adrenaline, I slept like a baby and awoke to the wonderful aroma of coffee. It took me a moment to remember that Lorenzo had stayed the night. I would definitely have to find a way to thank him later. But now what I wanted more than anything was a shower.

The water felt invigorating, and for the first time since I arrived home from the hospital, I actually felt like myself. Whether it was just the natural healing process or the fact that Bobbie was going to have a definitive answer for me today or the fact that the handsome Lorenzo Polonco was downstairs right now, probably searching my barren cupboards for food to feed to me, I felt like today was going to be a very good day.

I put a little extra effort into my morning beauty routine, covering up the greenish bruises with concealer and working loose waves into my blond hair.

Lorenzo was in the kitchen frying up eggs. He looked good, more than good, actually. It was the first time I had seen any kind of stubble on his usually clean-shaven face, and his hair was tousled as if he had just spent the early morning sailing on a yacht. I hadn't thought it would be possible for Lorenzo to get any better looking, but he had. My heart gave an involuntary lurch, and parts of me that had been dormant for days began to tingle.

"Good morning, Cinderfella," I said with a grin.

In answer, he pulled the pan off the burner, crossed the kitchen, and kissed me long and hard, his hands finding the small of my back and pulling me in close. "Good morning," he finally answered.

People say that laughter is the best medicine, but I beg to differ. There wasn't an atom in my entire body that was lingering on the injuries or events of recent days. Instead, I felt giddy and sexy and ready for anything. For one thing in particular, but that would have to wait.

"Coffee," he said handing me a mug. "I'm not sure how you take it, but I'm guessing you like it creamy and sweet."

I locked eyes with him and smiled. "That's exactly how I like it."

Lorenzo sauntered back to the frying pan with a smile. "Is it my imagination, or are you feeling a lot better than you were last night?"

"It's definitely not your imagination. I called the chief last night and told him about my late-night visitor. We're meeting this morning to make a plan."

Lorenzo slid the eggs onto two plates and set them on the table. "That's good. He believes you."

I took a bite of Lorenzo's eggs. They were almost as good

as Rosemary's eggs, and that was saying something. "Hard not to, considering." I looked at the clock. "We're meeting in half an hour at the Great Griddle. What's your day like today?" I asked.

"You know, the usual, running the empire." We finished off our breakfast quickly, and once I'd scooped the last mouthful of fluffy eggs into my mouth, he took the plates over to the sink. "Off to work, young lady," he said.

I felt my heart pull again. Together with Lorenzo in the kitchen, sharing breakfast, getting ready for work—it all seemed so normal somehow, like a scene from *Leave It to Beaver*. And I liked it. For a moment, I could almost forget that I was off to catch a dirty cop for a double murder and Lorenzo was off to run his various dens of iniquity. We walked out of the house hand in hand, both of us happy to pretend for a moment. I was snapped from my fantasy when I saw my Jeep. It was wallowing on its rims in four pools of rubber, looking like a mammoth in a tar pit. My tires had been slashed. I guess Detective Coleman had had the last laugh after all. I did the math in my head. It would cost almost two grand to replace them—probably around what it would cost Jay to replace his carpet.

"Well," I said grimly, "I guess I deserved that."

Lorenzo looked shocked. "In what universe do you deserve to have your tires slashed?"

I gave Lorenzo a bleak smile. "I kind of broke into Jay's house yesterday." Lorenzo raised his eyebrows at me, waiting for me to continue. "I ate his last doughnut and drank milk straight from the carton, no glass."

"So he slashes your tires?"

"Um…I might have also stolen some DNA samples and

left a big bloodstain on his shag carpet." Lorenzo's eyebrows shot up again. "From a steak!" I added hurriedly. "God, what did you think? I had to keep his dog occupied while I ransacked his house."

Lorenzo shook his head slowly. For a guy who was trying to walk the straight and narrow, I was probably starting to look like a bad bet. "What am I going to do with you? I'm going to have to send Bertrand with you twenty-four-seven. I'm just not entirely sure it's you that needs the protecting."

"Well, I might have deserved this, but the timing couldn't be worse," I said, turning my attention back to my Jeep.

"I can give you a lift if you like," said Lorenzo. I gave him a look, and he chuckled. "Yeah, I guess it wouldn't be the best idea to show up to your big meeting with the chief with the brother of the deceased."

"Yeah, probably not the best career move on my part. I'll see if Chief Thompson can swing by and pick me up. I'm sure he won't mind, especially when I tell him it was Jay who was responsible for my tires." I gave Lorenzo a parting kiss. "It would probably be best if you weren't here when he arrives."

"Gotcha," he said, climbing into his gleaming black Maserati. "Call me with updates. I want to know everything." And he drove away.

Fifteen minutes later, the chief pulled into the driveway and I climbed into his big black SUV. Not surprisingly, it was clean inside and out, and smelled like a mixture of Armor All and men's aftershave, an altogether not unpleasing aroma. I made a mental note to myself—next New Year's I was definitely going to make a resolution to keep my car clean. There was a bottle of water, a car charger, and a pen in the chief's center console. My center console was overrun with CDs, loose change, two different flavors of lip balm, chewing gum, and gas receipts. If you were brave enough to open the glove box, you'd find tampons, deodorant, a box of condoms, and a stash of emergency chocolate kisses that had melted and reformed so many times during the summer that they were probably inedible. I'd bet my left fallopian tube that I'd find nothing but the owner's manual, proof of insurance, and perhaps a bottle of Purell in the chief's glove compartment.

After my cursory inspection, I turned to look at the chief. He looked like a man on a mission today, tired, grim faced and determined. I couldn't blame him for being stressed out. When you found a dirty cop on your force, it cast a black cloud over the entire department. The public was always quick to assume the worst. They believed dirty cops were like peanuts: How can you have just one? Chief Thompson would be dealing with the fallout from this scandal for years to come. I didn't envy his position right now.

He was very cordial with me, though, even gentle. I couldn't be sure, but I wondered if, like Lorenzo, he felt a little bit responsible for my getting hurt, too. If that was the case, I wanted to stop that line of thinking immediately. The thought of going back to playground duty with Ken made me indescribably sad.

"Chief," I said, breaking the silence, "I want to thank you for giving me this opportunity. It's a dream come true, making detective, so…thank you."

Chief Thompson gave me an appraising look then offered a tight smile. "You definitely surprised people. I don't think anybody realized what a tough cookie you are."

Call me petty, but I was glad that somebody finally

noticed. I was sick of being treated like an invalid, or worse, a girl. "You know," he said, "nobody would have found the real killer if you hadn't been on this case. I owe you."

In a million years I never expected to get this kind of validation from the chief. In an attempt to hide the look of satisfaction I could feel creeping onto my face, I turned my attention to the passing countryside. It was dry. It hadn't rained in almost three weeks, so the roads were hot and dusty, and the acres of pasture flying by the window were speckled with patches of brown scrub grass. Everything was thirsty for water. It was only a matter of time before the rains came, though. You could feel it in the air — the humidity, the heat. It was barely past nine in the morning, and already the temperature was pushing its way into the nineties. Even the chief had made concessions to the heat today. His sleeves were rolled up to his elbows, revealing strong forearms with ribbons of plump veins crisscrossing their way down to his fingers. A freshly scrubbed scab on his arm made me wonder if he had a cat. The chief didn't exactly strike me as a cat guy, though.

The sound of Bobbie's ringtone pulled me from my thoughts. I looked over to the chief. "This must be it." I pulled the phone from my purse and answered, "Talk to me."

"You're not going to believe this," said Bobbie. She didn't sound happy.

"What? The results aren't in yet?"

"No, I've got your results," she answered, and my heart started its slow descent to the pit of my stomach.

"Did you get a positive ID on Coleman?" I asked, even though I knew what the answer would be.

Bobbie took a deep breath on the other end of the line.

"Sorry, Cass," she said. "It wasn't Detective Coleman."

My head was spinning. "Did you try all of the samples I gave you? 'Cause maybe the stuff on the towel wasn't his, you know?"

Bobbie stopped me. "I did, Cass. I matched Amber's fingernail against all the samples. He's not your guy."

"Shit." This was going to turn out to be a really bad twist on my career path. Thank God we hadn't broadcast our suspicions to the rest of the station. I looked over at the chief, who was appraising me coolly. He'd gone out on a limb for me, and I had just failed him. If I could have curled up into a little ball and blocked out the rest of the day I would have. Without saying a word, he reached for his water bottle and took a swig. Out of the corner of my eye, I saw a flash of something pink and shiny fall from the condensation on the bottom of his bottle and back into the cup holder.

"Hey, that's…" I stopped short. It was a pink crystal, the same sort of pink crystal that had decorated Amber's phone. The bottom of my purse was still littered with them. There was only one way that one of the crystals could have made it into the chief's cup holder, though. Well, two ways, but I couldn't imagine Chief Thompson or his wife carrying a pink bejeweled cell phone. I looked away as fast as I could, hoping that the chief hadn't noticed my discovery. I shot him a quick look just to be sure, and felt my heart drop. The chief was looking at the crystal. Then he slowly lifted his gaze to meet mine, his expression completely unreadable.

I tried to swallow, but there was no moisture in my mouth. I was in trouble. Deep down, I was certain of it. There was a feeling you got in the pit of your stomach when you were well and truly in danger. It's different than the jolt of adrenaline you get from a surprise attack. It's a deeper response, born of instinct and fear, the reason prey runs from predator. It started with a prickle at the base of your skull the moment you realized you were being measured, and traveled like an electrical current to the deepest part of your gut once you realized you were rapidly running out of options for survival. I finally realized what the flight part of the fight-or-flight response felt like. It felt like shit.

My mind started to race. Somehow I had to let Bobbie know that I was in trouble.

"Yeah, Roberta," I said, formulating a plan. "I'm with the chief now."

"What?" Bobbie asked sounding confused. Nobody ever called her Roberta—nobody but her mother, that is—and that had only happened when Bobbie was five and about to be punished. "What's going on, Cass? Are you okay?"

"No, actually, not at all," I answered, trying to mask my mounting panic with nonchalance. "We were on our way to the Great Griddle to wait for the results, but I guess there's no point now." I glanced at the chief. His knuckles were white on the steering wheel. He wasn't buying what I was selling, but if he was planning to take me somewhere to dispose of me, at least I'd make sure that they blamed the right guy this time. Up ahead I could see the turnoff to the Great Griddle. The chief blew past without giving it a second look. "Okay, thanks for the help," I said in as normal a voice as I could muster. "And whatever you do, please don't go running in this heat today."

"Cass, are you in trouble?" she asked quietly.

"Yeah, you bet. See you soon." I slipped my phone back into my purse without hanging up, hoping beyond hope that Bobbie hadn't disconnected on her end, and set my purse by my feet. When I looked up, Chief Thompson had his gun trained on my forehead. It was official. We were not pretending anymore.

His blue eyes were ice-cold, empty of all traces of softness. There was nothing left that I could hook into. I knew he wouldn't want to shoot me inside his vehicle. There would be no way to explain a Jackson Pollock of my DNA all over his spick-and-span leather interior. That would buy me a little time. That was the only thing going in my favor, though, that and the fact that he had to split his attention between the road and me. Still, at the moment I liked his odds better than mine.

"You just couldn't leave it alone, could you?" he asked, breaking the silence. He swiveled his head to look at me, as if he were seeing me for the first time. "You had to keep digging." He turned his eyes back to the road.

"I don't know what you're talking about," I whispered.

"Don't play dumb, Jones. I already gave you that opportunity."

It was my turn to see the chief with new eyes. He was the one who had almost killed me in my own home, the one who had killed Jimmy Polonco and Amber, the one who had tied Amber's body to the bottom of the floating dock on the reservation. He was a wolf, capable of killing, with cool detachment and a shocking lack of remorse—a wolf in chief's clothing. I would have smiled at the word play if I hadn't been so distracted by the fact that he intended to add me to his scorecard.

"Why did you do it?" I asked. If I was going to die, I wanted to have the details sorted in my brain first. I was going to have some serious explaining to do once I reached the pearly gates, and thinking back on all the strings I'd left untied would only serve to muddy the waters of my salvation. "You're obviously taking me somewhere to kill me," I prodded, "so just humor me."

"It wasn't supposed to go this way," he said quietly. "Leora came to me with a business proposition. I assumed that Jimmy was on board since Leora hadn't told me otherwise, but when I went to work out details with him myself, he lost it, threatened to expose me to the department."

"So you just killed him?"

The chief stared ahead at the road. "That was Leora's idea. She hated her husband, and I couldn't afford to have him expose me. And with Jimmy out of the way and Leora in charge of Jimmy's businesses, Leora and I would be able to resume a very profitable business arrangement."

I must have looked shocked because he explained, "I'm getting close to retirement. I've worked at this government job for thirty-five years, and I can barely afford to keep my house. I had to take out loans to put my kids through school. And I see these criminals move into town and make their fortunes. I just want my fair share."

"You didn't care how many lives you had to destroy to 'get your fair share'?" I asked, trying to keep the emotion I was feeling out of my voice.

"Junior Bloodgood is a useless piece of shit. He actually did *try* to kill Jimmy. I couldn't care less if he rots in jail. And Amber? That stupid stripper tried to extort money from me. I'd been paying her very well for helping me set up Junior. Then when the job was over, I met up with her at Double Down to give her her last payment, and she said she was going to go to the police if I didn't keep the money coming. She deserved what she got, too."

"You're Daddio," I murmured.

"Stupid slut," he spat out. "She was pretending she was a spy or something."

"And what about me?"

The chief trained his cold eyes on me again. "If you'd minded your own business and done what you were told, you'd be a local hero, a decorated detective. But you didn't. Shows me that you're even more stupid than Leora and I had hoped."

I felt like I'd been slapped. Somehow the idea that I was being driven to my very own murder scene paled in comparison to being called stupid by the chief. In one sentence, he had undermined everything I held sacred. I hadn't earned a promotion based on my merits. I'd been given a promotion on the assumption that I was a shitty cop. Something inside me twisted, crouched down in my gut like a coiled spring. In his eyes, and probably in the eyes of all the unevolved apes at the station, I was a stupid girl with a badge and a gun, and it made me angrier than I could even describe.

I could feel my pulse quicken, taste the fear inside me morphing into rage, that blinding, red-tinged rage that replaces all reason and drowns out all other emotion. And I welcomed it. If he wanted to underestimate me, so be it. But I wasn't taking my own death lying down. If he wanted my silence, he was going to have to work for it.

In one continuous motion, I unclipped my seat belt and grabbed onto my door handle as if I were going to jump out. The chief reached out instinctively, grabbing onto the collar of my shirt in an effort to yank me back. Instead of pulling away from him like he expected me to do, I tucked my feet up underneath me and used his pulling momentum to launch myself back into him, using my head as a battering ram. I heard a crunching sound and a grunt of pain. I had just broken his nose big-time. The SUV swerved, hitting the gravel on the opposite side of the road. Before he could throw me off, I turned and pulled on his seat belt with both hands. I felt a sharp pain in my ribs. He was punching me with his right fist. *At least I managed to make him drop his gun*, I thought to myself. I ground my knee into his groin as payback and wrapped the slack of the seat belt around his neck. Then I grabbed onto the tethered end and heaved with all of my strength.

The chief made a gagging sound as the air rocketed out of his windpipe, and I hung on, letting the seat belt take my entire body weight while I watched his eyes bug out in panic. His hands flailed like two flapping kites caught up in a tornado, seeking purchase on something solid. He finally found a handful of my hair, but before he could do anything, I released my grip on the seat belt and slammed my elbow down into his nose. If I hadn't already broken it with the back of my skull, I had sure as hell broken it now. Blood poured from the pulpy mass of flesh that had once been a fairly attractive nose. I raised my elbow to strike him again, but before I could deal him a second blow, he wrenched hard on the steering wheel, throwing me off his lap, and careening us into the loose gravel on the shoulder. I felt a moment of beautiful weightlessness as the tires surrendered their grip on the earth, until gravity took the reins, catapulting us sideways into the ditch, bulldozing us through the bulrushes, long grass, and dirt, and into a maple tree.

The SUV shuddered as if it were trying to heave itself up onto an elbow, then it gave up and settled into a dead heap. I opened my eyes in a daze, momentarily disoriented by my geography. I was lying on my back against the passenger side window, looking up into the cloudless sky above me. One knee was tucked up under my chin while my other leg was strewn across the center console. I had sustained some damage, that much I knew, but it didn't feel like anything was broken. My head felt like a horror show again, though, and I selfishly asked the universe to keep my brain from exploding before I could see the chief behind bars.

I smeared a mass of blood-streaked hair out my eyes to get a look at the chief. He wasn't moving. He was fettered in by the seat belt, held bolt upright in his seat like a cadet at military school, his tongue bulging out of his mouth. He was suffocating. I gathered my legs together underneath me as fast as my pounding head would allow, and scrambled to unwrap the chief's neck. Freed from his seat belt, his head lolled forward at an unnatural angle. He reminded me of a newly slaughtered cow that had been hung to drain. As if on cue, a stream of blood, earthbound by the laws of gravity, started to ooze from the chief's nose, landing on my collarbone and seeping its way down the front of my shirt. *Definitely not kosher*, I thought grimly.

I touched my fingers to his neck and found a pulse. It would be so easy, I thought to myself, to finish the job right now, put another hundred and twenty pounds on his windpipe. No one would be the wiser. I looked down at my hands, wondering if they would be willing to operate independent of my brain, but they didn't move. No matter how faint or far away my line in the sand, evidently I still had one, and as much as I would have loved to be rid of this particular monster, I knew deep down that I was no murderer. In fact, I actually believed with all my heart in the sanctity of the legal system. The woman in me desperately wanted to squeeze the air out of his unmoving body. The cop in me would never let her.

I heard a squeaking sound coming from under the seat, and a ribbon of relief coursed through my body. Bobbie had kept the line open.

I pawed under the seat for my purse and dug out my phone. "Bobbie!" I sobbed.

"Oh my God, Cassidy! Are you okay? What's happening?"

"Please tell me you heard?"

"Every word, and I hit record when things turned ugly, so we got that son of a bitch for real! What's he doing now?"

I looked up at the chief. "He's bleeding, mostly." He was bleeding a lot, actually, but he was moving now, too, and reaching for something by his foot — an ankle holster. "Hold on, Bobbie. I have to do something."

I kicked up at the chief's hand with my boot just as his fingers reached the grip of his gun. He let out a gargling sound of pain and turned his ruined face to me. His lips were pulled back in a grimace, blood dripping off his teeth as he strained to reach his gun. I gave him a twisted smile. "You just couldn't let it go, could you?" And I hoofed what was left of his nose.

Blood sprayed down onto the top of my head. It was warm like the water that first comes out of the sprinkler on a hot day, but it was red and slippery and tasted like dirty pennies. I gagged, willing myself not to vomit, and then I heard the sirens. The cavalry was coming. I put the phone, slick with blood, up to my face. "Was it you that called for backup?"

"I called Ken. I didn't know who else to trust."

"That was perfect, Bobbie. Thank you." I couldn't see much from the ditch, but I could hear more than one vehicle approaching. There was a lot of churning gravel, sirens blaring, doors slamming, men yelling. Apparently I'd found yet another way to upset a large group of people with minimal participation on my part. I looked up at the bloody heap that was the chief and conceded that perhaps my participation was slightly more than minimal on this one.

I felt the SUV rock, and then Ken's handsome face appeared through the window above me, and I felt a flood of relief. "What's a nice girl like you doing in a place like this?" he asked as he propped open the door. He reached his hand down to help me and I grabbed on with both of mine, using the chief's limp body as a stepping stool as I made my way inelegantly out of the chief's crumpled and dirty SUV. Ken helped me claw my way out of the ditch, and when I finally made it to the top, all talking and activity ceased. Detective Coleman was there with his partner, Watson. Officer Lisa Miller was there, too, and so was Bertrand. He must have been following me again, I thought hazily. I looked down at my hands. They were covered in blood, as were my jeans and my T-shirt. Out of the corner of my eye, I could see a clump of red matted hair. I tried to smooth it down, but it had already begun to crust. *I must look crazy.*

I looked back up at the crowd. They were still staring at me, probably waiting for me to either keel over or say something. With more bravado than I felt I said, "If you think I look bad, you should see the other guy," gesturing to the ditch with a nod of my head.

Everyone but Bertrand and Detective Coleman sprang into action. Bertrand, seeing that I was in one piece, gave an almost imperceptible nod of his head and drifted back to his truck to wait, leaving me alone with Coleman. I fixed Jay with a look of defiance. We'd accumulated a lot of history together in the last week, none of it good, and if he was planning on getting into it with me now, I wanted him to know I wasn't in the mood. To my surprise, he responded to my sneer with a tiny smile, which grew in magnitude as he crossed the gravel to stand in front of me.

He placed his hands gently on my shoulders and looked into my eyes. "You're a real pain in the ass, you know that?"

"So I've been told," I said.

"But you're okay?"

I nodded my head. Deep down I could admit that I appreciated the concern in his eyes, but I had questions that needed to be answered. "What was your involvement in all this?" I asked, turning the mood to something more serious.

Jay dropped his hands from my shoulders and shoved them into his pockets, then looked over his shoulder to make sure that we were still alone. "A few months ago Internal Affairs came to me. They'd gotten an anonymous tip that someone high up in the department food chain was getting their hands dirty."

"You think the tip came from Jimmy Polonco?" I asked.

"That'd be my bet, seeing as how he turned up dead," he answered. "Anyway, the investigation was pretty slow going since we weren't given any specifics."

"How did you know it was the chief?"

Jay gave a little chuckle. "Well, let's just say I've learned not to trust anyone who drinks too much or too little, and the chief is a hard-core nondrinker."

"You're definitely not going to trust me, then," I mumbled.

"Why, you don't drink, either?"

I raised an eyebrow at him. "Please. I'd give my left fallopian tube for a bottle of tequila right now."

"Good to know." We shared a sliver of a smile, and he continued. "Anyway, I'm following him for about a week and nothing happens. Then one night, I think I'm following him home, but instead, he heads over to Double Down, and I see him meet up with this stripper."

I nodded my head. "Amber…"

"That's right. But it just didn't sit right with me. I mean, why would a straight-as-an-arrow teetotaler like the chief be meeting up with a stripper? She never danced for him. They weren't sleeping together. So I decide to strike up a friendship with her best friend, Candy, to see if I could get more information out of her."

I nodded. It was all making sense so far. "But why didn't you tell me what was going on when you…saw me at the club?"

He cast me an intimate look. I had given him a very thorough and enthusiastic lap dance in that club, a dance that neither of us was likely to forget anytime soon. I looked away, waiting for the flush in my cheeks to cool, and he cleared his throat in an effort to redirect his thoughts back to our original conversation. "I couldn't tell you," he said quietly. "Believe me, I was as surprised to see you as you were to see me that night. I'd heard you'd been promoted to detective, but I didn't know the details, and then when I saw you at Double Down, I thought…"

"You thought I was in on it with the chief."

"I didn't know, but I had to add you to my list."

I nodded again, absorbing the information. "I get it. When I saw you there, I assumed the worst about you, too."

"Yeah, you did," he teased, rubbing his top lip. "You ripped my mustache off."

"When did you realize that I wasn't involved?" I asked.

"The night you ended up in the hospital. I saw the chief's truck on the road out by your place. I could have tied him to it, but I didn't have enough to pin the murders on him, too." He looked at me apologetically. "I came to the hospital to warn you, but you wouldn't let me anywhere near you."

I thought back to the hospital when I'd had him kicked out, thought back to the station when he stopped me in the hall. I shook my head. "I guess I can be a little stubborn," I muttered.

"Yeah," Jay laughed. "Just a little." He looked at me appraisingly. "Good stubborn, though. You were the one who found the missing piece of the puzzle. I had it figured out, but I couldn't prove it." He gave my shoulder a squeeze. "I never thought I'd say it, but you impressed the hell out of me…and you deserve the promotion you got. Remember that."

Before I could respond to his heartfelt admission, we were interrupted by the arrival of more vehicles—two ambulances and a shiny black Maserati.

Lorenzo jumped out of his car and loped toward the swarm of activity, frantically scanning the landscape. When his eyes found me, he stopped dead in his tracks. I'd forgotten that I looked like Carrie on prom night. He recovered his composure quickly, though, and hurried over, concern etched onto his handsome face. "What happened to you?" he asked, drawing me in for a gentle hug.

"Just another day at the office," I said into his chest.

I caught Jay's eye, and he smiled at me. "If you think she looks bad," he said, "you should see the other guy." I smiled back. Truce.

As if on cue, four paramedics wrestled the chief to the top of the ditch on a backboard, and I could feel the smile on my face evaporate. "Excuse me for a moment." I limped over to the chief's stretcher. His face was a pulpy disaster, his nose all but obliterated. His eyes were swollen shut, and his neck was collared for whiplash. "Why isn't he cuffed?" I asked sharply.

Lisa rolled her eyes. "I don't think he's in any condition to do anything."

"Is he breathing?" I asked, directing the comment to the paramedics. They nodded yes. "Then he's in a condition to do something," I said back to Lisa. I pulled up the chief's pant leg, relieved him of his secondary weapon, and handed it to her with a look that told her she'd been sloppy. I left my bloody hand out and wiggled my fingers at her. "Cuffs?" She handed her set to me, and I leaned in over the chief as I secured his hands. "Who's the stupid one now?" I hissed.

I straightened up to find that once again people were looking at me with stunned surprise, maybe wondering how a hundred-and-twenty-pound woman had been able to an-nihilate a man like the chief, or maybe wondering about the depths of my violent side.

I shrugged. "I get really mad when people mess with me." That would probably keep them guessing, I thought to myself.

Jay chuckled and held my gaze for perhaps two seconds too long, then turned away to find his partner.

Lorenzo walked up and slipped his arm around my waist. He was staring at the chief, the man who had murdered his brother. He gave me a squeeze. "Thank you," he whispered into my hair.

"I'm Kevin bloody Costner," I slurred in return.

Chapter Nineteen

I had argued about going to the hospital, but the fact that I'd only recently been released from the emergency ward with trauma to the brain and had just been pulled out of a car wreck covered in blood seemed to trump any "I'm fine" argument I tried to make. That and the fact that Lorenzo believed I actually thought I was Kevin Costner. He had so much to learn about me. Eventually, I realized it would be faster to let them have their way, so I relented and let them load me into an ambulance. Lorenzo had wanted to come to the hospital with me, but the cops needed to talk to him about his sister-in-law Leora, the chief's partner in crime. It was just as well, I thought to myself. The lighting in the hospital was awful, and I knew without even looking into a reflective surface that I needed all the help I could get today.

Tests and scans completed, Dr. Massey eventually confirmed my "I'm fine" diagnosis and released me into Bobbie's care for a second time.

"Oh my God! I'm so glad to see you in one piece," she said grabbing me into a hug. She pulled back and inspected me from top to bottom. "Damn, you're a mess. Let's get you home and hose you down!"

It had only been two days since the last time we had pulled up my long driveway in Bobbie's big white Escalade, fresh from the hospital. This time felt different, though. This time I knew I was safe. This time I was a real-life, bona-fide, murderer-catching, badass detective. This time Lorenzo was waiting for me on the front steps with a Styrofoam takeout container in his hands and a heart-melting smile on his face. And it felt good.

I turned to Bobbie with a smile. "Wanna come in?" I asked.

Bobbie laughed. "Oh my God, you're so sweet, but I don't think I want to get in the middle of that right now." She nodded to Lorenzo, who was making his way over to the truck.

He looked good, and my heart did an involuntary flip-flop. He had changed out of his bloodstained clothes into faded jeans and a white V-neck T-shirt. I looked down at my own ensemble. I was wearing the same blood-soaked jeans I'd been wearing when they dragged me out of the car, but the blood had hardened into a delightful crust during my hours of forced hospital confinement. Bobbie had brought me a clean T-shirt, the only extra clothes she'd had at work. It was pink and tight with a cartoon bunny on the front whose thought bubble said, "I didn't slap you, I just high-fived your face." I pulled down the visor and looked in the mirror. It wasn't good. I'd managed to get most of the blood off my face and arms, but my hair was still a rooster comb of the chief's DNA.

"I look like shit on a stick," I moaned.

"Here," said Bobbie, holding out her giant Chanel sunglasses. "These worked last time."

I stuck them on my face and took another look in the mirror. "I look like Liberace!"

Bobbie stifled a giggle. "Yeah, I don't think they're helping this time."

I gave Bobbie a hug and a kiss on the cheek. "I love ya!"

"I love you, too. Call me tomorrow."

Lorenzo opened the door and helped me down. It was a gallant gesture, and one that I wasn't accustomed to. I did a lightning-fast scroll through my sexodex. I guess I hadn't dated a lot of gentlemen. Lorenzo gave me a buttery smile. That was about to change.

When we got inside, Lorenzo popped the lid on the Styrofoam container. Nestled inside was a giant slab of carrot cake with a pillowy blanket of cream cheese frosting. "Roger thought this might make you feel better."

I grinned and stood up on my toes to press a kiss against Lorenzo's lips. "I think I'll save it for breakfast tomorrow morning."

"You don't want to feel better now?" he asked, returning my kiss.

"Oh, I do," I whispered into his mouth, "but there's only one thing that's going to make me feel better right now, and it has nothing to do with cake."

About the Author

Victoria has spent her adult life playing superheroes and cops on television and in movies. Her alter ego writes magazine articles and screenplays in her home in the Hollywood Hills. This is her debut novel.

Printed in Great Britain
by Amazon.co.uk, Ltd.,
Marston Gate.